Midnight Queen

by

Anne Stevens

A Tudor Intrigue
Tudor Crimes: Book 2

And wilt thou leave me thus,
That hath loved thee so long,
In wealth, and woe among?
And is thy heart so strong,
As for to leave me thus?
Say nay, say nay!

Sir Thomas Wyatt, ambassador and poet

§

In 1529, a new ambassador to the court of Henry VIII has been appointed, and becomes a supporter of Queen Katherine in her fight to remain as the king's legal wife. Cardinal Wolsey has fallen from power, and new factions are forming within the court.

Eustace Chapuys, the Spanish and Holy Roman Empire's new ambassador, becomes embroiled in court intrigue and, in 1531, is forced into an unlikely alliance with Thomas Cromwell, now a member of the king's Privy Council.

Friend and foe become confused as the great men of England vie to gain King Henry's ear. Sir Thomas More is the new Lord Chancellor, and he is pressing for an annulment of the royal marriage, whilst the influential Pole family want Katherine reinstated, and her daughter Mary declared to be next in the line of succession.

Thomas Cromwell moves between each camp, trying to further his own ends. He is intent on reforming the church, using his influence with Henry to break the power of Rome, and on providing a male heir to the throne.

Throughout, Katherine of Aragon remains aloof from every plot and machination, keeping her own council, and fighting against fate from her tenuous position. She must rely on Chapuys to guard her honour, and Tom Cromwell to guard her life. The queen watches from the shadows, wondering when, and where the blow will fall.

If Anne Boleyn is to assume the role of King Henry's consort, in the full light of day, then Katherine of Aragon is surely becoming a woman of the shadows... the Midnight Queen.

1   The New Spanish Ambassador

The wax candles have burned low, and a few have spluttered, and died. The first fingers of what promises to be a cold, grey dawn are making their way, languidly, across the cobblestone courtyard outside, and Katherine, daughter of the House of Trastámara, once a princess of Aragon, and now Queen Consort of England watches from her small, barred window. She turns at a small, almost apologetic noise behind her.

"Your Majesty has not slept well?" the woman asks, in Spanish. She is dressed in the Aragonese fashion, and speaks the Spanish of the noble classes.

"No, not well, Maria."

Katherine answers in an English flavoured with her mother tongue's accent. Over thirty years in England, the queen thinks, and she still struggles. "You must speak English to me, even when we are alone. The king does not like to hear Spanish spoken in his court these days. It makes him feel uncomfortable... as if we are speaking against him."

"Yes, madam," Lady Maria Willoughby says, suitably admonished. She has been in Katherine's service since 1505, and for almost a quarter century, they have been the closest of friends. "What about

4

conversing in French? His Majesty speaks that language well enough."

"Do not make fun of him," the queen tells her. "He does not deserve it."

"He does *not* deserve you," Maria says, almost spitting the words out. She slips into her native Basque tongue, and says "*Erregeak txerri bat da!*"

"Enough of that!" Katherine is suddenly angry. It is difficult to make people understand that she still loves the man, and cannot bear to hear him slandered. The king, she assures her closest friend, is *not* a pig. It is Cardinal Wolsey who is dripping poison into his ear. It is always the malevolent old cardinal, weaving his wicked plans, like a spider constructing its web.

Maria sniffs, and starts to prepare her queen for the day ahead. She will dress her in a subtle mixture of English, and Spanish fashion. There will be no French influence. For *la puta* dresses that way, showing her shoulders and her *pits nus,* to any man who cares to look.

"Maria, do not sulk," says Katherine. "It will make your face red. Is everything prepared for today?"

"Everything has been done," Maria confirms. "All of your ladies have been warned to be at their best, and the household staff have their instructions. Except for the

Moroccans, of course."

The queens household numbers about two hundred and twenty five souls, ranging from two dozen ladies in waiting, to two personal cooks, a master of horse, twenty three maids, eight cleaners, and a physician. They are all of Spanish blood, except for the two gigantic Moroccan slaves, given to her by Princess Isabella of Portugal, her devoted sister.

They stand at six feet, and look splendid when they are in their national costume, with their muscles oiled. There is no useful purpose to be served in keeping them, but they can look menacing, if need be, and seem to be devoted to the queen, who treats them like pets. They understand some Spanish, and a few of the more vulgar English words. Orders are usually conveyed by signs and mime, and are often misunderstood, or completely ignored.

"I will speak to Abdul and Hakim," Katherine tells her. "I shall have them standing on either side of me. It will impress the new ambassador with my majesty, don't you think, Maria?"

"What do we really know of the gentleman, Majesty?" Maria asks. It is not out of prurience. Maria de Salinas, Lady Willoughby, no longer has any real interest in men. She has been married, and widowed, and her ten years of dull wedlock has left her unimpressed with the male sex. It has also left her with a fine English title, a couple of nice houses, and an income of over a thousand silver marks a year.

"So little," the queen says. "I am informed only that he is coming, and wishes to pay his respects to me. He saw the king a few days ago, and asked his permission. I am told he is a young man for such an important post, and is a clever speaker. My nephew must think highly of this *Señor* Chapuys."

"His name sounds to be French, madam," Maria says, carefully. "He might have some sympathy with the ... that woman."

"I believe he is a Savoyard by birth, and therefore a loyal subject of my dearest nephew, Charles," Katherine explains. Savoy, like most of Europe, is under the banner of the Holy Roman Empire, and Charles V is its undisputed head. His power stretches from the Germanic provinces and the Netherlands, through Austria and Hungary, then down into Spain, where he has been acknowledged as the first true Christian king. He has control of most of Italy, and the New World colonies, and is rivalled only by the French on one side, and the Ottoman Turks on the other. His wealth is equal to that of all of his rivals added together.

"I pray Ambassador Chapuys is an improvement on the idiot he is replacing,"

Maria mutters. Katherine pretends not to have heard, but says a silent 'amen' in agreement. The outgoing ambassador has been of little use. In over two years, he has done nothing but strut about the court, giving, and taking, offence at every turn. Cardinal Wolsey has turned him about and about, until he has as little influence as a low born jester.

Time will tell, the queen thinks.

*

Eustace Chapuys pulls his cloak tightly about him, and approaches the entrance of Westminster Palace. There are guards, of course, but mostly for show. England is at peace, and has been for over forty years now. They salute, and uncross their halberds.

The ambassador sweeps past them, with King Henry's toady at his heels, twittering away in poor French. Edmund Carlisle is a mincing fop, whose duty it is to deflect Chapuys from his aims, and pamper him into compliance with the king's wishes. He is of limited intelligence, and does not know how to handle a man of such wit, and perspicacity.

"You have but to ask, sir," the young gallant is saying, "and I am commanded to be of service."

"Excellent. Please be so good as to

wait here for me, and I will try to think of a service you may do me," Chapuys tells him sharply. Master Carlisle makes as if to follow, but the ambassador steps across him, firmly. "No sir. Enough is enough. I have been granted a private audience with my master's aunt, the Queen of England, and so it shall be. Now sir, I pray that you desist your pursuit, and wait here for me."

He sweeps on down the corridor, ignoring the young man's scandalised pleas. His French is truly most deplorable, Chapuys thinks. He, himself can speak German, French, Spanish, Italian, Latin, and enough Flemish to get by on. Then he has a smattering of Arabic, Polish, and Russian. He can also speak quite good English, but for the moment, that is his particular secret.

Men will say much, if they believe you are unable to understand, and there is much to learn before he can perform his duty to a satisfactory standard. He comes to a door guarded by an attractive middle aged woman, and bows. He notes the style of her dress, and speaks to her in Basque.

"Pray, have the kindness to present me, madam. I am Eustace Chapuys, ambassador of Spain, and of the Holy Roman Empire."

The woman is taken by surprise, and smiles.

"I am Lady Maria Willoughby, sir. You

speak the Basque dialect well, I perceive."

"Well enough, my dear lady," Chapuys replies, then slips into more fluent Castilian Spanish. "You are Maria de Salinas ... the Lady Willoughby? I am told that you are Her Majesty's closest friend in England?"

"I have that honour," Maria replies. "She has few, at the moment, and none in court, Señor Chapuys. I pray you will redress that imbalance." She waves the guard aside, pushes open the door at her back, and ushers Chapuys into a large room.

At the far end, under a canopy of red silk, sits the queen. She is flanked by two enormous dark skinned men, standing with their arms folded. As he advances, the new ambassador removes his hat, and executes an elaborate bow.

"Most gracious Majesty," he begins, in Spanish. "I have letters of introduction from your loving nephew, The Emperor Charles, and words of friendship from your many relatives in Spain, and Portugal. You are still remembered with love in Aragon."

"Your Spanish is excellent," the queen tells him, "but we must speak in either French, or English, sir. My husband, the king, insists on it." She emphasises the word 'husband' and Chapuys gives a slight nod to show he understands. The entire thrust of his mission is to be aimed at establishing the legitimacy of the queen's marriage to Henry. No matter what, her right to be known as queen, is paramount, and not open to negotiation.

"Then let us converse in the French tongue, my dear lady," Eustace Chapuys says, "for English is a barbaric language, far beyond my poor understanding. I would not wish King Henry to receive an unfavourable report of my conduct."

Katherine knows that some amongst her ladies have loose tongues, and some are even married to English noblemen, and have sharply divided loyalties. It is best to keep any public conversation as neutral as possible.

"I agree, Señor Chapuys. His Majesty is currently in a state of confusion, over a certain matter." Katherine can hardly bring herself to discuss so loathsome a matter as the validity of her marriage. "It has been put into his head that our vows are worthless, because of my unconsummated marriage to his brother, Arthur."

"A patent nonsense, of course, but still a matter which is exercising the minds of many people, Your Majesty," he replies. "I have heard that Cardinal Wolsey is under a dark cloud at the moment, and that your dear *husband* is most displeased with his actions."

"Wolsey promised him a quick annulment," Katherine explains. "It is the cardinal's first false step in twenty years."

"It is said that he languishes in his Esher house, and is banned from the royal court. Even so, madam, we must remember the tale of the scorpion."

"Ah, Chapuys, you have only been here a few days, and already know more than your predecessor," the queen says. She is pleased at his perception, and his confirmation that Wolsey has fallen. "Should we be pleased that the Cardinal's influence over my husband is broken?"

"There is a difference between a great fall, and a mere stumble," Chapuys mutters. "The scorpion might yet have a sting in its tail. I advise you to wait; bide your time, and see what happens."

"But if he is finished?" Katherine asks again.

"Your husband, the king, must have many other very able advisors, madam," Chapuys tells her. "I believe that he has turned to the Boleyn father, and the Duke of *Norfook*." He stresses the latter part of the duke's name, and someone titters in a corner of the room at the pronunciation.

The queen looks at the source of the noise sharply, and it cuts off. She does not understand the humour, but it will spread throughout the court that Chapuys has invented a new, rather comic, even lewd sounding, pronunciation for Norfolk.

"The Boleyn family are not my friends, Señor Chapuys," she says. "They will do me the greatest harm at every turn, if they can."

"I do not think they bear you any personal malice, my Lady," the ambassador replies, soothingly. "It is just that they seek advancement, and fear you, because you stand in their way. They know you will fight against them."

"To my dying breath," Katherine mutters.

"And mine," Chapuys confirms, bowing. "I believe you have a Spanish doctor, madam? Can you recommend him, as a good man?"

"There are many competent doctors at court," Katherine says, offhandedly, then catches herself. The man is, indeed, very cunning. "Though few speak Spanish, of course. If you are unwell, I will send my Doctor Vargas to you. He is a most dependable sort of man, though a little dull, conversationally. He shall treat your ailments, no doubt."

"You are too kind, Your Majesty." Eustace Chapuys stares into her brown eyes, willing her to understand his true meaning. "I have some small, but regular ailments, and would appreciate a consultation with your man… on a *regular* basis."

"Of course. I have just found you, my

dear Chapuys, and wish you to continue in good health. My doctor will call on you once each week."

"A most agreeable arrangement, my dear madam," Chapuys tells her. Then curiosity overcomes him. He asks about the towering bodyguards, who loom over them.

"They are Abdul, and Hakim, my loyal Moroccan giants," the queen explains. "They seem to understand nothing, but a few words of Spanish, and my hand signs."

"Ah, I see," says Chapuys. He turns to Abdul, the older of the two men. "*As salaam aleykum*". The big man steps back in surprise, then grins, and replies. The ambassador speaks slowly, his knowledge of the eastern tongue being much inferior to his grasp of the many European languages.

"You speak our tongue well, for an *ajami*, My Lord," says Hakim. Ajami is the nearest he can come to describing Chapuys and his like. It means 'Persian', and is usually meant as an insult. The ambassador smiles, and explains why.

"I was once an envoy to the great Suleiman the Magnificent, when he was encamped outside the gates of Vienna."

"Bless his name,"Abdul mutters, touching his chest and forehead, reverently.

"My master, Charles, defeated him, and turned the infidels back." Chapuys feels he must say as much, in support of his faith.

"You win some, and you lose some," the older Moroccan says, shrugging his great shoulders. "Another day, and it might be your master who has to flee. It need not worry small men, such as we, sir."

"Indeed not." Chapuys cannot help but smile. "Guard the queen well, and I will see you well rewarded."

"Your gold will strengthen our devotion tenfold, master," Hakim says, and he grins at the little Savoyard diplomat.

The queen is both amazed, and delighted by this sudden flurry of incomprehensible chatter, and asks what Eustace Chapuys has told her huge bodyguards.

"I greeted them, my Lady," Chapuys tells her. "Then I said they must guard you with their lives. They say they love and revere you, and will lay down their lives if need be." This is a fair approximation. The ambassador greeted them simply, and has promised them a few gold coins if they do their sworn duty. "Hakim agrees that they will be ever watchful, and do their sworn duty to you.

"This is splendid, Chapuys," the queen says. "You must ask them something for me. They came to me as slaves, you see, and I do not know their histories. Are they brothers, or is one, perhaps, the father or uncle of the other?"

Eustace Chapuys asks, and they both grin, and the older man explains their close relationship, which the ambassador cannot, in all politeness, repeat to the queen. After a little thought he says, diplomatically: "They say they are just good friends, Your Majesty."

"And how did they come to me?"

Chapuys asks Abdul about their past, and receives a garbled tale of treachery and deceit. An uncle of their cousin has stolen their birthright, and sold them into slavery. They long to return home, slit his fat gullet open, and recover the herd of camels he cheated from them. Then they will return to being honest farmers again, and praise Allah for their deliverance.

"Shall I ask the queen to free you?" the ambassador asks, trying to hide a smile. "Then you may sail back to your far away land, and live happily once more." The two men are utterly aghast at the suggestion, and swear that they want to stay with their queen for ever more.

"After all," the older man confesses, "it was only a *very* small herd of camels!"

Eustace Chapuys understands. Home is often a mythical place that is better kept in the heart, and left deep in the past. The two guards have no wish to go home, and their mistress, Queen Katherine feels exactly the same. Her heart is Spanish, but her roots have grown deep down into England's rich dark soil, and back home, she would be nothing but a passing curiosity: an ageing, casually cast off monarch, unable to hold on to her king.

"I look forward to our future meetings, Your Majesty," he says warmly. "God preserve and support you in your time of tribulation." He bows, and walks backwards from the room as a sign of his devotion. It is not just diplomacy. He sees that the queen has right on her side, and will move heaven and earth to keep her seated on the English throne. That Anne Boleyn, a protestant whore, seeks to dislodge her, is an affront to him, and to his faith.

As he leaves, one of the younger ladies in waiting slips away, and meets with her lover in the Chapel garden. He pulls her into a quiet corner, and lets his hands rove over body. She tilts her head back, and lets him kiss her lips. Later, she will allow him all the freedom he wishes.

"Well," George Boleyn says, running a finger down the side of her face, "what did the new ambassador have to say for himself?"

2   The Invitation

Gilbert Guyot's English is good. He is from Provins, a small market town a few miles south of Paris, and has been educated by the redoubtable local nuns. They broke many a rod over his back as a child, but have failed to beat out the devil. He can speak English, French, Languedoc dialect, Italian, and some Spanish, due mainly to his need to travel a lot.

Gilbert is an acrobat, and juggler of some note. He has his own small troupe, and tours the continent, and England, entertaining at country fairs, and the homes of the rich. The Vernay brothers, Jehan and Claude, complete his ensemble, with their knife throwing, and tumbling prowess. They are all clever cut purses, and know a hundred ways to turn a dishonest penny. Sometimes, if the money is right, they even turn their hands to murder.

"I must have my expenses, of course," he tells the willowy Englishman. "Half in advance, and the rest on completion. Is this to your liking?"

"What proof do I have that you are the right man for the task, Guyot?" the English gentleman asks. Asking for written character references is not an option, and he is wary of throwing away hard earned gold.

"Give me a name," Gilbert says, casually, "and he will be dead before sunset.

There will be nothing to bring the matter back to your door, my friend. Each bag of gold will buy you another death."

"It is a long list."

"Then, I pray you have enough money," Gilbert Guyot says, taking a bite from the hunk of bread that came with his broth.

"More than enough," the Englishman replies. "My master is rich enough to scour England of this traitorous filth."

"What of the mother and daughter?" the Frenchman enquires. "They will cost more, of course."

"Do not concern yourself with them," his co conspirator tells him. "There are special arrangements for them."

"No matter," Gilbert says. "If things do not go to plan, you can always call on Guyot, and his amazing tumblers."

*

Cardinal Thomas Wolsey has been dead for three long months, and the order of things, unbalanced by his epic fall, is beginning to right itself. Eustace Chapuys has kept his head down, waiting to see who emerges as Henry's most favoured councillors. Every pack of dogs must have a leader, and the vying for position has been amusing for him to observe. Who will sit at Henry's feet, and who will have to be content with the scraps from his table?

In his reports to the Emperor Charles, he draws word pictures of each man of influence, and gives his opinion as to their worth, and capabilities. He is also able to pass on messages from Katherine, having established a link between them both, via her dull little doctor.

The dour faced Spaniard, Vargas, arrives each week, takes Chapuys' pulse, feels his throat, and delivers, parrot-like, his mistresses memorised words. The man's accent is hard to place, and Chapuys tries to draw him out as to his family history. It is important to know about the people you are forced to trust. Vargas admits to being from a small village on the southern border with Portugal, which accounts for the accent, and says he was sent to Salamanca, as a small child, to study medicine, paid for by the benevolence of the Catholic church.

He is therefore their man. He must repay their investment, by going where he is told. The Bishop of Salamanca is a cousin, twice removed to Katherine, and has decided that his illustrious relative must have the best physician possible. The grim faced doctor is a relative newcomer to the court, and has been in England for less than three years.

"Will they ever let you go?" Eustace

Chapuys asks. The church owns the men she advances, and Rome can be a harsh mistress. Often, the church will demand half a man's salary, and a further fee to release his soul.

Dr. Vargas shrugs, He is indentured … that is to say, bonded to them for another five years, when he will be free to choose his own path. By then, he might have enough to buy his freedom, return to Spain, and open his own hospital.

"For the poor?" Chapuys asks, and a slight smile turns up the corner of the doctor's mouth. He shakes his head.

"No, of course not. It will be for those who can pay. There are already too many poor in this world," the doctor explains. "Why prolong their sad existences?" Wealthy men, it seems to him, deserve to live longer, and will they will pay most handsomely for his knowledge.

The ambassador listens, and believes he understands what it is that motivates the man. He is from a poor background, and fears living in poverty. This fear binds him to the queen, his benefactress, and will ensure his loyalty to her, until he has enough gold saved to fly the nest.

Each week Dr. Vargas comes and delivers the queen's carefully memorised words. Chapuys selects the relevant parts, and passes them on. He writes two reports each month, knowing that the blander one will be intercepted by English spies, secretly opened, and read, before forwarding.

The second, more informative document, he hand delivers to a certain Lombard banking house in the city. For a small fee, it is sent by courier, mixed in with their usual banking transactions. As an added precaution, Eustace Chapuys writes in a complicated code, that can only be deciphered by reference to a particular book in the Emperor's extensive library.

In this way, the ambassador has managed to avoid having to adopt any partisan relationships, and has kept on friendly terms with Norfolk, Suffolk, the young Earl of Surrey, and diverse members of the king's privy council.

Then this! Chapuys is outraged to be confronted, outside his very own house. He is stopped in the street, and accosted by a tall young man, who is armed with a fine sword, and looks as though he knows how to use it. The little Savoyard does not flinch, but stands his ground, his head barely reaching the man's chest, and glares.

"Have I the pleasure of addressing myself to the Honourable Ambassador from the Holy Roman Empire, Eustace Chapuys?" the rogue says, in good French, even though they actually know one another, if only by sight.

"You have," he says, answering the young gallant in the same language. "I am very busy, sir. What is your business, and why do you bar my passage?"

"Pardon my poor French, sir, but you do not have any English, I'm told. My master, Thomas Cromwell, requests the presence of your esteemed company at dinner tonight."

"You must thank my neighbour for me," Eustace Chapuys replies, "but I am far too busy. Inform him that I will call, and make my formal introductions, another time. Now, step aside, sir, and let me get about my business."

"Your house lies adjacent to his at Austin Friars, sir," the young man says. "These last few months, you and he have waved, in passing, and It seems churlish that you now refuse to eat a hearty dinner. My master will be most aggrieved."

Damn him to hell, Chapuys thinks. Cromwell is getting ever closer to the king, but has powerful enemies. It will not do to seem too friendly towards the low born fellow. He tries to conjure up an escape from his present predicament.

"Perhaps another night?" he suggests.

"Master Cromwell bids me say your presence will be most welcome… *tonight*. He has also asked Sir Thomas More, Stephen

Gardiner, and Charles Brandon, the Duke of Suffolk. It will be a merry night."

Merry indeed, Chapuys thinks. Both More and Brandon are against the annulment, but for differing reasons, and Gardiner, a distant relative of the king, is the coming man, and might soon have Henry's ear. He performs a speedy mental about face. Such men will make good allies to Queen Katherine's cause, and could even help bring the Boleyn clan down.

"Very well," he says. " I shall eat with your master, and his illustrious friends. At what hour?"

"My master's servants will come and light your way, sir," the young man says. "Until then…. Adieu." Chapuys bows, and resumes his passage. "Sir, beware of the dung!"

The ambassador steps deftly to one side, avoiding the steaming heap, and is almost at the front gate of York Place, the king's new courts, when he realises that the young man has warned him in English. He is angry at his stupid error, then smiles. It is not often that he is outwitted, and it is a lesson in humility.

A second, even more humbling, experience awaits him, once in the outer halls of Henry's court. The king is far too busy to grant him an interview today, being much preoccupied with a new pair of falcons.

Hunting before diplomacy, Chapuys decides, is the English way. So, he loiters about, passing the time of day with any who have a moment to chatter.

The king's main friends, and senior gentlemen of the court are off with the king, of course, but information is still there, waiting to be gathered. He has a few words with one of the king's physicians, and asks after Henry's state of health.

"Robust, sir," the doctor answers, dutifully. "If the rest of the court were as healthy as His Majesty, I should starve through lack of fees."

"God be thanked for His Majesty's fine constitution," Chapuys says, dropping a few coins into the man's hand. "Do mention to the king that I always wish his good health continues, my dear doctor."

"Charlatan," one of the musicians says, seeing the transaction. "His Majesty's continued good health is not due to that gentleman's ministrations." He holds a hand to his chin, and wags the fingers in a gesture that is meant to signify a grey beard and an age addled brain.

"Ah, Master Paisley, you have no time for the court physician then?" Chapuys offers a slight bow.

"They are all thieves," Paisley replies. "They charge huge fees for a few herbs."

"Is it then your soothing music that makes the king so sprightly?" Chapuys asks, with a sly wink. "Henry is only two years younger than I, yet he prances about like a thoroughbred Spanish stallion."

"I put it down to these fine fillies the king chases, Master Ambassador," Cuthbert Paisley replies. "Mistress Anne is a quite remarkable woman."

"Then they share a bed?" Eustace Chapuys smiles, and drops his voice. "Come, come, my dear Paisley. I have no time for half of a tale. Remind me, did I ever pay that gambling debt to you? Ten shillings, as I recall."

"Surely, was it not fifteen?"

"I believe it was," the ambassador agrees, loosening his purse. "You were saying?"

"The idle talk around the court is that poor Henry has yet to storm that particular castle keep, sir," the musician replies. "The lady is all for saying 'yes', then says 'oh no' at the very last moment. The king is left with nothing, and no-one, to warm his long, dark nights."

"What of her sister, Mary?" Chapuys has paid, and will demand every ounce of news in return. "She is willing enough to tend to his baser desires, I hear."

"Even Henry would not go so far,"

Cuthbert Paisley says, slightly shocked at the risqué suggestion. "To pay court to Lady Anne, whilst tupping her sister would be a dangerous game... even for as bold a king as our Hal."

"And yet...." Chapuys leaves the statement hanging in the cold morning air. He decides, instead, to follow another line of enquiry. "What do you hear about the attempt on Henry's life, the other week."

"Less than you, sir," Paisley says, trying to pull away. He is suddenly frightened by the overly knowledgeable Spanish envoy, and wishes to be elsewhere.

"Really? I hear that one of his young gallants was taken with a concealed dagger, ready to strike the king dead. Am I then informed wrongly?" Chapuys asks, ingenuously, and several small silver coins change hands again.

"I really cannot say," the young flautist, Herbert Paisley tells him. "Though a few faces have gone from court. Harry Cork, one of Cromwell's fellows, is no longer about the place, and the king's pet Jew banker, a dog called Mordecai, seems to have left England, never to return. Does that mean anything to you, sir?"

It does, but he holds his tongue. Eustace Chapuys has been piecing together small slivers of gossip, and is led to believe that a young devotee of Queen Katherine has been foolish enough to make an attempt on the king's life.

Harry Cork has not been influenced by the queen, who loves Henry still, despite his heavy handed attempts at having their marriage annulled. Rather, he was misled by a group of people loyal to Rome, and keen to see the king out of the way. The young man has failed, and another man has died in Henry's place.

The ambassador is given to understand, by his many Lombard banking friends, that the Jewish moneylender, Master Isaac ben Mordecai, is dead, and that suspicion has fallen, like a black cloud over Henry's court. This lack of trust has left Henry's coffers light, and his people are trying to lure the rich Italian banking families back, to trade in England once more. They are coming, of course, for a profit is a profit... but they come very slowly, and most grudgingly.

Harry Cork, a young gentleman of the court, was little more than a paid servant, working for both the royal household, and Thomas Cromwell. Prior to that, he is known to have been in the pay of the Duke of Northumberland, who is now in disgrace, and banished to the northern parts of England.

Young Cork is named as the old Jew's murderer, and his opportunistic attempt to slay the king has, mercifully, failed. Success would been the worst outcome for all concerned, and sides would have to have been taken. It would have meant a bloody civil war again. Eustace Chapuys knows that these things are never cut and dried, of course. There are always many possible outcomes.

With King Henry dead, Katherine is left as queen, and will return to the bosom of the Roman faith. Or so the assassins might reason. They are misguided, of course. With Henry gone, the great lords will form themselves into armed factions. Some for the old Plantagenets, some for Princess Mary, and some for themselves.

Norfolk, Suffolk, Northumberland, and the papist Pole family will rip England apart. The Boleyn faction, lacking any legal claim, will side with Lady Anne's uncle, the Duke of Norfolk, and form a powerful alliance.

Chapuys thinks that Charles Brandon, the wastrel Duke of Suffolk, lacks any real wealth, but could side with the northern barons, because of his hatred of Anne Boleyn. The lady distracts Henry from the hunt, gaming, and general roistering that usually bonds the two men. Friendship, especially with kings, is a fragile flower.

Harry Percy, Duke of Northumberland, allied to the lords who rule Cumberland, Lancashire and Cheshire could raise an army of fifty thousand men. With Suffolk by his side, they could match Norfolk and the Boleyns', man for man. The Poles have no real power, but their name still evokes memories of Plantagenet rule, and men would flock to their colours, if it meant a return to the true church. Add to this the sure knowledge that the irascible Scots, led by Lord Erskine, would sweep down from the North, to raid and plunder, and that the Welsh princes would want a true Tudor on the throne, and the mixture becomes ever more volatile.

Then, there are always the rich and powerful commoners to consider. Chapuys wonders just how well placed Thomas Cromwell is, and whether he might consider an unholy alliance with Sir Thomas, the new Lord Chancellor of England. No, he decides, Sir Thomas More and Cromwell, are oil and water. They cannot mix, and are thus lessened in their effectiveness. Austin Friars will never side with Utopia.

All this is mere conjecture, he says to himself. The king is still very much alive, and in firm control of his realm. Cork, whomsoever he worked for, has failed, and, no doubt, paid the price. He moves on, amiably chatting to any who will pass the time of day with him, and all the while, he wonders... just what is Thomas Cromwell up to?

"Ah, Will, there you are." Tom Cromwell says, looking up from the confusion of documents on his desk. "How has your morning been?"

Captain Will Draper, has been at Austin Friars for a little over three months, and is happy with his lot. He is trusted by Master Cromwell, has a good income, and a beautiful new wife. Miriam comes with her own small fortune, and a strong willed young brother called Moshe. The young men of the establishment call him Mush, and pretend that he and his sister are not of the Jewish faith, but have Spanish blood in their veins. This accounts for the dark good looks, and the odd dropped word in a foreign tongue. Few can speak either Spanish or Hebrew, so cannot tell the difference.

Jews are forbidden to live in England, on pain of death, so an elaborate set of forged documents exist, created by Master Cromwell, to safeguard the family. On occasion,, Miriam tries to thank him, but he deflects her with his usual dry humour, asking that, in return, she and her brother must not corrupt his saintly staff of young lawyers, and tough bodyguards, from their devoutly Christian beliefs. The young men of Austin Friars are notoriously absent from church, and count themselves to be whatever religion Cromwell might specify.

Will Draper reports that his master's dinner invitation has been, after a long verbal struggle, accepted by the new Spanish ambassador, and that the man speaks reasonably good English. He explains his simple subterfuge, and Tom Cromwell smiles at its simplicity.

"That was cruel of you, Will," he tells his special agent in these matters. "Though I suspected as much. A man who can speak Spanish, French, Latin, German, and Italian, yet knows not a word of English, stretches even my elastic credulity. I have it from one of Queen Katherine's cooks that he even chatters away to her pet Moors."

"Perhaps he is a secret Turk," Draper says, grinning at the idea. "They say that followers of the Prophet may have over a hundred wives. I wonder he has enough time to eat."

"Your wit will cut you yet," Cromwell replies. "Keep your silly stories for Rafe and the others. Make sure that four of our best men collect him. He is to be shown every honour due his station, and I want him overwhelmed with our warmth, our kindness, and our goodwill. Is that plain enough?"

"Yes, sir," Draper replies, then hesitates, as if wishing to speak.

"What is it?" Cromwell asks.

"I don't understand, sir. Chapuys is a Spaniard, and is for Queen Katherine. His master is the Holy Roman Emperor, and the nephew of Henry's wife. Why do we treat him so cordially? It would be better to starve him of knowledge, and make his stay in England as uncomfortable as possible, would it not?"

"That is one point of view," Thomas Cromwell says, "but not mine. I wish to hold out the olive branch of peace to him. See that Eustace Chapuys is well tended."

He could explain his thinking to the young soldier of fortune, but there are not enough hours in the day. Eustace Chapuys is a very clever man, and clever men always find ways to prosper in their allotted tasks. Close down one avenue of advance, and they will try harder to find another. No, Chapuys must be courted, not repulsed. In this way, Cromwell hopes to gain an unwitting ally in his quest to see Henry settled. The king is restless, and that is bad for England, and Europe too.

Cromwell is looking forward to the evening's meal, when he will entertain probably the most educated man in Christendom, Sir Thomas More. Stephen Gardiner, a lawyer priest, who is a close advisor to Henry will also attend, along with Ambassador Eustace Chapuys, and Charles Brandon, the Duke of Suffolk, a man of great influence, but little brains.

Brandon owes him a fortune, and is still the king's closest friend. Because of this, Suffolk is the perfect conduit to the king. He has but to whisper an idea into Brandon's empty head, and the man takes it as his own, and drops it into his next conversation with Henry. A few days later, and the king is espousing Cromwell's idea as his own, and asking for a candid opinion of it.

"A most excellent idea, sire," Cromwell usually says. "How do you think up such clever notions?"

Now, the lawyer, and Privy Council member, considers how he shall seat his guests for best effect, aware that they are like oil and water. It promises to be a heady mix. He thinks how Will Draper would deal with such men, and he smiles. The soldier of fortune is a shrewd enough fellow, but still lacks that concentration that makes a clever man into something more.

Draper has made two mistakes in but one short statement to Cromwell. First, he thinks Chapuys to be Spanish, whereas he is a Savoyard, and secondly … he refers to Katherine still as a queen.

"Small things, my boy," he mutters, "but it is the small things that get you hanged!"

3   A Meeting of Minds

Miriam Draper, *nee* Miriam ben Mordecai, is working on a delicate piece of embroidery which, once finished, will fetch a good price at the Flanders market. There is no need for her to work, as her inherited fortune, and Will's steady earnings, give them a comfortable life, but she is driven to make the most of herself. They have been married but a few of weeks, and she is already keen to move out of Austin Friars, and build a nest of her own.

"Master Cromwell will not like it." Will uses his master like a first line of defence, giving himself a moment to think.

"It will free up our room," Miriam replies, persuasively. "He will not mind you finding your own house, as long as you do not leave his service."

"Leave his service?" Will cannot comprehend such a foolish act. Cromwell has restored his lost savings through his connections with the Lombard banks, made him his senior secret agent, at a very good wage, and treats him like a favourite nephew. "That I shall never do, my love. We are his people... and I am pledged to his service for evermore."

"Goodness, but that is a long time," Miriam replies. "You are sworn to Master

Cromwell then… no matter what happens?"

"Yes, of course." Will answers, and sees that he has walked into his wife's little trap.

"Then we can look at houses close by?" Miriam asks, and smiles at him. "I don't see why not," Will says. "Looking can do no harm."

"There is a lease for sale, down by the river," she says, the very moment her husband relents. "James Whitcombe, the wool merchant, says we can have it, if we like."

"I see, and do we?" Will Draper asks. He is used to campaigning in Ireland, and sleeping under wet canvas. It will be nice to have their own home, of course, but it is not an essential to him. He lets Miriam have her head, because she has a fine eye for a bargain, and he trusts her judgement.

"Yes. It has a private jetty, four good bedrooms, servants quarters, and a block of stables. There is a neat little garden, and the mooring rights are included." Miriam replies. "We might be able to have a small rowing boat … or a skiff. Apart from the good sized upper bedrooms, there are several downstairs rooms, for entertaining our friends. The garden is modest, but very pleasant. We'd need two or three of servants though."

"That is hardly a problem, my love," Will tells her. "Master Cromwell's house is full of waifs and strays. I'm sure he'll let us employ a couple of them. Young Mark is a willing lad, and little Mary is a hard worker, and can bake."

"Then I am to give word?" Miriam asks.

"What, you haven't already?" her husband says, and smiles at her innocent face "That is rather slow of you, mistress."

"He would not let me sign," Miriam explained, blushing in annoyance. "He says you must guarantee the transaction. I explained that it was *my* fortune, but he said that, under English law, I am your property, and that the money is yours."

"Why yes, that is so, my sweet," Will says, grinning at her unease. "I had not thought. Perhaps I should have it locked up in Master Cromwell's strong room, and only give you a few silver shillings, as I see fit."

"You would not!" Miriam flares up, then sees he is merely mocking her. "You beast... you are too kind to treat me so."

"And I do not wish to wake up with your brother's knife at my throat," Will replies, thinking of the practicalities. He pulls her to him, and kisses her on the lips and forehead. "I trust you to make the right choices for us. I shall earn it, and you shall manage it."

"Truly?"

"Truly, my love. I have no head for

business, and trust you to invest wisely. You are the prettiest banker in all Christendom. Tell James Whitcomb that he had best deal with you, for if not, I shall call on him with Master Cromwell, and drive a very much harder bargain. What are his terms?"

"He will grant us a twenty year lease, at twenty pounds a year," Miriam explains.

"Will he indeed?" Draper smiles. Cromwell has taught him one thing, above all else. Never take the first offer. "Insist on thirty years, with an option for another twenty, and offer him fifteen pounds a year, payable quarterly, in advance."

"I will make the offer, and threaten him with your unpleasant company, my love," Miriam replies. In truth, she has already squeezed the man, and made an even better bargain, but does not wish her new husband to feel redundant. "Master Whitcomb shall give me the documents for your signature, and everyone shall be happy."

Will Draper adores his new wife beyond measure, and feels compelled to tell her the truth.

"You must make us a fine home, my dearest one, but keep it always in your mind that I am at Master Cromwell's bidding, night and day. I may not be home often, or for long."

"Then we must make the best of the few hours we do have," Miriam says, slipping the bolt on the door. "Hurry, my husband, duty demands your *immediate* action."

*

"*Afanya't, gos mandrós*," Eustace Chapuys loudly curses, and slams his fist on the table. Normally the most benign of masters, he is becoming annoyed with his servant. Luis Gomez, resentful of being labelled a lazy dog, pretends not to understand his master's instructions, and brings the wrong embroidered jacket from the huge travel chest.

Chapuys, pushes him aside, and finds what he is after in the box. It is a fine velvet doublet, with fashionably slit sleeves, and a soft, rabbit fur lining. He holds it up, and smacks the recalcitrant servant on the back of the head with his free hand, but gently.

"Oh, *señor!*" old Gomez gasps, and cowers back in a suitably frightened way. "Your father would never treat his poor Luis so. He never raised a hand to me."

"My late father was ever too soft with his servants," Chapuys grumbles. "Fetch me my hose, and the new hat, the one with the goose feathers. Tell me you cannot find it, Luis, and I will have you flogged through the streets of this perfidious city."

He will not, of course, and Luis Gomez, who has tended Chapuys since he was a child, knows it. Having started out as a stable boy with the father, Luis has guarded young Chapuys for many years, and grown old in his service. He usually knows just how much he can get away with, but tonight, Chapuys is nervous, and quick to lose patience. All because he must go to dinner with some English lords. It is not like him to be so easily flustered.

Gomez does not understand the finer points of the dinner invitation, so does not understand the inherent dangers. He is an old man now, and looks always for the quiet path. If only Eustace Chapuys would learn to settle down, and avoid meddling in things that need not concern him.

The ambassador is to dine with a table full of men, not unsympathetic to the queen's cause, and the host is Cromwell, one of the most dangerous men in England. Recently elevated to the Privy Council, the lawyer, a son of a blacksmith, is Henry's man in all things, and should not be promoting such a convivial meeting of minds. There is obviously some mischief about.

The ambassador feels rather like a mouse, invited to dine by the local cat. Whatever the motive is, at some point, the cat will unleash its sharpened claws. Chapuys has asked around about Cromwell, and finds the man to be quite unfathomable. Some men hate him, many more fear him, and quite a few say he is the most amiable of men, keeping the best table in London, and the finest cellar outside of Rome. He treats his friends well, and his enemies politely, is the oft used phrase. In short, the ambassador is about to dine with an enigma.

With Master Thomas Cromwell, it seems the knack is to know which you are to him. Friend, or foe. The man is a melting pot of opposites in Chapuys' estimation. His capacity for kindness and cruelty seem to exist in equal measure, and you are never sure which face he will show at any given moment.

"*Señor*," Luis Gomez calls, from the window. "There are men with blazing torches outside." Ambassador Eustace Chapuys sits the hat on his head, and descends to the lower floor. He orders a second servant to throw open the heavy, oaken, barred door. A slight young man with ginger hair and pointed beard steps forwards, and bows low.

"Ambassador Chapuys," Rafe Sadler says. "We are here to guide you to dinner. I am Rafe Sadler, Master Cromwell's chief law clerk. If you please?" Rafe bows once more, and waves for his three friends to take up their stations. Chapuys studies their faces, and finds himself missing the presence of Captain Will Draper.

"Where is the dangerous one tonight?"

he asks, out of simple curiosity. "The one who looks like Satan might cross the road to avoid him." Rafe smiles. Will Draper, the man who scares the very devil away with his doleful looks, according to Chapuys. It will make a good story around the Austin Friars breakfast table.

"Captain Draper does not do escort duty, sir," he tells the dapper Savoyard. "He is Master Cromwell's *special* agent. His task is to ensure my master's will be done."

"I see. Then I did well to accept his invitation," Chapuys replies, falling in with the torch lit party. The men hedge him in cosily.

"Indeed, sir," Richard Cromwell mutters, "else he might have tied you up in a sack, or rolled you in a rug. My uncle's dinners are famous throughout the city sir, and must not to be missed, I assure you. Even if you must be kidnapped."

"Wait. Who goes there?" One of their number calls, and produces a short, stout club from beneath his cloak. His companions move hands to hidden daggers, or sword hilts.

"My Lord Suffolk's men," comes the haughty reply. "Name yourselves, gentlemen, or face the worst."

"Cromwell's men, and we *are* the worst!" Rafe Sadler replies without sounding arrogant. "Walk with us, sirs. We are well met, my dear Lord Suffolk."

"Rafe Sadler, is that you?" Charles Brandon steps out of the shadow, slipping his wrist knife out of sight. He means to give Thomas Cromwell's favoured young man a hearty greeting, but he sees the ambassador, and gives him a cursory sort of a bow instead. "I could eat a horse."

"One is roasting, as we speak," Richard Cromwell calls back, and they all laugh, except Chapuys. He is not a lover of horse meat, and he fails to grasp the humour of it. "Don't worry, *Señor* Chapuys, it is only a small horse!"

*

Thomas Cromwell greets them at his great double fronted door, and ushers them into the main hall, where a huge log fire is warming every corner. A thin, sour faced man, is already seated at one end of the table, with a tall man, dressed as a cleric, but with rings on every finger, at his side. Charles Brandon is a little taken aback by their presence, but smiles and bows, politely to them both.

"My dear Lord Chancellor," he effuses, then to the other he says a terse "Gardiner." Sir Thomas More acknowledges Suffolk's polite greeting, and hopes he will not be seated next to him. He thinks Charles Brandon is the stupidest nobleman in Europe, and has no conversation worthy of any note. He sits opposite, whilst Cromwell takes great pains in putting Ambassador Chapuys next to the great man.

"Ah, Thomas," Cromwell says, heartily. "Have you met Eustace Chapuys, the Holy Roman Emperor's ambassador to the royal court? I see you have, if only in passing. Stephen, why so glum, have I put you in the wrong place? I thought sitting on More's left hand side would suit you rather well."

"A rose between two thorns," Brandon says, amiably. He is unaware of the unintended insult, and pulls a wicked looking knife from his sleeve. Chapuys is startled, until he realises it is for eating purposes only. The use of cutlery is still not widespread in England, and gentlemen often carry a sharp blade, in case the lamb is too tough to chew. "I see you still dress yourself up like a bloody priest, Master Gardiner."

"I am in holy orders, as Your Lordship knows only too well," Stephen Gardiner tells him. "I am a Doctor of Canon Law, sir."

"Oh, are you? I wondered, what with you being friendly with the Bulstrode girls. Margaret and Jane are such a lively pair… are they not, Master Gardiner?"

"You listen to idle gossip," Gardiner replies, tartly. He dislikes Brandon, who is an upstart, only placed in a high position because of his friendship with Henry. This vexes the cleric, who has claims, if only illegitimately, to being a distant cousin to the king. "There are those who are ever ready to do the devil's mischief."

"Gossip, you say? Not so, sir," Brandon says, raising his voice to include the whole company. "It was I who saw them leaving your company, my dear Stephen. They often perform their immoral arts *a deux*, I hear."

"Only hear, my Lord Suffolk?" Thomas Cromwell says, quietly, and Brandon sinks into silence. He is in debt to the blacksmith's boy for more than money, and has no wish to cause any lasting offence at his dinner table. "My information is that they give you a special price, such are your skills in that way."

"As you say, Master Cromwell." Suffolk reddens and bites his tongue. It is a sorry thing when an earl of England cannot jest about carnal matters when in the company of gentlemen, but he stays silent.

Ah, Chapuys thinks, that is why I am here. Master Cromwell wishes to display his hold over these men, the better to thwart any move before it is begun. Suffolk is under the man's thumb, and trembles at the slightest rebuff. Interesting. He wonders about the other guests. Servants appear, moving softly on house slippers, and serve up large bowls of a delicious smelling soup.

"My cook roasts the vegetables first, then stews them until they turn to liquid. At the last, he stirs in some herbs, and a ladle filled with sour cream." Cromwell seems delighted at his ability to impress with his knowledge of the culinary arts. "Though I ask, the man will not tell me which herbs he uses."

"Flog him," Stephen Gardiner says. "Or threaten to break him with the rack."

"I am not the Lord Chancellor," Cromwell replies, smiling at Thomas More. Chapuys senses a sudden undercurrent. "Is the soup to your liking, Thomas?"

"I prefer plainer fare," More snaps back. "I have simple tastes, often dining on bread, and a little watered down wine."

"That is why you lack friends," Cromwell replies. "And that is also why I have invited Ambassador Chapuys along tonight. He is the Holy Roman Emperor's man, and a close friend of the infamous Bishop of Rome."

"The Pope," More says. "You're discourtesy clearly shows you up as what you are, Cromwell."

"I say 'the King of England'," Cromwell retorts, "so why not 'the Bishop of Rome'?"

"You speak like a heretic," More replies, pushing his barely tasted bowl away.

"You must take care, Master Cromwell, for I am the king's man in matters of the church."

"As I now am in more secular ways," says Cromwell. "I hear you have taken up some good men this week past."

"Ah, I see. You wish to plead for them." More smiles now. He feels to be on safe ground. "One of them, John Vesey, was discovered with proscribed books in his house."

"Foolish of him," Cromwell says. "Proscribed by whom? Who has the power to forbid? He should have visited the king's excellent library, and read them with impunity. Henry, God bless him, condemns no man without knowing the facts."

"Yes, he has read Tyndale. The better to understand why we must destroy the Protestant influence." More is being watched attentively by the entire table. They have seen the trap, and are surprised when the Lord Chancellor blunders into it. "He has asked my opinion on points of church law, many times."

"And you were able to explain the heretical nature of Tyndale's writings?" Cromwell raises one eyebrow, and his voice assumes an inquisitive tone.

"Of course. I am the foremost expert in Europe on this wicked heresy." Stephen Gardiner gives a small cough, and taps More's ankle with his, but it is far too late. The Lord

Chancellor has allowed pride to blind him to the path Cromwell has picked out for him.

"What is the offence, sir," Cromwell asks, "possessing these books, or reading them?"

"Both, of course."

"Then both you, and His Majesty, stand accused," Cromwell tells him. "For you both own to having these books in your possession, and have read them thoroughly."

"We must, to determine the heresy," More replies, and almost bites his tongue at his folly. He has allowed Thomas Cromwell to win an easy victory.

"Then the men you have arrested may not be heretics at all, but simple people who wish only to discover if Tyndale is a true heretic," Cromwell says, holding his splayed hands out to his guests, as if in supplication. "They are guilty only of curiosity. A curiosity they share with both yourself, and the king."

"It is not their place to be curious." More is on the defensive, but will concede nothing to this upstart lawyer. "The church forbids…"

"What about you, my Lord Suffolk… have you read Master Tyndale's notorious tomes?" Cromwell turns his stare onto Charles Brandon.

"Well, yes. The writings are freely available around the court," he replies, "but I found his arguments to be … ill founded."

"Thank God," Chapuys tells him, "for that means you are not a heretic, My Lord. I too have read many such tracts, from Martin Luther to William Tyndale, and am not at all persuaded by them. This, I assume, absolves me of heresy too?" The several guests turn and look at the man in surprise, for he has spoken to them in a very passable English.

"You are a fast learner, Ambassador Chapuys," Cromwell says, grinning. "I too have read Tyndale. Stephen, I know, has, for he borrowed my copy. I deduce from this that we have all read the good man's writings, and remain resolutely untainted by the devil."

"The sin is in believing," More says. "They hide the books to evade capture, and they evade capture, because they have adopted heretical views."

"Then if any of these men recant, and swear they are faithful to Mother Church, you will let them go free?" Cromwell asks, just as the next course, duck, roasted and served with a poached pear sauce, arrives.

"Of course," More says, sniffing at the fragrant dish set before him. "They must recant, and mean it. Then they will go free."

"And how will you know they mean it?" Eustace Chapuys is beginning to enjoy the cut and thrust. "Who can tell what is in a man's heart, let alone his mind?"

"You speak wisely," Sir Thomas More tells him. "They will be put to the question, of course. Under duress, a man will tell the truth."

"Or lie, to stop the pain of being broken," Thomas Cromwell says, coldly. "You cannot torture a man to confirm the 'truth' you wish to hear. It is despicable."

"You call me despicable? My actions will save this country from heresy," More replies, hotly. "Men will not return to the wrongful path, if they fear the dreadful consequences. Yet, if they insist on holding to their belief in this abominable new English bible, they are condemned out of their own mouths."

"You will torture the innocent, and burn those you deem to be guilty?" Cromwell shakes his head in disbelief. "The king will hear of this, and he will not allow it."

"Really?" More gives his host a crooked smile. "Henry does not want to split from Rome. He fears for his immortal soul. Once he is reconciled with Pope Clement, his annulment can be looked at once more. That is all the king desires."

"Can it?" Chapuys asks, startled at so frank a statement.

"It can," the Lord Chancellor replies, once more feeling he is back on solid ground. "Queen Katherine cannot provide a male heir.

It is her duty to step aside, and enter a nunnery. There are many precedents to support this action, I assure you. Henry must have a new, younger queen."

"*La Boleyn?*" the ambassador says.

"Lady Anne is but a passing frivolity," Sir Thomas More tells him, confidently. "She will surrender that which the king wants of her, as did her sister Mary, before her. He will lose interest after a few weeks, and look abroad for a new consort."

"I see you have it all planned out," Cromwell says, biting into his duck. "May I ask the name of the king's future bride?"

"That is down to diplomacy," More explains. "He must seek out an alliance with either France, or the Emperor Charles. I make no mystery of where my aims lie, Ambassador Chapuys. Your master is dear to Henry, and will make a good ally."

In one sentence, Sir Thomas More has stated his intent to marry England to the Holy Roman Empire, the moment Queen Katherine is gone. Chapuys' breath is taken away by the audacious way the proposal has been put to him, in front of Cromwell and the others.

Then he realises why. Charles Brandon, Duke of Suffolk, is Henry's best friend, and can be relied on to convey the gist of the conversation back to his king. Henry will be tempted, and the Emperor Charles might well consider substituting one Spanish princess for another, more fertile one.

All that would remain, is for the queen to retire to holy orders, refute her royal claims, and abandon her daughter Mary to the king's tender mercy. Mary will be set aside, declared bastard, and her claims to the throne ignored. It is an attractive, insidious and deeply wicked idea, which Eustace Chapuys will fight with all his ability. He understands that there is a long, difficult diplomatic battle to be fought, and prepares himself for the struggle to preserve the current *status quo*. For the moment, he must reply to More in as ambiguous a way as possible. Diplomacy is the art of saying nothing, cleverly.

"My dear Sir Thomas…" he starts.

There is a sudden, insistent pounding on the front door, and a loud voice booms out.

"Open up… in the king's name!"

4   The Strange Alliance

Thomas Cromwell raises a hand, stilling the disquiet that has sprung up. There is another loud knocking, and both Suffolk and Gardiner start to rise to their feet, casting nervous glances at the door. After a few moments, Rafe Sadler appears. He is grinning mischievously.

"There are two young gentlemen demanding entry, Master Cromwell. They are in their cups, and can hardly stand. They wish to be fed and watered, and claim this to be the most hospitable eating house in all of London."

"Damned impertinence!" Sir Thomas More stands, and looks as if he is about to issue orders for their immediate expulsion.

"At least it is not the king's men, come to burn my English bible," Thomas Cromwell says, calmly waving More back into his chair. "Who is it, Rafe?"

"Young Henry Howard, the Earl of Surrey, and Master Richard Rich, sir."

Thomas Cromwell raises an eyebrow. Richard Rich, a rising young lawyer, and the Duke of Norfolk's fifteen year old son and heir, are not noted as friends, and he is intrigued enough by this development to allow them entry. Besides, he thinks, Tom More hates the dissolute young Earl of Surrey with a vengeance, and it will vex the wretched man to share his meal with him.

"Show them in, Rafe," Cromwell says, and Rafe is taken aback, having expected them to receive a curt dismissal.

"A fine evening, Master Cromwell," Richard Rich says, staggering in, arm in arm with Surrey. "You know Henry Howard, I believe?"

"My Lord Surrey," Cromwell replies, and elbows More, who has refused to bow to the boy, as is his due. "Is your father keeping well?"

"The old bastard is as fit as a fighting cock," the young earl pronounces, so bitterly that Suffolk almost gags as he stops himself from laughing aloud. "He has installed a powdered strumpet in the family home, and thrown my dear ageing mother out into the wilderness. Though, I must confess, Master Cromwell, his mistress is a rather comely little wench, and seems to saddle up well enough."

"Have you not found out for sure yet?" Master Rich says, and laughs at his own ribald remark. It is the humour of young rakes, and Richard Rich is desperate to be accepted amongst the court's younger bucks. Henry Howard, though only just fifteen, is wealthier than them all, so is their acknowledged leader. They fawn over his every word, and hang on his every gesture, no matter how drunk he is, or how empty headed he sounds.

Surrey guffaws at Rich's coarseness, and flops into the chair vacated by Stephen Gardiner. He sees the abandoned duck, and grabs at it, eating greedily. Thomas Cromwell swiftly rearranges the seating order, and puts the ambassador as far away from the two intoxicated rowdies as he can.

The level of conversation changes. More is now sullen, and annoyed at being displaced by a callow fifteen year old, who makes no bones about his violent dislike of the parsimonious Lord Chancellor.

"Damn me, More," young Surrey sniggers. "The food is much better than the filthy slop you serve. My father says you make a virtue of parsimony, and can count your loose change without removing it from the purse. I hear you have taken to breaking men's bones over this new Tyndale book. Is it true that anyone who reads it, is now declared to be a heretic?"

"We have been over this muddy ground already, My Lord Surrey," Cromwell tells the young drunkard, "and it seems quite clear that there are certain exclusions to the rule."

"I pay no mind to it," Surrey replies. "Reading never quite took with me, d'ya see? I leave it to mealy mouthed preachers, and stick dry scholars to write for me. A *real* gentleman can have too much education, can't he Dick?"

Richard Rich winces at the use of the diminutive, but does not correct his new friend. If the price of entry to the boy's clique is to be known as 'Dick Rich', then so be it. He refrains from mentioning his own excellent education to Surrey, which has left him with a fine, though devious, legal mind.

"Then these rumours are true, Master Cromwell?" he asks, glancing at Sir Thomas More.

"That the Lord Chancellor is to begin torturing free men to see what they are thinking?" Cromwell replies, raising his voice over Surrey's drunken chattering. "I fear so, my young friend. I suggest you go home tonight, and destroy anything in your library that might offend him."

"You go too far, sir," More mutters, angrily.

"I pray *you* do not," Cromwell replies, smiling thinly. "I have many friends, throughout Europe, who have read the various translations of William Tyndale."

"His books are banned," Sir Thomas insists. "What will it take to get it through your thick blacksmith's skull? To even possess a single copy, is an act of high treason."

"Treason?" Cromwell asks. "Against whom, sir ... King Henry, or England?"

"They are one and the same in this

matter," More tells him, smugly. "My mind, and Henry's, are one and the same when we consider the filth that Tyndale spews out."

"Save your breath, Thomas," Cromwell snaps. "You will find no friends under my roof, and no supporters of your twisted theological outpourings!"

Chapuys consoles himself that, though the evening is now spoiled, he has a better idea of English politics than he had before the soup arrived. Despite their outward show of open handed fairness, the English are complex, and have more skins than an onion. He finds it strange that men of such opposing views, can still like, and even admire one another.

Cromwell and More strut around like two prize fighting cocks, each looking for an opening, but there is more to this than meets the eye, the ambassador thinks. The Lord Chancellor is a most learned man, and has a set of principles that he will not abandon, whereas Thomas Cromwell is the new cockerel in the pit, ready and willing to change his mind, as easily as he would change his coat.

Several more courses follow, each consumed with varying degrees of gusto, and the talk turns from contentious religious texts, to cock fighting, bear baiting, and card games.

"I saw Sir Peter Hawbrey wager ten pounds on which way a falcon would turn last week," Henry Howard declares, wiping his mouth on his sleeve. "I was there, and the king called him an addle pated fool, for we all know the bird well, and have seen it *stoop* often."

"Fascinating," Cromwell mutters. "I trust he learned his lesson?"

"Hardly," Surrey says. "I took another twenty off him playing '*Find the Lady*'. He has as much sense as a head louse!"

"If that," Cromwell guesses. "How is your dear mother , the Duchess Elizabeth, taking her enforced separation?"

"No idea," young Howard replies. "I haven't seen her since Christmastide. She is a frightful old bore over money, lectures me like she was a priest, and resents father having a little fun."

Cromwell makes a mental note to look into the matter, and ensure that the discarded Duchess of Norfolk is provided for. Rafe can arrange for a small pension, until Norfolk takes her back. She is yet another cousin of the Tudors, and must not be left to starve, whilst old Norfolk dallies with a painted whore. Henry will not approve of his actions, for it only enflames an already contentious state of affairs. The putting off of wives is a serious business, and one better left to kings.

At last, the gargantuan meal comes to an end, and the company make ready to depart. Cromwell has learned a little about Chapuys, and has used the occasion to demonstrate Sir Thomas More's callous disregard of human life. He hopes the lesson has not been wasted on the broader company, and that they might oppose so radical a solution as torture to find the truth.

The Lord Chancellor breaks away from the main company, and relieves himself against the stable wall. Cromwell is suddenly beside him.

"My apologies, Tom," he says. "Had you requested it, I would have found you a golden chamber pot to piss in." It is a direct reference to Thomas More's famous book 'Utopia', which has such silly ideas within its pages.

"I see you have read my book," More sneers. "Then you will see I recommend golden fetters for those who abuse their perfect society. Mock my writing, if you will, Cromwell, but it is printed in Latin. Unambiguous Latin. The language is that of Holy Mother Church. The language of prayer, and scriptures."

"Unreadable by the common man," Cromwell replies. "Do you need one of my men to light your way back to Utopia?"

"I am the light, and the way, our lord said," More snarls. "I need nothing from you, sir. Grow as powerful as you might, but beware the flames of hell. You are a heretic, Thomas, and I will not stand for it."

"Then we must fight," Cromwell sighs. "A pity, for I so enjoy your company."

"My God must come before my friendship for you," More concludes. "Take care."

More is a dangerous zealot, and will put the world to the stake, if it dares disagree with his narrow minded view of Christianity. Why Henry has raised him to high office is a mystery, but it is so, and must be dealt with. Cromwell will slowly undermine the Lord Chancellor, removing a spade full of sand here and there, until his strong walls crumble. It is a bad day that sees Englishmen being tortured over what they read.

Eustace Chapuys has but a short distance to walk. He puts on his cloak, and is almost out of the door, when he is called back by Rafe, who has found his splendid new hat abandoned in the cloakroom. The gentlemen in the company compliment him on his flamboyant style, and Suffolk examines the item, before handing it to Rich who passes it on, until each man has admired the beautiful feathered cap.

The ambassador, smiles and nods, realising that he is being mocked, but only in a friendly way. Overall, the dinner has been an enjoyable affair, and the company has been jovial, interesting, and often a little bawdy. He is pleased that there were no ladies present to hear the ribald comments, and talk of fornication, and mightily sated lust.

He is back in his own house, and undressing, when his old servant ambles in without knocking. There is a fold of parchment in Luis' right hand, and the new hat is in his left. He holds both up for inspection by his master.

"This was tucked into the hat's lining, *Señor* Eustace," he explains, and hands it over to his master. Chapuys is puzzled. Inside his hat? Placed there by one of his fellow diners, or by one of Cromwell's servants, he wonders?

The paper is of a fine quality. The writing is small, neatly scripted, and to the point.

There is a plot made. It is to murder Katherine, her daughter Princess Mary, and many of her closest followers. Look to Thomas Cromwell, sir, and be ever on your guard.

A Well Wisher.

Chapuys is used to intrigue, and is not unduly shocked by the contents of the note. He would be more surprised if there were not plots, and counter plots, surrounding the queen. It simply saddens him that what was meant to be a genial dinner has provided the means for someone to pass on so dangerous a warning.

He has been Katherine's loyal supporter since his appointment, and has been on constant watch, ensuring her safety to the best of his abilities. The two huge Moroccan bodyguards never leave her side during daylight hours, and her best friend, and loyal companion, Maria Salinas, shares her nights.

"Look to Thomas Cromwell," he mutters, then smiles as he unravels the true meaning. "Luis, stop standing there like a lout, and fetch my cloak again, and a torch."

"You are going out again?"Luis asks.

"Yes, you fool," Chapuys snaps. "Why else would I need my damned cloak?"

"Then I shall come with you," old Luis says. "You are not safe left to your own devices."

"I am only going next door," Chapuys tells him.

"Then I will bring a knife, and a stout cudgel," Luis tells his master. "For that can only mean trouble!"

*

Rafe Sadler is on his rounds, checking window catches and extinguishing candles, when there is an insistent knocking at the door. He shakes his head in disgust, sure it will be Henry Howard, covered in vomit, and unable to find a boat to take him home. He calls out, begging a moment, and fetches a solid looking club from the cloakroom. He works for Cromwell, and because of that, one never knows who might be knocking on the door in the dark of the night.

As he unbolts the door, Will Draper appears on the staircase, half dressed, and with a business-like looking dagger clenched in his right fist. The sudden late visit has also aroused his curiosity.

"Have a care, Rafe," he whispers.

"Ambassador Chapuys!" Rafe steps back, and the little Savoyard steps in, out of the drizzle that has just started. He gestures for his servant to wait outside, in the covered porch, with the blazing torch.

"Forgive my unquestionably bad manners, Master Sadler, but I must speak with Thomas Cromwell… at once."

"The master is in his bed," Will Draper says.

"Lying is a sin, Will," Cromwell says, emerging from his library. "My dear Eustace, I hoped you might pay me a further call… but so soon?"

"I received this," Chapuys says, slipping into Latin. "A casual reader might suspect you to be a murderer."

"Not you though?" Cromwell replies. His Latin is better than the ambassadors. "I respect your wish for secrecy, but Rafe speaks Latin well, and Captain Draper is the bastard son of a bishop."

"My God," Chapuys gasps, and reverts to English. "You are having one of these English jokes with me... yes?"

"Yes," Cromwell replies. "He was only a priest. Now, come into my library, and we will talk. Rafe, bring us some good wine, and then make sure we are not disturbed."

Chapuys takes the offered chair, and admires the well stocked library. He has an idea of the cost of so many books, and guesses that Cromwell is already a very rich man.

"You like books, I see."

"Knowledge is power," Thomas Cromwell says with a casual shrug. "How was the note delivered to you?"

"My old servant, Luis, found it tucked into my new hat," Chapuys explains. "It can only have been put there during my visit to your home."

"Has it occurred to you that I might be the leader of this prospective plot, sir?"

"No, not really," Chapuys says. "It says that I should look *to* Thomas Cromwell. Not look '*at*' him, you see. And an accuser would not bother to use your given name. He would say something like... 'Look at Cromwell', or 'Beware of him'. The message is clear to me. My unknown friend is advising me to look to you… for help."

"Have you no inkling as to the note's author?" Cromwell is going over the evening, wondering when the warning was put in place, and can think of only one chance.

"I have not," the ambassador replies. "My hat was out of sight from my arrival, until my departure."

"It would be in the cloakroom, by the side door," Cromwell explains. "The room is in plain sight of my servants, and a man would be foolish to try to slip in without detection. I think it was put in your hat as you left. Who handled the hat?"

"Everyone," Eustace Chapuys says, and his shoulders slump. "I think every guest touched it as it was admired, and several of the servants too."

"I can assure you, it was none of my people who placed the note," Cromwell tells him. He makes a quick calculation. Suffolk, Surrey, More, Gardiner and Rich each handled the hat, and each could have slipped the fold of parchment into the hat's lining.

"Then who?"

"You are missing the point, my dear Eustace," Thomas Cromwell explains. "We have been warned of a plot, and must uncover it. The death of the queen, other than by natural means, would be a disaster for England."

"Then my secret friend was right. I must look to Thomas Cromwell for help. I cannot protect Her Majesty with my slender resources. Will you join with me, *Señor*?"

"Thomas... or Cromwell will do," Cromwell says. "Yes, I must. If Queen Katherine's life is at risk, we must save it, and uncover the plotters."

"The queen has many loving friends," Chapuys says, diplomatically, "but also many enemies. Where shall we start, Thomas?"

Cromwell understands all about plots, both real, and imagined. They all have points in common. To have a plot, you must have plotters. Usually several come together, in the hope of strengthening their hands, but this is a fallacy.

The more plotters there are, the more likely that there will be a Judas amongst them. A man who, enticed by the intrigue, suddenly realises the danger. To murder a queen is treason, and to even think about it is likely to lead to the block. So he tells what he knows.

The plot unravels quickly, heads roll, and rewards are given to the turncoat plotter. Cromwell knows this, but is still uneasy about some things. Why warn Chapuys, instead of himself, directly? Why write in French, and why conceal their name? An anonymous man cannot be rewarded.

"The note warns that the queen's

followers are to be killed too," Cromwell says, at last. "The plotters fear them, and want them out of the way. The king is innocent in this matter, for he has no need of intrigue. One word from his lips, and a dozen Dukes would fall over themselves to kill his enemies."

"He would do this?" Chapuys asks.

"No. He believes in the due process of the law. It never fails to find in his favour. His enemies would be charged, found guilty in a court of law, and legally executed."

"Then where do we start?" the ambassador asks a second time.

"I think we must set a hound on the trail of these would be queen killers, and sniff them out."

"Ah, I see," Chapuys nods his understanding. "Your man, Draper. I have heard certain stories about him. Is he really so dangerous?"

"He is clever, and loyal," Cromwell replies. "He can read motives, and has a nose for seeking out wrongdoers. We must give him what we have, and let him run off his leash."

"Does he love the queen?"

"Really, Eustace!" Cromwell smiles. "We all love the queen... whoever she may be."

"A lawyer's answer."

"I *am* a lawyer," says Thomas Cromwell. "Let me call Captain Draper in, and appraise him of the situation."

Will Draper comes at once. He is now fully dressed, and is expecting orders. The sudden appearance of the Spanish ambassador must mean trouble, and that is what he is paid for. He takes the note, and reads it carefully.

"The writing is that of a well educated man, sir," he tells Cromwell. "His French is excellent. The inference is that Master Chapuys is to seek your aid. The writer knows you, and believes you will resolve the matter."

"Is it a hoax?" Chapuys asks, hopefully. Will Draper shakes his head. Apart from the fact that it is in too bad a taste to be faked, the note hits upon a truth that even Cromwell does not yet know.

"It speaks of the queen's followers, sir," he tells Cromwell. "I was sifting through reports this afternoon, and saw that Sir Jeremy Clayton died in a hunting accident this morning."

"Ah," Cromwell says, and sighs. He turns to Chapuys, and explains the meaning of this. "Sir Jeremy is known to be a supporter of Katherine. He has spoken out in parliament about the annulment, and is close kin to the Pole family."

The Poles are of Plantagenet descent, and are thought to have a very strong claim to the throne. They have kept their heads down for decades, hoping that the Tudors do not decide to nullify their claim with the sharp edge of the axe. If the king is forced to keep Katherine, they would only grow in power.

"These Poles might threaten the position of my Lord Norfolk," Chapuys says. "Was it not his brutish son who dined here earlier?"

"Uninvited, I assure you," Cromwell replies. "Besides, why would young Howard reveal a plot that can only benefit his family? The Howard clan hate the Poles, and wish them nothing but harm. They will be rejoicing at poor Clayton's sudden demise."

"We should investigate the death, sir," Draper advises his master. "If only to confirm it as an accident. His estate is only a couple of hours ride from here."

"It is my wish that you look into the matter for me, Will," the lawyer says. "Smell out who is involved, and end their plotting."

"Am I to compile a list of the guilty, so they might be tried?" Draper asks. Knowing something is not the same as proof, and Will wonders what evidence might exist, beyond mere word of mouth.

"You must act as you see fit," Cromwell replies. "If the life of the queen, Princess Mary, or any of her friends is threatened, protect them... to the best of your ability."

"You are condoning murder,

Cromwell," Chapuys mutters to him in Spanish.

"I am saving your queen's life," Cromwell snaps back, in equally good Spanish. "Are we agreed on this alliance, or not, sir?"

Eustace Chapuys has no choice. He is committed to protecting his queen. He holds out a hand, and clasps Cromwell's tightly.

"To the death!" he says, melodramatically.

"Oh, surely not, Eustace," Cromwell replies. "Let me pour you some more of this rather excellent wine. We have much to discuss."

"You must forgive me if I seem a little slow," Chapuys apologises, "for I am not used to such crepuscular activities, sir."

Cromwell smiles. Most of his business is conducted at unholy hours, often before dawn with some frightened informant, or after midnight in conversation with one of his murkier agents.

"I too am tired," he says, "but this insidious plot must be tackled at once. Can you stay awake for another hour or two, my friend?"

"My servant is waiting outside." It is not an excuse, but a sudden remembrance. The old man will be frozen half to death, and Chapuys to blame for it.

"I will have Rafe take old Luis to the kitchens, and feed him well, Eustace," Tom Cromwell says. Then adds mischievously, "He is overly fond of our lentil soup."

Chapuys wonders if Cromwell has spoken without thought, or is trying to show the ambassador the extent of his reach, and the depth of his low born cleverness.

5   The Necropractor

Adolphus Theophrasus is part Greek on his father's side, and part Jewish through his mother's long bloodline. This manifests itself by giving him an olive skinned, and exotic appearance; ideal for his chosen profession, where patients choose a doctor for his ostentation, rather than his innate medical skill. He has a medical practice, situated in a small house near to London Bridge, and is much sought after by those rich idlers who enjoy following the latest trends. Some call him a quack, but others claim he is the greatest anatomist since Leonardo Da Vinci learned his trade on the battle fields of Italy. He is the most knowledgeable physician in London, but his dubious family tree leaves him open to attack.

The Lord Chancellor's officers are on to him, and would like to expel him from England, on the grounds that he has Jewish blood in his veins, but find they cannot. It seems that, on enquiry, the good doctor's closest blood relatives are from a small town in the depths of rural Cornwall; a fact attested to, and confirmed by documents uncovered by some of Thomas Cromwell's legal people. They are forgeries, of course, but of such fine quality that they surpass the originals in many ways.

"I find myself to be irrefutably English, thanks to your master," the doctor tells Will. "A Cornishman, in fact. So, tell me, young master, what I can do to help you?"

Will Draper tells him, and watches as the colour drains from the man's fleshy face. He wrings his hands together, and then tugs at his voluminously cultivated beard.

"Are you utterly mad?" he says to the tall young man who has come to see him. "What you suggest is against the law. I believe the penalty, as for so many crimes, is death by hanging. Besides, the family will never allow it."

"The family will not know about it," Will Draper assures him. "We will visit the family vault, and examine the body in secret."

"I might have to perform a full necropsy on the man," the doctor explains. "There will be scars. Someone will know, if they ever uncover the tomb again."

"Why would they do that?" Will Draper is toying with a heavy purse hanging at his belt. "We open the tomb secretly, examine the corpse, and close it up again. All Master Cromwell needs to know, my dear doctor, is what really caused the poor man's untimely death. There is some doubt, and Cromwell wishes to get to the truth of things."

"A riding accident, you say?"

Adolphus Theophrasus shakes his head. It is a common enough cause of injury and death amongst his better off patients. The gentlemen of England seem to think it best to be roaring drunk before climbing on a horse. "Almost certain to be a broken neck... which tells you absolutely nothing, my friend. I might be taking your bag of silver for nought. It also occurs to me that I might also end up swinging on a very high gallows. You Englishmen are a pious lot, and not adverse to stringing up a suspected Christ killer. Even half a Jew is unwelcome on these shores!"

"My master is a very powerful man," Will says. "He will not allow anything to happen to either of us. What say you, Doctor Adolphus? Twenty pounds is enough money to buy the lease of this house for you."

"Only a mad man would do such a thing."

"Twenty five pounds then?" Will says.

*

"I must be mad," the middle aged physician grumbles, as he approaches the stone clad mausoleum of the Clayton family. "We are dealing with dark forces, young man. What if the body is protected with strong spells, or haunted by a dybbuk, or a daemon?"

"I do not believe in magic spells,

daemons, ghosts, boggarts, or hobgoblins," Captain Will Draper mutters. "As for a dybbuk … I neither know, nor care, what one is."

"A restless ghost, waiting to invade the living body of the unwary," the doctor explains. "It binds itself to the soul, twists itself about your mind, and causes madness."

"Your knowledge fascinates me, sir." Draper says, hiding his annoyance. It is still daylight, and there is a small chance of detection, but it is a chance he must take if his mission is to be successful. The doctor will need as much light as possible for his grisly work. "If an apparition wishes to spring up, I will run it through with my blade, or serve it with one of Master Cromwell's famous legal papers. Now, for God's sake, sir … hurry on!"

The door is barred, but not locked. Will wonders at this strange need to imprison the dead, as if they might rise from their cold beds, and walk about in the cold night air. He eases the wooden bar up, and pushes open the doors. They creak, and the sound causes him to look about him. There is no-one to hear.

He enters, and looks around. There are two small, stained glass windows in the end wall, and the interior is well lit with the cold, late afternoon sun. Will beckons to Adolphus Theophrasus, urging him to follow in his footsteps. The man hesitates on the threshold, then steps inside the chill room.

The doctor is eager to be done with the morbid task, and gone. He touches the magic amulet hanging at his throat, crosses to the newest coffin, and tries to open the lid. It does not yield, and he casts a doleful glance at Will Draper, who draws a knife from his belt. The soldier of fortune forces it under the edge of the lid, and levers the coffin top up, and off. Sir Jeremy stares up at them, with an astonished look on his face. Will fancies that it is a look of surprise, as if he does not know he is dead yet.

"Is he stiff?" Will asks. He has seen many dead men on the field of battle, or killed in the heat of the moment, but never one formally laid out, and ready for his place in heaven.

"No. The corpse stiffens at death, but the rigor mortis passes after a goodly number of hours. I do not understand why, but think it is the moment the soul finally departs. Now, hold your tongue, young fellow, and let me get on with the business in hand. I do not wish to be caught here by some passing yokel."

The doctor has practiced anatomy in both Italy and France, where it is not so heavily proscribed, and he makes a thorough external examination of the body first. Will stands by, patiently, waiting for him to produce a sharp knife, or a saw, and begin his gruesome task.

He is surprised when the doctor makes an exclamation, and beckons him forward. The older man points to the dead man's pale face, and smiles.

"There… do you see?" he asks. "The evidence cannot be any clearer, my friend!"

*

"*Sine ut mortui requiescere*," Eustace Chapuys intones in a grave voice. *Let the dead rest.* It is a wise injunction, and should be obeyed, without question. He is completely horrified at what Will Draper has done. To defile the resting place of the dead is a mortal sin, he tells Tom Cromwell, and he shall surely burn in the fiery pits of Hell for it.

"Yes, yes, Master Chapuys," Thomas Cromwell says, somewhat testily. "We will deal with Captain Draper's immortal soul at a future date, my dear friend. I shall buy it back from Old Hob himself. Tell us, Will, what is the verdict?"

"Murder, sir," Will says, perching on the edge of the great oak breakfast table. Chapuys has been invited to supper, and the seats are filled with Cromwell's young men, all eager to hear of his latest adventure.

"On whose word?" Cromwell, ever the lawyer, asks. "Or did he have a dagger sticking in his heart?"

"Nothing so crude, sir," Will explains. "The doctor was able to deduce the cause of death in a matter of minutes. You see, Clayton had a broken nose."

"The bone in his nose was broken?" Eustace Chapuys is mystified. Surely, he thinks, this can happen when you take a tumble from your horse.

"No, sir." Will Draper marshals his thoughts, and imparts knowledge he was unaware of, until that afternoon. He raises a finger and presses it to his own nose. "What you call the nose bone is but a piece of gristle. The doctor says its purpose is to keep the nostrils open, so we may breath."

"And Clayton's was broken?" Cromwell says. "Was it not as a result of the sudden fall?"

"No, it was not," Will replies. "Sir Jeremy fell backwards from his mount. His horse must have been badly startled by something ... or someone ... and reared up. He landed, heavily, on his back, as attested to by the cut to the rear of his head. Doctor Theophrasus spoke of how blood settles if the body lies in one position too long, and there were dark bruises on the man's back and buttocks. The nose came after the initial fall. The dead man was on his back, stunned, when he was smothered."

The table is silent in anticipation. A

dozen pairs of eyes are now fixed on Will Draper, as he demonstrates murder by placing his hand over Rafe Sadler's face.

"A strong, gauntleted, hand driven over the mouth and nose… so." Rafe flinches. "The upward force breaks the gristle, and closes the airways. The heel of the hand crushes firmly down, over the mouth, causing marks in the mouth where the teeth press into the soft flesh. Death, my doctor tells me, comes in seconds."

"My God," Chapuys is horrified. "How can he be so sure of this?"

"The great force exerted pushes the lip down onto the teeth," Will tells them again. "This results in bruising to the inside of the lip. It is a clear indication of death by smothering."

"You saw this for yourself, Will?" Rafe, not usually the squeamish sort, shudders at the thought of his friend rummaging around in a damp crypt, surrounded by the dead.

"The good doctor peeled back the upper lip," Will Draper replies. "I saw it with my own eyes."

Rafe wants to ask more questions, but one of the boys is at the door, beckoning for him to come outside. He crosses the room, and follows him out.

"Is there any clue at all, as to how the crime was committed?" Chapuys is fascinated, but cannot see how this news benefits them, other than confirming that a plot exists.

"I spoke to the wife, and other members of the household," Will replies. "She tells me that her husband is out of favour in the court, thanks to a speech he made, which disgruntled the king. So, they went to stay in their country house at Christmastide, and they decided to stay on."

"A wise move," Cromwell says, ushering them into his library, where a good fire has been set by Miriam Draper. "Sir Jeremy Clayton was foolish enough to make a disparaging comment about Lady Anne Boleyn, likening her to the Whore of Babylon, and she has a very long, very spiteful, memory."

"They gave a few dinners, and tried to keep themselves to themselves," Will Draper continues, "but it was his birthday, and they decided to celebrate the event with a small gathering. They invited thirty guests, laid on a feast, and provided entertainment. A touring troupe of men performed acrobatic tricks, and were a great success with everyone, I am told. Next morning, Sir Jeremy went for his usual ride in the forest, and never came back."

"The first victim, it seems," Eustace Chapuys says, crossing himself. "How do we proceed, Captain Draper?"

"We must draw up a list of likely targets," Will tells the ambassador. "Then, we watch them."

"There are too many Pole family members, or friends of the Poles," Cromwell says. "They are spread the breadth of the kingdom, and I would need more than a thousand young men to protect them all."

"Then we must wait for the killers to make a mistake," says Will. "As each murder takes place, we will find more evidence as to whom we seek."

"*Mon Dieu*," Chapuys mutters. "How can you fight an invisible enemy, Master Cromwell? We do not have their names, nor do we know where they will strike next."

"St. Albans." Rafe Sadler re-appears. He is at the library's open door, holding a report, freshly delivered. "Lady Anne Pole is dead. She was found, drowned in a stream this morning."

"Our opponents are fast workers," Cromwell says. "The lady is known to me. Her husband, Sir Anthony, is currently in France, trying to raise money, and sympathy for the queen, and her daughter, Mary. It seems these conspirators have sent him a very harsh message. What do we know of the business, Rafe?"

"Nothing more, sir," Rafe says. "The news is scant."

"Then you must ride to St. Alban's at once, Will," Cromwell says. "Find out what you can for us."

"The assassins may already be back in London, sir," Will says. "Or chasing down their next victim in Kent or Sussex. I might spend a year criss-crossing England, without any luck."

"I know," Thomas Cromwell replies, "but it is all we have, for the moment."

5   Stolen Away

Gregory, Thomas Cromwell's only living child, has brushed Moll down, watered, and fed her. She is standing patiently by the front gate when Will appears, buckling on his fine German made sword. St. Albans is a fair distance away, and he will have to stay the night at some inn, or wayside lodgings.

"God's speed, Captain," Gregory says. He is not yet eleven years old, and longs to be a man such as the captain. His father, however, is intent on making him into a fine gentleman, with dancing, hawking and jousting skills.

"And to you, young fellow," Will replies as he mounts the sturdy Welsh Cob. "I hear your father is sending you off for more schooling. In Cambridgeshire, is it not?"

"Yes. I am to be turned into a gentleman, against my own nature; learning how to turn a pretty phrase, ride to hounds, and write romantic poetry," Gregory explains. "I fear that my father wants me to join the court and thus enhance my position in life."

"Not a bad thing," Will says. "Life is all about position and power."

"And love?" Gregory asks. "Do you place your love for Mistress Miriam above, or below position?"

"A good question," Miriam Draper says, stepping out into the courtyard with a parcel food under her arm. "What say you, my dear husband?"

"I place you above the stars in the sky, my love," Will responds, without a heartbeat's hesitation.

"A good enough answer." Miriam smiles, and blows a parting kiss. "Bring me something nice back, and I might start to believe you mean it."

Will Draper grins, and urges his horse, Moll, out onto the muddy street. He wonders if a pair of kid gloves will suffice, and calculates if he has enough silver in his purse. Gregory stands, waving, as he canters away towards the north road.

Daylight is almost gone by five o'clock, and he is forced to stop at a small village a few miles short of his destination. The tiny huddle of neat, thatched cottages surround a village green, where a few dozen sheep graze. The land, Will is told, is owned by Lord Stafford, son of the disgraced, and duly executed Duke of Buckingham. Amongst his friends and relatives, there were Plantagenets. He finally paid for his royal family connections, with his life.

Will buys a bed for the night, and sees Moll is well enough stabled, before turning in. There is food to be bought, and a passable wine to drink, but Will has little appetite, and wishes to keep his head clear for the morrow.

The following morning sees him back on the old Roman road to St. Albans, and another mysterious death. The morning is dry, but there is a cold breeze blowing, which makes him wish for a heavier cloak. He arrives before the burial has taken place, and is able to view the deceased. She is laid out in the great house's large reception hall.

Her casket is made from well jointed planks of oak, which have been caulked to keep out the wet. The woman herself is dressed in her best gown, and has fresh flowers woven into her long hair.

"Are you a family friend, sir?" An aged man asks of him. He is the dead woman's eldest brother, and is somewhat suspicious of strangers. "Forgive my bluntness, young fellow, but these are strange, and trying times."

"I am here on Privy Council business," Will replies, offering a prepared half truth. Thomas Cromwell is a member of the council, and he is here by his leave. "My interest is in how your poor sister died, sir. I bear the family no ill will, and my investigation has nothing to do with her, or her absent husband."

"She drowned, sir," the brother tells him. "Though I'm damned if I know how. My sister was found in a shallow stream on the edge of our south pastures. She had been out, attending a wedding on the estate."

"A wedding?" Will feels the hair on his neck bristle. "One of your people?"

"Young Dan Fairclough," says the brother. "The son of our land agent. He wed an estate girl yesterday. My sister attended the festivities, set off for the house, and vanished from our sight. We found her in the stream."

"Was she not attended, sir?" Will asks. "What of cut purses, or vagabonds, intent on outraging some single woman?"

"On our own land?" the man says, and shakes his head at the idea of it. "There was no perceived danger. My sister is a veritable saint, sir, beloved by all of our people. Apart from her obvious cause of death, she was unmarked... and unsoiled. Unfortunately, I left before the entertainment began, so am unsure of the exact train of events."

"Entertainment?" Will asks. He knows what the reply will be, and offers up a small prayer of thanks. A clue has fallen into his lap, at last.

"Yes. Tumblers, and a juggler," the brother replies. "Some damned foreigners, touring the countryside. I paid them ten silver shillings for the day."

*

"Someone is asking questions," the Englishman says, huddling back into a dark corner of the tavern. "It might threaten our endeavour."

"Have you a name, Sir Edward?" Gilbert Guyot asks. "Give it to me, and I will kill him."

"Captain Will Draper," the Englishman tells him, "but that will avail you nothing. He is a Cromwell man, and the whole of Austin Friars is at his back. Hack off one head, and two more grow in its place. I fear we must stop, or face dire consequences."

"Ah, you English are so dramatic," the Frenchman mutters into his ale pot. "Give me all of the details, and I will make sure these Austin Friars people stop meddling, for ever."

"You can't kill them all." The Englishman is horrified at the prospect of mayhem spreading across London. His master's instructions were, after all, quite clear on the matter. Secrecy, and subtlety, were to be the watchwords. "They are like a small, indefatigable, army."

"*Mais non*, Sir Edward," Gilbert says, smiling. "Sometimes, you only need to lop off one little branch to affect the whole of the tree. Leave the pruning of this bush to us!"

*

Lady Anne Pole's cold body can, thankfully, remain unmolested. Will Draper has found his connection, and is riding hard for London, where he will organise a search for his new found suspects. Gilbert Guyot, travelling in the company of two unknown men is meandering across England, murdering anyone who claims friendship with Queen Katherine. They have the perfect excuse to be close to great houses, and important people, in so far as they are summoned, and paid for their skills.

Anne Pole's brother is of little help. He does not know where the troupe came from, or where they will go next. It is up to the excellent young men at Cromwell's disposal to put out feelers, hoping to ensnare the murderers, before they can kill again.

Moll is a sturdy Welsh Cob, taken from the leader of a gang of border bandits, after Will relieved him of his head in single combat. She is capable of covering very long distances at a steady pace, but her master is pushing her too hard. As he reaches the outskirts of the city, her wind goes, and he is forced to dismount, and walk her the last couple of miles.

*

There are still more than two dozen friars living at the Austin Friary, and they often cross Thomas Cromwell's land to get to the river, where they fish for eels. He grants them free access, and does all in his power to ensure they remain untroubled in these troubled times. If they are ever disbanded, the lawyer will make provision for them, so they do not starve.

He refuses to acknowledge his actions as a sign of kindness, saying instead that he does it so that his enemies cannot accuse him of persecuting the Roman Catholic church. In truth, he likes the old men, and often discusses matters of philosophy with their leader. It fascinates him that there are men who do not crave advancement, or seek monetary gain in the world, and he admires them for it.

Miriam Draper does not understand why men would want to live a life of chastity and poverty either, but always drops a freshly baked loaf, or a large game pie in their wicker baskets whenever they pass by. Her faith teaches that man must ever strive towards God, and she sees that this is just their way of doing that.

So it is, that when she sees the two black coated friars sidling past, she hurries out with a small offering of food.

"For the brothers," she tells them, then turns to let them be on their way. The cloak is heavy, and engulfs her almost completely. For a moment, she is shocked, then opens her mouth to scream for help. Jehan Vernay drives his fist into the side of her swaddled head, and she slumps, unconscious, into his brothers arms. It is all over in a moment. The two men carry their bundle through the main gate, deposit it onto the back of a low ox cart, and drive off.

"Did you leave the note?" Gilbert Guyot asks.

"As you wished," Claude Vernay replies. He is the more stupid brother of the two, and often has to be told everything several times. He still does not understand why they are killing people, but the money is very good, and that seems to satisfy him for the moment. "Why are you telling them who we are?"

"They already suspect who we are, Claude," his brother snaps. "For the love of Saint Jean... pay attention to what you are told. Our friend here, Gilbert, will make everything well, as he always does."

"But why don't we kill this one?" Claude asks, and the leader, Gilbert Guyot, grins as the smarter brother curses his siblings thick headedness.

"She is a surety," Gilbert says, patting the unconscious bundle at his feet. "As long as we have her in our power, no one at Austin Friars will try to harm us."

"Oh, I see. Who is she, then?" Claude asks his comrade.

"I don't know," the leader confesses, "but she lives there, and is dressed up like a rich lady. She might be this Thomas Cromwell's woman, his mistress, or his daughter."

"No matter," Claude concludes, for he understands now, and is eager to show it. "She is now our hostage, and they must bend to our will."

"Did you get a good look at her, brother?" Jehan Vernay says, with a knowing smirk. "She's certainly one I'd like to *bend* to me."

"You must keep your brains inside your codpiece," Claude sneers. "The girl is worth more untouched, is she not, Gilbert?"

"For now," Gilbert replies, but the truth is, he has seen the girl, and finds himself in agreement with the cleverer of the two brothers. "If they do not back off, we can all have a taste of her, eh, lads?"

*

It is a while before the Austin Friars household become alarmed. Some think Miriam is in the kitchen with the cook, and the kitchen maids think she is above stairs, embroidering. It is Rafe Sadler who sees the pie lying in the mud outside. He picks it up, sees the muddle of boot prints, and understands, at once, why it is there.

"Are you sure?" Thomas Cromwell is just back from Henry's court, and wants all of the facts.

"Not sure, master," Rafe says, "but there is some strong circumstantial evidence. A pie on the ground, as if dropped. Mistress Miriam often gives alms to the friars. They grow fat on our charity, but not this time. I sent word, and they say none of their people are abroad today."

"Proof, Rafe. I need proof!" Cromwell is vexed. Miriam is as dear to him as Rafe, his nephew Richard, or his own son, and he is beginning to fear for her life. A fat, slovenly man is hovering by the front gate, trying to catch someone's eye.

"Who is that fellow, hanging about my gate?" Tom Cromwell asks. His eyesight is poor, ruined by too much reading by candle light.

"Luis Gomez, sir. Eustace Chapuys lazy old servant."

"Bid him come over," Cromwell says. "He seems as agitated as I. Ah, Luis … what is it, my dear friend?" The last he says in fluent Catalan.

"Forgive me, *Señor*, but I was afraid my master might see me talking to you, but he has just gone out."

"What is it, man?" Cromwell demands.

The old Spaniard has been in his pay since arriving with Chapuys, and is well known to decorate the truth in the cause of increasing the reward.

"I saw two big friars carry out a heavy bundle," he tells them. "They put it on the back of a cart, and drove off towards the great bridge. Is this of use, my lord?"

Cromwell translates, and Rafe almost strikes the man to the ground in frustration. It would have been of more use at the time.

"You dolt!" he cries, and clenches a fist. "One word of warning, and we could have saved all this!"

"What's this?" Will Draper calls, walking his tired horse into the yard. "Beating other men's servants now, are we Rafe?" He sees their faces, and senses trouble. His smile fades. "Dear God, tell me the worst."

"They've got Miriam, Will," Cromwell says.

"What do you mean?" Will Draper says, but knows now what is amiss. His wife has a sense of where he is most times, and is usually waiting at the gate for his return. He jokes with her, saying that it is witchcraft, but she just shakes her head, and says 'no, it is simply love'.

"Where is she?" he asks, and as if prompted, one of the small errand boys gives a shout as he retrieves a folded note from the muddy wheel ruts by the gate. He dashes over to Cromwell and offers the find up for his inspection. Cromwell holds it up close to his eyes.

"It is the name of an inn," the lawyer reads. "The Red Dragon, and it says 'come alone'. These people want me, it seems."

"I'll go." Will holds out his hand for the paper, but Cromwell refuses to surrender it. The last line threatens murder, if not obeyed, and Cromwell does not wish to burden Will with such a terrible prospect.

"No, they demand I go alone... and I shall," Cromwell folds the note, and slips it into his belt pouch. "We might find out who these creatures are, and so save our precious Miriam."

"I already know," Will says, and explains what he has found out. Rafe and Cromwell listen in silence, before offering their ideas. The three men talk for a few minutes more, and arrive at a course of action.

"How do I get to this Red Dragon?"

"Horse is the fastest," Rafe volunteers. "It is south of the river, and very dangerous territory, master."

"I have faced danger before," Thomas Cromwell replies, testily. He has fought the Spaniards in Italy, for the French, and lost, but it counts as experience. "I suspect they are holding Miriam in Southwark, else why cross the Thames?"

"You must go armed," Will tells his master. "A sword to keep casual footpads at bay, and a concealed blade in the sleeve. They might take the sword, but miss the backup weapon. If they threaten violence, and you get close enough, aim for the gut."

"Don't fuss so," Cromwell says. "I will bring our dear Miriam back to you, Will. I swear, on my honour."

"We should flood the area with men," Rafe tells them. "I can raise fifty men within the hour, Master Tom."

"No!" Thomas Cromwell snaps. "We will stick closely to our plan. Agreed?"

"Agreed," Will says, but in his heart, he knows that he shall do murder if Miriam is harmed in any way.

*

"Wine, *Monsignor?*" Thomas Cromwell is in the habit of wearing black, and is easily mistaken for an abbot, or a parish priest, but on this occasion the title is used ironically. "You look thirsty, Master Cromwell."

"You are French?" The man has spoken in French, and he sounds like a native of that land.

"I was born near Paris, but now, I

travel the world, plying my trade," Guyot says.

"Would that be murder, or abduction, sir?"

"Take a seat," Gilbert Guyot says, gesturing to a plank set across two empty barrels. "We have much to discuss."

"You wish for money?"

"No. I wish to be left alone, unmolested by your pack of hunting dogs," the Frenchman replies. "One of your men is trying to upset my business, and I want it stopped, now."

"Why should I listen to you?"

"Because I have your daughter, or your wife... or perhaps your mistress?" Guyot tells him. "She is very beautiful, so I think it is the last. Stop your interference, and I will let her live. She will be released, as soon as my task is done."

"Why don't I have you taken captive, and simply rack Miriam's location from you?" Cromwell has little to bargain with, but tries his best. "My men will make you scream within the hour."

"A good idea, except for my companions, you see," the Frenchman replies. "The Vernay brothers are loyal to me. If I am not back inside the next half hour, they have orders to cut her throat. Of course, they might delay long enough to use her first. As I say, she is a very attractive young thing."

"You have my word," Thomas Cromwell says, as if resolved to defeat. "Release her, and my people will turn a blind eye to your plot."

"Really?"

"Yes, really. I have no love for the Pole family, or any other enemy of the king."

"I am told that Master Cromwell is an honest man," Gilbert Guyot says, "but I cannot accept your kind offer. You will desist, and I will send her back, but at another time."

"How can I believe you?" Cromwell asks, then smiles and nods. "I have it. To ensure Miriam's safety, I shall call off all of my men. Further, I will pay a sum of money to you, when she is finally released. How does five hundred pounds sound?"

Guyot is stunned into silence. He is being promised a huge fortune, just to let a girl live. He considers the offer, sees there is no longer any profit in killing her, and agrees.

"She will be handed over to you, once my little list is completed," he tells Cromwell. "Another three names, and she goes free."

"Free, and unmolested," Cromwell insists. "Touch her, and the money is off the table!"

"Hah! I knew she was your mistress." Guyot made a rude gesture with his hand. "You don't want anyone else to squeeze the fruit, eh?"

"Agreed?" Thomas Cromwell spits into his palm, and offers it to the Frenchman. They shake on the deal. "I wish you God's speed in your mission, as I sorely am missing the girl."

"You are a fool, my friend," Gilbert Guyot murmurs, as the lawyer leaves. "For five hundred pounds, you could buy a thousand such whores." He waits for a few minutes, then gets up to leave. No one else rises, or makes a move to follow. He is safe, and knows that Cromwell will not take a chance with the girl's life.

6   The Daisy Chain

As Gilbert Guyot leaves the Red Dragon, Richard Cromwell, dressed as a street hawker, complete with his heavy swag of cheap goods, falls in behind, and follows him for a couple of streets. The moment the Frenchman glances back, he stops, and begins unfastening his bundle, as if he is about to set out his wares.

The narrow highway is crowded, and Guyot's eyes flick warily from one face to another. No one is following, and no one seems interested in his progression. A young, ragged street urchin, who has been lounging against a door jamb across the street falls in behind him, and continues following.

Guyot is, with good reason very wary, and pauses a hundred paces on, as if to button up his doublet. The small boy, Adam, saunters past, fingering his nose. He continues walking away from his target, only stopping when he is met by another boy further down the street.

"East or West?" Adam asks of his new companion. The second boy, whilst pretending to chatter with him, watches the Frenchman over Adam's left shoulder.

"East, back towards the river," Mark says. "We can cut through the chandler's yard and pick him up further on his way. If he carries on the way he is going, Master Rafe will pick him up near the wharves."

The Frenchman takes another look behind, confirming that he is not being followed, and cuts down towards the old boatmen's wharf. As he comes out onto the busy river bank, a skinny, red haired sailor is sitting on a lobster pot, whittling away at a piece of driftwood.

Gilbert Guyot walks past Rafe, unseeing. The 'sailor' puts away his knife, and slowly follows, until the Frenchman comes to a ramshackle fisherman's boathouse, which he enters. Rafe strolls past, and memorises everything he can see about the seemingly deserted building.

He turns a corner, and Will is there, waiting with Richard Cromwell and the two boys, Adam and Mark. The lads have equipped themselves with solid, wooden staves, and are ready for a bloody fight. Will places them by the front entrance, and orders them to stay.

"If any escape past us, you may set about them with your sticks," he tells the willing boys. "Let no one escape, lads."

"There is a side door, leading down to the water's edge," Rafe tells them. "Else wise, it is in through the front, up the stairs, and rush them."

"They are sure to be armed," says Will. "Three tough men, who handle knives for their livelihoods. They might hurt Miriam before we overcome them."

"Do you have another idea?" Richard says. Just then Mark, who has slipped away, reappears with an armful of hay from a nearby stable.

"That's the job," Adam says, exposing himself. "Here, let me piss on it, and it will smoke all the more. Do you have flint and tinder, Captain?"

"A splendid idea, boys," Will says. "We shall smoke them out. They'll fear a fire, and try to escape."

"What if they don't..." Rafe's words die away as the urine soaked fodder starts to billow thick, grey smoke. The time for words is over. Minutes pass, and the building fills with smoke. Will stands, sword in hand, but no one comes. At last, in desperation, he plunges into the house, and races up the rickety old stairs.

*

Eustace Chapuys has set himself a mission. He is unaware of Miriam's abduction, and has decided to uncover the author of the warning note. He reasons that each of the men at Cromwell's dinner will be loitering around Henry's court, and determines to seek them out. He will string them along, like a daisy chain, he thinks, until he has the truth of things.

The king has taken over all of Cardinal Wolsey's old houses, and the grandest of them is York Place. His Majesty has moved his base from Westminster Palace to the new address because it is bigger, and more sumptuously appointed. He is already adding to the near one thousand rooms, and plans to lay out more gardens, and a new, central courtyard.

King Henry is uncomfortable with the old name of the place, as it reminds him that he stole the palace from Cardinal Wolsey, who was also the Bishop of York during his long, illustrious career. He has taken to calling his newest residence 'The White Hall Palace' or, more usually, just 'Whitehall'. There is some talk of Lady Anne Boleyn being given a suite of rooms within the new palace, to ease problems of access to the king.

The ambassador has hopes that this means she is about to surrender her virtue to Henry, who, like any man, will lose interest, once the prize is taken. Lady Anne will join the long list of the king's discarded lovers, and the business of royal politics can assume centre stage, once again.

Eustace Chapuys arrives at the main entrance to the palace, and is challenged, belligerently, by one of the guards. He is new, and eager to be seen to do his duty. The Sergeant at Arms, Billingsley, comes rushing out after him, and orders the bemused younger man aside.

"This good gentleman is the Spanish Ambassador, Private Porlock," he explains. "You can pass him through, without delay, whether it be day or night."

"Too kind," Chapuys mutters, dropping a shilling into each open palm. "Is the king here?"

"Bless me, sir, but he don't let us know generally," the older man says, chuckling. "King Hal rarely stops for a chinwag these days. The rest of the rascally crew are here though. The lords Norfolk, young Surrey, and Suffolk, came in together, with their heads together, as if up to some real mischief. And then, Lord Percy turned up an hour since, creeping in like a little mouse, hoping to avoid the cat."

"The Duke of Northumberland is in court?" Eustace Chapuys is a little surprised, as rumour has it that Harry Percy is much out of favour with the king these days. "I wonder what he is after?"

"Come to have his aristocratic arse kicked again, sir," the guard says, jovially. "Bless him, but he was ever in trouble, even as a nipper. Men like his lordship are a constant worry, and need their bums booted on a regular basis. It might save him from the block, if he is kicked hard enough."

"Your insight quite fascinates me, Master Billingsley," the ambassador tells him. "Perhaps I should employ you as my assistant. It would save me coming into court myself."

"Why thank you for the kindly offer, sir," the Sergeant at Arms says, straight faced, "but I've done twenty three years with good King Harry, and I've my pension to think of. It will be enough to buy me my own pub, and afford a decent wife... a big, jolly lass, with great kissable *baubies* on her!"

Eustace Chapuys smiles at the man's simple needs in life, and enters the huge building. The older guard watches him until he vanishes from sight.

"Now, that's a gentleman, my friend," he tells his subordinate, and Porlock nods his head in ready agreement as he pockets his shilling. "There's a few here today who might take a page from Master *Charpooses* book, an' no mistake. He never leaves home without a purse full of change, in case he meets up with a friendly face. When was the last time you saw so much as a bent penny from that old miser Norfolk?"

"Never," Private Porlock replies, and spits on the hard ground. "They say the bastard's purse ain't been opened since the king's father was a lad."

"Tight arsed bastard,' the sergeant agrees, and they both spit, as if confirming the truth of it.

*

The Duke is used to being talked about. He thinks he is the most important man in England, save for the king, and believes everyone to be fascinated by his aristocratic magnificence, and regal bearing. If he was ever told how disliked he was, he would simply not be able to believe it.

"Harry Percy, you young puppy," he booms across the outer court. "It's pleasantly surprising to see your thick head still on your thin neck. I thought Henry told you to go north, and never show your ugly pudding face here again."

"You thought wrongly, Norfolk." Harry Percy has no wish to speak with the older Duke, and does not explain that his reprieve is due entirely to a generous gift he sent to Anne Boleyn, and a touch of masterly grovelling to her brother, George. Flattery has its uses, he thinks, and thanks God he has a talent for it.

"Come to my London house tonight," Norfolk says. "I have a new cook. We can talk about my new stables. They rival even the king's."

"Then be wary, sir," Harry Percy replies, with shrewd observation. "For the king does not like to be bettered, not in any way."

"A good point, well made," Norfolk

says, chuckling. "It was you who once tried to better him over my niece, as I recall." Percy goes white with fear, and tries to shush the older man into keeping a more judicious silence about the sad affair.

"Enough, I pray you, My Lord," he stammers, and looks about for fear someone might overhear. "I was very young, and made a foolish mistake."

"Claiming to have wedded, and bedded Anne Boleyn was certainly that," Norfolk replies, enjoying his ability to make the younger man squirm. It is an old tale, and it gets better with each telling. "As if she would let a useless young whelp like you tup her, Percy. Why, she would as soon part her legs for a thatch cutter!"

"May I join you, gentlemen?" Ambassador Chapuys has appeared by their sides, as if from nowhere. The two men exchange worried glances, wondering what he might have overheard, then nod rather than bow to him. "Though in truth, it is your delightful son I seek, my Lord Norfolk."

"He's lallygagging in the courtyard, trying to talk some young lady into an indiscretion," Norfolk says. "If you find the *'delightful'* little milksop, tell him I will not pay out my good gold for any more of *his* ill gotten bastards."

"If you wish, My Lord *Norfook*,"

Chapuys says, bowing, and he adds in Spanish, "The son should not follow in his father's footsteps too closely." He bows to them, and retires from their presence. The story about Percy and Anne is an old one, and the little Savoyard gives it little credence. Were it true, Percy's head would have been on a spike many years ago. Unless, Chapuys thinks, someone has convinced Henry to disbelieve it. He wonders about Cromwell, but recalls that the man was but a clerk to Cardinal Wolsey back then. He shrugs, and goes in search of Norfolk's boy.

*

The younger Howard, the Earl of Surrey... Henry... or Harry to his few friends... is standing by the sundial, watching one of the numerous ladies in waiting walk away. She is proving an elusive quarry, but he senses the end is near. Even though he is only fifteen, he has bedded several older ladies, and knows just how to charm them into bed. In his case, it seems to be with the promise of money, or the odd jewel or two, and a lot of begging.

"Ah, there you are, my Lord Surrey," Eustace Chapuys says, offering a cheery wave to the young man. "Your father sends his warmest greetings, and asks that you sire no more children out of wedlock. He says he will not pay."

Howard's face is a picture of surprise, then he throws his head back, and roars laughing. In truth, it is but one bastard, sired on a plump wench of lower birth, when he was thirteen. Since then, he has been careful to stick to whores, or married women who can pass the child off on an unwary husband.

"The old man can put a billy goat to shame, and should take his own advice," he says. "He puts my mother aside, for a girl little older than I!"

"Yes. Advice is very cheap, young sir." Eustace Chapuys is wondering how to broach the subject of the concealed note. "You admired my hat the other night, as I recall. Did you examine it well?"

"Your hat?" Surrey frowns, trying to recall the evening through a haze of drink. "Oh, yes. The monstrosity with the silly feathers in it. I dare say it would suit a bumptious foreigner, sir, but it is a little out of place in England. I fear your milliner has advised you badly, Ambassador Chapuys. Ask for your money back… that is my advice… old fellow."

"I admire your frankness," Ambassador Chapuys says, though he thinks the callow youth has little sartorial taste. The young nobleman shrugs his indifference. He is the heir to the oldest, finest family in the realm, and speaks very much as he wishes, without thought for anyone else's feelings. He has even been known to criticise the king… but not too often, and only when he is very, very drunk. "I found a certain letter, after I left Master Cromwell's house."

"Yes?" Surrey is fast losing interest, and wants to be off, after his next intended victim.

"May I ask… how came you to Austin Friars?"

"By *palanquins*, as I recall," Surrey replies, without a hint of sarcasm in his voice. "We picked them up by the bridge. The chair carriers overcharged us, or tried to… and I chased the snivelling bastards off with my sword. Bloody cheating peasants, they are not fit to breath the same air as us!"

"You misunderstand my question, my Lord Surrey," the Holy Roman ambassador persists. He tries again. "I believe you received no invite?"

"Oh, that!" Surrey explains, as if the little Savoyard is a child who understands nothing. "Norfolk is the most powerful noble in England, and I am his one legitimate son. I can turn up wherever I damned well please. People are always happy to set another place or two, at my request. It is considered an honour amongst honours to feed a great

Howard."

"Then it was you whom decided to visit Austin Friars?" the little Savoyard persists, and Harry Howard frowns and scratches his noble backside.

"Damned if I can remember," he says, at length. "When was this again?"

"You were with Master Rich."

"Who?"

"Richard Rich, My Lord?"

"Oh, Dick?" Surrey smirks. "That one would put his own sister under you, for advancement. I like the fellow!"

"You were with him?"

"I was?" The head is shaken again, and Chapuys sighs at his lack of progress. He feels as if he is trying to swim through a sea of tar. Surrey's mind is in a state of constant alcoholic confusion, and he cannot be relied upon to recall anything with any degree of certainty. He bows to the youngster, and slips away.

*

The ambassador must go in search of a more receptive intellect, in the shape of the redoubtable Stephen Gardiner. Chapuys asks after him, and is told that the cleric seldom leaves his chambers, which are set in the west wing of the sprawling environs of Whitehall.

The tall, perpetually nervous looking cleric is, indeed, in his chamber, which is situated within the court precincts. Henry is often in need of his scholarly advice, and likes to keep him close by. It has taken him almost forty years to reach his present post, and he often bemoans the success of newcomers, like Thomas Cromwell. Born on the right side of the blanket, but with a father who was the illegitimate son of a male cousin, on Henry's mother's side, his position in life is somewhat ambiguous still, and joining the church has, at least, given him a recognised station within the court.

Henry is usually friendly towards him, and on one occasion even called him 'dear cousin', but he was drunk at the time, and might well have called his horse the same, given the chance. However, Gardiner is a shrewd lawyer, and specialises in canon law… which makes him useful in the important matter of the king's divorce. The lawyer cum cleric sits on the fence, and acts as devil's advocate… swaying gently in the political breeze, and hoping it does not turn into a religious storm.

Eustace Chapuys knocks, and hopes that his unannounced visit is not deemed to be intrusive. A servant answers the summons, and goes to see if 'the master' is available for callers. Chapuys thinks he will be rebuffed but, to his relief, he is invited in with a degree of cordiality he does not expect.

"This is a great honour, sir," Stephen Gardiner says, clearing papers from a stool. "Pray, be seated. Can I have them bring you a glass of wine, or something to eat?"

Eustace Chapuys declines all offers, politely, and comes straight to the point. He has more interviews to conduct, and time is of the essence. He asks if Stephen Gardiner enjoyed the dinner at Thomas Cromwell's house. The man places his hands in his lap, and composes himself to answer. Never rush it, he thinks, and never give an opinion until you have an idea of what is expected of you.

"To a point," the cleric replies, warily. He judges that the ambassador is a staid sort of man, and a devout catholic, so feels happy to speak against Norfolk's unruly child. "I thought the tone went down a little, after that pipsqueak Surrey, and Richard Rich turned up. I spoke harshly to Richard afterwards, whom I thought of as a solid sort of a fellow, and he apologised for the intrusion, most profusely, saying that the boy, Surrey, had been most insistent that they visited Austin Friars that evening."

"Really?" Eustace Chapuys frowns at this snippet of information. "You found the wider conversation stimulating, I trust?"

"What ever was said over dinner, was said amongst friends, sir," Stephen Gardiner replies, carefully. "Thomas Cromwell sets a good table, and it would be remiss of me to blackguard any of his guests too much, though I fear Sir Thomas More is going too far, of late. He thinks the king is his friend, and that is enough to keep him secure."

Stephen Gardiner sees a chance to ingratiate himself with Eustace Chapuys by disparaging the Lord Chancellor. It shows that he does not fear More, and is leaning towards Cromwell, politically speaking. Besides, they are alone, and he can always deny whatever is said later, if necessary.

"How so?" Chapuys is interested in Gardiner's view. He recalls More threatening to rack a few heretics, and wonders why it has caused so much anger. In Spain, and the rest of the Holy Roman Empire, a week does not pass without some bunch of heretics being hanged, burned, or beheaded. The English are far too soft on these people.

"The people he threatens are friends of mine… and of Thomas Cromwell's too. Decent men, in trade, who make this country wealthy. Perhaps they are a little misguided… but breaking their bones on the rack is abhorrent!"

"Then his crime was to bring the matter up in polite company," Chapuys replies. "For heretical beliefs are a canker in the churches side."

"Protestant thinking has gained a

foothold in many places," Gardiner says, "but I think making them into martyrs is not the answer. The king wishes to remain on good terms with Rome, and allows More some leeway, but it cannot go on."

"Why not?"

"Because Henry wishes to be perceived as a modern, benign ruler," Gardiner says. "He wishes thereat of the world to admire him."

"Yet he wishes toast off his legal wife?" Chapuys says, and regrets the words at once.

"That is for the lawyers to decide," Gardiner says. "Now, how might I help you, sir? I assume your visit is not simply a social one?"

"No," Chapuys replies, with a watery smile. "I was wondering... did you like my hat?"

*

"Thank God, I thought I'd lost you," Will Draper cries, as he cuts through Miriam's bonds. "Are you unhurt, my dearest love?"

"Except for my pride," she replies, hugging herself into her husband. "How could I have been so stupid?"

Richard and Rafe have rushed up a ladder that leads to the roof. The three men have jumped from rooftop to rooftop, with an agility born of their particular talents, and escaped the trap. Richard contemplates the twelve foot gap he must leap, if he is to continue the pursuit, then turns back, and goes down to the next floor.

"They are gone," Richard Cromwell curses. "They leaped away like startled harts in a hunt!"

"At least we have our Miriam back safe, and under our wing once more," Rafe says. "The master will be relieved at your release, my dear."

"Just so, but it leaves us no further forward," Will Draper tells them. "They will keep out of sight now, then strike when they feel safer. They might even speed up their killing, so as to earn their fee, and get safely abroad. We must get back to Austin Friars, and confer with Master Cromwell, at once. He will know how best for us to proceed."

"What of little Chapuys?" Richard Cromwell asks.

"He is of no real use to us," says Will. "We must leave him to his own devices, whilst we run these creatures down, and kill them."

*

Eustace Chapuys has much to digest, and ever more to understand about the English way of things. Gardiner, Cromwell and More actually seem to like one another, and often work together on affairs of state, but there are certain, invisible, boundaries. Each man thinks he is doing his best for the king, even when they disagree with one another, and it makes for some feisty altercations when they meet up.

All three are for the king, and therefore against the queen, but Sir Thomas More wishes to achieve King Henry's desire without hurting his relationship with the church in Rome. This means he is set dead against the new protestant movements, and will use brutal force, if necessary, to quell them.

Cromwell is, Chapuys believes, an adept of the new heretical faith, and does not, in the least, mind upsetting the natural order of things. Given his head, he will convert the whole of England to the new form of religion, and the king along with them.

Stephen Gardiner is sitting on the fence. He does not wish to hurt anyone, yet wants everyone to get their own way. In his world, it seems possible that More and Cromwell can, like the lion and the lamb, lie down together. It does not cross his mind that neither man will surrender an inch, and that, eventually, blood must flow.

He is a true diplomat, even to the point of lying about the ambassadors hat.

"Quite... delightful," Stephen Gardiner says. "Is it new?"

"I wore it at Master Cromwell's splendid dinner, just the other night," Chapuys replies.

"Oh?" Gardiner wishes to turn back to his heap of documents. "I don't recall. Nice feathers, my dear Eustace. I do feel that they add a certain... dignity... to a ... hat."

"But you do not recall handing it to me?" Chapuys asks.

"Handing it to you, my dear fellow?" The cleric frowns, and shakes his head. "Surely, would that not be a servant's task?"

"Everyone held it, at one point or another."

"They did?" Stephen Gardiner smiles at him, a little vacantly. "How nice for you, my dear ambassador!"

"Then you handed it on, so that I might take it with me," Chapuys says.

"Well, it was your hat, was it not?" Gardiner replies with a smile. "Who else would wish to wear it in your stead, my dear fellow?"

7   A Meeting of Minds

In quick succession, Chapuys confronts Suffolk, Richard Rich, and Sir Thomas More. He is met with a blank stare from Charles Brandon, who is always terrified of saying the wrong thing these days. Thomas Cromwell owns him financially, and has warned him not to speak of the evening... or about anything that was said, particularly to Henry.

"You have lost your hat, sir?" Suffolk says.

"No, my Lord Suffolk," Chapuys persists. "I say only that it was admired as it was brought to me. You, yourself examined it, I believe."

"I did?" Charles Brandon furrows his brow, and tries to remember. "No. It's gone. Sorry, old chap. These days, I can scarce remember my own name. Why, just the other day, I had a tryst with one of Boleyn's ladies in waiting ... the plump little one with the big gourds ... and forgot all about it. The little slut took it rather badly, and slapped me in front of George Boleyn!"

"Perhaps you might consider hiring a social secretary, sir?" Chapuys suggests. "I am sure Master Cromwell can recommend a suitable young man for the post."

"I think I am indebted enough to that

fellow," Suffolk moans, then frowns at the little Savoyard. "I trust you will not repeat what I say, sir?"

"On my honour, My Lord," Eustace Chapuys replies, and bows himself away.

*

Richard Rich recalls much of the evening, and apologises again for young Harry Howard's appalling behaviour at the dinner table. He knows it has left a bad taste in powerful men's mouths, and placed a black mark against his name in Thomas Cromwell's carefully kept books.

"I tried to dissuade him, really I did, but he is used to getting his own way," Rich says, casually. "Though God alone knows his motive. He hates Sir Thomas More, and thinks Master Cromwell is nothing more than a jumped up blacksmith's boy."

"He sneers at the whole world," Chapuys concurs. "He eschews good manners, yet expects everyone else to fawn over him, just because of an accident of birth. He should thank his mother for ensuring his legitimacy!"

"Oh, you have heard the rumours then?" Rich says, maliciously. Surrey's legitimacy is in no doubt, but his mother's subsequent morality certainly is.

"Rumours, sir?" Chapuys asks.

"Never mind," Rich tells him. "He is a prickly sort, and no mistake."

"And he bites the hand that feeds him," Chapuys says. "Whether it be his father, or poor Master Cromwell."

"You must understand, *Señor* Chapuys, I do not share his views about Thomas Cromwell. I admire the man's brilliant rise from obscurity, and wish to do the same. That is why I hang around the wealthy pups of great and powerful men. I seek only to use the drunken, licentious rogues ... not like them. God forfend!"

"I admire your honesty, Master Rich," Chapuys tells him. "I am also from much humbler seed. I truly believe that clever men will always rise. Do you remember my hat?"

"Your hat? Why yes, I do. I found it to be quite exquisite, sir. Is it in the French style?"

"You passed it to me."

"Did I?" Rich frowns, then nods. "Rafe Sadler came out with it, and I passed it to Surrey. He made some fatuous comment before handing it on. I think it was admired by everyone there, even Sir Thomas examined it."

"Ah, Sir Thomas More," says Chapuys. "The man is an enigma. He endows a great university with one hand, and flogs a heretic with the other. I am told he pets stray dogs and the very small ... what is the word...

niño… yes, childs."

"Children," Richard Rich says, correcting the Savoyard's quaint English. "He is a cold man on the outside, but a seething volcano inside. If pressed, I would look to a fairer minded man as a patron."

"Wise words, sir." Chapuys actually likes the young man, and appreciates his candid words. He is for Cromwell, and is as good a man as the society he moves in allows. "Now, I must find the volcano, and scale its steaming slopes."

"Take care, Ambassador Chapuys," Rich says. "You will find him in the chapel at this time of day. When he is not persecuting honest men, he wears his knees out, praying to God."

"He is a pious man then?"

"You have not heard him pray then, I take it" Rich says with a smile. He clasps his hands in prayer, and rolls his eyes up unto Heaven. "O, Lord, I am still waiting for a response to my last list of demands. Amen."

"Ah yes, I am familiar with that style of worship, Master Rich," Chapuys replies. "I wonder God's ears are not worn out with listening to such nonsense."

"Quite so," Richard Rich says. He has nothing to do, but does not want the ambassador to think he is at a loose end, or under employed. "I am a busy man, Señor

Chapuys, but if I can be of any further service... do not hesitate to send for me."

"Too kind, Master Rich," Chapuys replies, and bows. This is a young man, he thinks, who will rise high and, hopefully, not on a gallows.

*

The Lord Chancellor's chambers are guarded by several dour looking clerks, and it seems, at first, that he is to be brusquely turned away. One of the clerks, however, recognises the ambassador, and hurries off to seek further instructions from his own immediate superior. This man suspects it must be important, for a Holy Roman ambassador to call, unannounced, and slips into the main chamber, where his own master is hard at work.

"Señor Chapuys, this is a nice surprise," the Lord Chancellor says, once the Savoyard has gained entry. He means, why have you not first begged for an appointment, Eustace Chapuys translates to himself. "What can I do for you?"

"A point of clarification, Sir Thomas," Chapuys says in a casual manner. "Concerning the queen."

"Ah, the annulment." More sits, and gestures for Chapuys to join him.

"I am told it will not happen."

"By whom, Tom Cromwell?" The ambassador returns a bland stare. Let him wonder at his sources. "The Pope will grant the act of annulment in the next few months, and the king will be free to marry, as his conscience dictates. Your own master must have several promising candidates to put forward."

"The Emperor Charles is not accustomed to the strange way Englishmen pick wives, sir." More raises an eyebrow at so sharp a response. "The process, over here, seems to be similar to a cattle market."

"Will you write to him?" More asks.

"I am sure you will know what I write, even before my master," Chapuys says. "My letters are all intercepted, read and forwarded."

"Not by my office," More lies. "That sounds more like Tom Cromwell's game. He has spies everywhere, except in my own private household."

"Then I must look at Master Cromwell most carefully. You think he aids the heretics?"

"Undoubtedly," More says. "He holds high office, and is close to the king, which makes him feel safe, but it is a false sense of security. I will follow the devil into every nook and cranny, rooting out his evil. Tyndale will go to the stake, as will every misguided soul he has corrupted."

"You would move against Master Cromwell?" Eustace Chapuys asks. "I thought you two were close friends."

"We are," More says, "but friendship is outweighed by duty, and it is my duty to cleanse England of heresy, and reunite us with Rome. Do you agree, sir?"

"I wish our respective countries to be firm friends," Chapuys says, truthfully. "The Emperor Charles, once acquainted with all the facts, will hold out the olive branch to his dear cousin, Henry."

"And you, Chapuys?" More stands, and fixes the ambassador with a stare. "The time for sitting on the fence is a thing of the past. Will you join the fight when Cromwell finally shows his true colours?"

"Of course," Chapuys replies, failing to specify which side he will favour. "Though I am, primarily, here to attend to the queen's needs. Will she be allowed to go to a home entirely of her choice?"

"Yes, of course she will… if it be set within England's borders." Sir Thomas More's face is stone-like, and his true thoughts are carefully masked.

"Will she be honoured in *all* ways?"

"As the widow of Arthur, and as the Dowager Queen of England." More does not waver from the true point, and adds: "She must remove herself from this false marriage cleanly, and acknowledge the rights of any new queen."

"And what of poor Princess Mary?"

Chapuys asks.

"She will be honoured also, but must realise she will likely as not, never inherit the crown. Henry will sire healthy male children, and her importance will be diminished with time. It is, I regret, the fate of all royal females. For you will know, if you read my book, Utopia, that I advocate equality between the sexes."

"I found your book to be ... most edifying."

"Thank you."

"Then all that will happen, is a modest change of title?" the ambassador asks, ingenuously. "The simple addition of the word 'dowager' before the title 'queen'?"

"That is it, in a nut shell, my dear Eustace. I may call you that, may I?"

"I shall consider it an honour, Sir Thomas. I must thank you, in advance for your complete honesty, and for the warmth you will show to my dear lady, Queen Katherine, and her daughter. My master will be soothed by your words."

"I am but a public servant, sir," More tells him. "Here to smooth the way in all matters political."

"You are doing an admirable job, Lord Chancellor," Chapuys replies. "You offer two courses of action to the queen. She can either request her release from the marriage, and enter a nunnery, or admit her marriage to Arthur was legitimately consummated, and become the Dowager Queen of England."

"And keep her castles and lands, of course."

"Of course." Chapuys says. There is no mention of the one, glaring fact; Princess Mary is the only surviving legitimate child, and must be declared a bastard if all this is to come about. "Now, where did I put my hat? It is the one you admired so much at Cromwell's house."

"This one?" The Lord Chancellor half rises from his seat, and produces the battered headwear. "My apologies, Ambassador Chapuys, but I appear to have sat upon it ... quite accidentally."

*

Chapuys drains the glass of wine, and holds it out to be refilled. He drinks it, but slower this time, and frowns at the wicked story Thomas Cromwell is telling him.

"Kidnapped, from your very door?" He is horrified at yet another nasty occurrence. The world of diplomacy is becoming a changed place, and he does not much like it.

"They dressed as friars, and put her in a sack," Cromwell concludes. "She is now in her own bed, and resting from the entire, harrowing ordeal."

"Thanks be to God your people were

able to recover the poor girl," Eustace Chapuys says, with a sincere ring in his voice. "It is a pity the felons escaped."

"Yes, or Will Draper would have killed them, to a man."

"Would that be a bad thing, my friend?" Chapuys asks.

"It would. We need a live person to tell us what is going on…. and who is behind all this wickedness."

"That is why I am here," Chapuys says, smiling at his own cleverness. "I have visited the royal court, and spoken to everyone suspected of handing me the note. I discount your own people, of course… for they would simply tell you directly, rather than send me chasing about the place."

"Yes, one of my young men reported this to me a half hour since. Would that I had known what you intended, my dear friend, so I might have put you in a sack too!"

"I don't understand what you mean," Chapuys says, deflated at Cromwell's harsh reaction to his news. "What have I done to so offend you?"

"You have alerted the world to our actions, my dear Eustace," Tom Cromwell explains. "Everyone at court is gossiping about why you have been questioning eminent people about a certain be-feathered hat."

"I was, perhaps, a little indiscreet?"

"Even my cook's boy knows," Cromwell replies, "and he is stone deaf!"

"Oh, sorry." Chapuys bows his head, as if to hide his reddening cheeks.

"Let us not cry over spilled milk." Cromwell refills their glasses again. "It is a Flemish vintage. I prefer it to the French stuff, and the current batch of German wine is fit only for washing one's feet. What can you tell me?"

"What do you need to know?"

"I don't know, until I know it," Thomas Cromwell replies, smiling. "Just talk, Eustace, and let me find my own way through your day."

"Very well. May I speak in French? I find it a subtler tongue when discussing fine distinctions."

"You can speak in any language you wish.... Just start!"

"*Le Duc de Norfook* was there." Cromwell suppresses a smile at the funny pronunciation, which might only sound amusing to an English ear. "He was goading Lord Percy over a girl. I only caught a little of it, but it seems that the young lord had married badly, or had sought to, and was in some sort of trouble with the king's people."

"Ah, an old tale. It was going the rounds back in my dear Cardinal Wolsey's day. Harry Percy was not a duke then. He fell into the clutches of a scheming young vixen, and made a rash promise to her, a promise that he should not have. The king decides who shall marry whom amongst his nobility."

"The impetuosity of youth," Eustace Chapuys says, sighing for days gone by. He has an adolescent son, back in Savoy, born out of wedlock, and sympathises with the dissolute Lord Percy for a brief moment. Young men often follow their loins at that age, and young girls are often bent on mischief, he thinks.

"It was Anne Boleyn."

"Dear God!" The story takes on a new meaning for the ambassador, and he wonders how he can use the knowledge to good effect. "Does Henry know about this?"

"He did not, until Percy became jealous of la Boleyn's growing relationship with the king. He went on a drunken trawl of London taverns and, hardly able to stand up straight, made a few silly statements. Unfounded rubbish, of course, but mixed in with enough half truths to lose him his stupid head."

"What did he confess to?"

"He boasted that the king was but one in a line of lovers, and that he and Anne had been betrothed, some years ago. By the time I found him, he was telling butchers, and cobblers apprentices, how hard he rode the girl on their wedding night, and that he found her to be… already *well* broken to the saddle."

"You found him?" Chapuys absorbs this, greedily.

"My agents did. He was in a very low place, more of a cheap brothel than a tavern. They took him quietly aside, and waited for me to come. Cardinal Wolsey was as furious as hell about the entire business. He already knew about it, you see. A few years before, he got wind of the romance, and told the old duke to take his son back up north, Then he told Thomas Boleyn to control his daughters, or face financial ruin, and expulsion from court life. The cardinal had another bride in mind for the Percy heir. The Boleyn family came from yeoman farmer stock, you see, and were not grand enough for the Percy family. That the father was wed to Norfolk's sister made no difference."

"How things change." Eustace Chapuys can see that the Percy family would want a much more advantageous marriage for their son, back then. "So, it was nipped in the bud, before anything happened?"

"Exactly. Young Harry was married off to Lady Mary Talbot, Lord Shrewsbury's daughter. He never forgave Wolsey for meddling in his life… the ungrateful bastard."

"Ungrateful, Thomas, how so?" Eustace Chapuys is confused.

"As a small boy, Percy was a page boy

in the cardinal's household. He was shown nothing but the greatest kindness."

"He also bit the hand that fed him, then?" Chapuys thinks back to young Surrey, and shakes his head in despair. Why do the young know everything, he thinks, and yet make so bad a fist of things?

"You might say so … and more than once. Anyway, one day, Anne Boleyn is not fit to marry Harry Percy, and the next, she is the king's favourite, and Henry wants her in his bed… but as a wife, not a mistress. It suddenly becomes rather important that we establish Anne's virtue. There is a qualification needed to make the girl Henry's next queen. Her virginity must be intact, and her maidenly honour beyond any doubt at all."

"Ah, yes. Caesar's wife." Chapuys refers to the old saying which demands the greatest virtue from the greatest of women.

"Exactly." Cromwell smiles, for he thinks of Claudius Caesar's queen, Messalina… and her four hundred lovers.

"So, you spoke with him?"

"I did." Thomas Cromwell's brow furrows as he recollects the event. "I took his thick head in my two hands, thus, and banged it on the table. Twice. Very hard. Then I explained the error of what he was saying, and told him that the king would be furious, and might even do him so very great harm."

"What did he say?"

"The sudden impact of his solid head with the sturdiness of the oak table top seemed to have cleared his mind. He quickly recanted, saying that he spoke only out of childish jealousy at the king's good fortune in finding such a young, beautiful... utterly intact... lady to love."

"No wonder Norfolk derides him so wickedly. He is the girl's uncle, after all, and must have been affronted."

"Percy must endure, and watch his step," Cromwell concludes, for the king's jealousy is a byword at court, and can flare up because of one wrong word.

"Oh dear." Chapuys recalls something one of his spies has told him. A piece of gossip that he had not thought of any importance. "Percy sent Anne a present last week. A piece of jewellery, I believe. Let us hope Henry is understanding."

"I too have sent such a gift to Lady Anne," Thomas Cromwell says. "She has a weakness for yellow stones. I sent it to procure her *platonic* friendship."

"Does Percy know what platonic means, I wonder?" Chapuys asks.

"He sent it, so she might intercede for him with Henry, and get him recalled to court. He hates having to live up in Northumberland with a vengeance. Once, he swore to burn

Durham down, and replace it with a forest, stocked with boar, deer, and wild wolves. He claims that animals are better than people... who cannot be trusted to keep faith."

"Then he is on a tightrope," says Chapuys. "Henry must accept that the gift, whatever it may be, was made in all innocence, else why let him come back to court?"

"Keep your friends close, but keep your enemies even closer," Cromwell tells him, with a knowing wink of the eye.

"I see. And how close are you keeping me, my dear Thomas?"

"You must stick to me like tar to a shoe, my friend," the lawyer replies. "I have yet to drain your mind of what you know. Pray, continue your illuminating discourse."

"I also met with Charles Brandon. I found him to be the sort of man I could pass time with. Pleasant, but shallow. He is weak natured, of course, and seems to have a strong regard for you."

"He is not your man," Cromwell says, emphatically. "He is in debt to me, to the tune of thirty five thousand pounds, and is fearful I will call in the loans. So, he would run to me if he heard a whisper, rather than slip you a note. The poor fellow wants only to be loved... and supported financially, in a goodly style."

"Then he is a bought soul."

"Yes. A pity really, because I like the fellow too, and wish he had a stronger character. Did you see Stephen Gardiner?"

"I did." Chapuys recounts details of the meeting, and Thomas Cromwell nods. He likes Gardiner too, and doubts he is involved. "One day, he must choose a side."

"You know about his sisterly mistresses?"

"A rumour," Chapuys admits. "Will it get him into trouble with the king... or the church?"

"Not when the Bishop of Rome has sired three bastard children, and even dear Wolsey kept women. Besides, Stephen will be going away soon," Cromwell tells the ambassador. "We need a reliable man in France. A couple of years should do it. I want him far away from court when the trouble starts."

"What trouble?" Chapuys is alarmed.

"The king will have his way, Eustace. Do you agree?"

"I regret this is so," Chapuys replies. "Charles is just the same. He is an emperor, and he must be obeyed."

"Your Emperor Charles controls the pope," Cromwell replies. "Which means, like it or not, Pope Clement must be set to one side, and his edicts ignored. Henry will be rid of his wife, either by annulment, or a writ of divorce."

"Divorce?" The Spanish ambassador is suddenly aware that the ground has shifted under his feet again. "There are no possible grounds for such an outcome. The lady is utterly blameless."

"What grounds do you wish?" Cromwell decides that the ambassador will be more useful if he understands what is going to happen over the next couple of years. "Here is how it works, my friend. The king wants a certain thing... so, he tells me, or Sir Thomas More, or Stephen Gardiner, and we arrange matters to his liking. The king, however, does not want people to speak unkindly of him, so we go along to his elected parliament, and pass a law. Say that the king is too fat, or has poor dress sense, and we can charge you with treason. You cannot act against the king's wishes, or even speak badly of him without causing an offence. We are writing the statute into the law books, even as we speak."

"I don't believe it." Chapuys does, of course, believe every word. Thomas Cromwell is breaking the mould of political life in Europe. He is making Henry Tudor all powerful with his clever new laws, and it is a dangerous thing to do.

"Yes, you do. England is a strange country, Eustace. In France, if the king desires something, someone does it for him, even if it means killing a few people. In Spain, the common people have no rights anyway, and must obey their monarch ...the Emperor Charles, on pain of death."

"It has always been so," Chapuys replies.

"We are a different sort," Cromwell tells him. "Anglo Saxon, Norman, or Welshman, we *must* have the law. So, we will write a law to suit that which Henry wishes. There will be no power on earth that can be placed above the king."

"The church will disagree." Chapuys is a shrewd man, and can see where this is leading. It is a frightening prospect, but one he cannot stop coming. "The Pope is God's voice on Earth."

"If the church disagrees, they are committing treason by their wilful disobedience. Even to appeal to Rome shall mark them down as traitors. Henry's new law will punish them severely."

"The Pope is head of the church."

"Not so. He is the Bishop of Rome, my dear Eustace. Let the Italians, Spaniards, and French, bow down to him. We Englishmen like our freedom." Cromwell smiles, crookedly at the Savoyard diplomat. "The people ... *all of them* ... will swear the Oath of Obedience to King Henry, which places him above even Pope Clement."

"The Oath of Obedience?"

"Yes. I think it a rather catchy title," Cromwell says. "My young man, Rafe Sadler thought it up. You see, obedience is absolute. You obey, or you do not. It will separate the wheat from the chaff. The Bishop of Rome will not be able to command in England any more, unless the king allows it."

"He will excommunicate Henry."

"No, Eustace. It is *we* who will excommunicate the corrupt Roman Catholic church," Thomas Cromwell declares. "The king, once he is prised away from Tom More, will see the sense of it. The Boleyn woman already has provocative, protestant views, and will help the cause."

"I am drinking with a heretic!" Chapuys shrugs, and raise his glass. "Tell me no more, sir. I know you will win, Thomas, because you are that kind of man. You and Captain Draper are of the same blood. Strike him, and he will strike back, harder. Draw a blade, and he will have a bigger, sharper, one. Cross him, and he will move heaven and earth to best you, in any way he can."

"Think carefully on what I say, Eustace," Thomas Cromwell tells him. "Use what I tell you wisely. It is possible to serve both Charles , and Henry, without making either man into an enemy."

"And what of Queen Katherine?"

Eustace Chapuys asks.

"Now, what of the last two guests?" Cromwell asks, ignoring Chapuys' last question. "I regret my agents could not get close enough to give me a written report of all that was said."

"Richard Rich is a clever young man, and fears the Lord Chancellor. He claims that the Earl of Surrey suggested they turn up for dinner, and was most apologetic about the whole thing. He seeks to use young Howard as a key to a golden future."

"Then he is a damned fool. Surrey has no future... golden or otherwise. What about Sir Thomas More?" Cromwell pours another round of drinks. "He is like a father to me. My own father was a blacksmith.... A good one, and sold ale out of a house on the edge of the common."

"Was he a good father?"

"On the whole... I must say yes. He hated me for not wanting to become a smith, and beat me once when I was about fourteen. I told him I was going to see the world, and he slapped me so hard, I almost went deaf. He was disappointed in me, you see. I left the same day."

"You ran away?"

"Yes. I worked as a farm labourer, then a deck hand, until I set foot on French soil. I wandered like a lost Jew, learning many useful things. Law and banking came very easily to me, and I prospered."

"Then you came home?" Chapuys is surprised at the candour of Cromwell's digression.

"Yes… home. You were saying … about More?"

"If he is indeed a father figure, then he is a rather cruel one," Chapuys tells his friend. "He is a dangerous man, and he lies with practiced ease. The man swore that Queen Katherine will be allowed to choose where she wishes to live, and Princess Mary too. If only they relinquish their birthrights."

"A generous offer." Cromwell purses his lips. "Will you consider it?"

"No, not for an instant, my friend. He lies. His aim is to put a new, malleable Spanish princess on the throne. That means Boleyn, Katherine and poor little Mary must go. Two Spanish queens is one two many."

"What are you suggesting?" Cromwell asks.

"Nothing. Though I can tell you this much." Eustace Chapuys pauses, for the full dramatic effect. "I know who sent the note!"

"Bravo, my dear friend," Thomas Cromwell replies, grinning like a schoolboy. "So do I!"

8   Pebbles in the Water

Austin Friars is part of the old friary grounds, and it is well situated, a little north of the river, and in easy walking distance of both Westminster, and Whitehall, the king's newest palace. It is a solid, well constructed house, which has been much extended over the previous decade.

The great, limed oak, timber framed, building was once an annex of the four hundred year old friary, but has been leased out for many years now. Although now a large, comfortable house, spreading over several floors, it is also the primary place of business of the burgeoning Cromwell empire. Most of the dozen upper rooms are bedrooms, and the ground floor is taken up with a large kitchen, an impressive entrance hall, and a sumptuous dining room. To one side of the splendid oak panelled entrance, is Master Thomas Cromwell's splendid library.

The room is large, measuring ten good paces by twelve, but seems smaller, thanks to the almost floor to ceiling book cases, each of which is filled with volume after expensive volume. The books are mostly about either the law, or religion, but there are many more that might be termed frivolous, especially by a man like the current Lord Chancellor of England.

There are stories about King Arthur,

and Celtic legends, side by side with hand illuminated bibles in Latin, and tracts explaining the varied legal issues surrounding the transfer of land, or common law. Master Cromwell's household has an eclectic taste when it comes to literature. Many books have over spilled onto the floor, or onto the great work desk.

The desk fills one corner, and looks more like the lair of a wild bear, and faces the only wall not to support bookshelves. This wall, plastered with a dung and horsehair mixture, and then whitewashed, has a great, carved fire place set in it. Stags chase through trees, and vines twist up, forming a great mantlepiece cut from the heart of a mighty oak tree, a hundred years before. There is a yew wood chair, and three sturdy stools in the room. Any more than three, or four occupants, and the master's study will start to feel a little cramped.

This evening, Thomas Cromwell is seated behind the broad desk, and the stools are taken up by Eustace Chapuys, Will Draper, and Rafe Sadler, his right hand man in legal matters. Leaning against the solid, carved mantelpiece is the huge figure of Richard Cromwell, the establishment's chief enforcer. He is hungrily eyeing the pewter platters on the oak desk top.

Miriam, wishing to be useful, yet

barred from this council of war, has prepared a lavish supper. Thick slices of boiled mutton, honeyed ham, and broiled chicken legs fill the plates, alongside some freshly baked bread, and a wedge of hard Dutch cheese. On the mantelpiece itself, there stands a large jug of English ale, One of fresh goat's milk, and two bottles of good, Flemish, red wine.

"Your dear wife fears we are going to be in here all night, Will," Cromwell says with a broad smile. "How shall we manage to consume so much fine food?"

"Have no fear," Rafe quips, "for, if that is not thunder, Richard's stomach is rumbling already. I can hear it from here!"

"And the rest can go to feed the beggars at our gate," Will adds. Austin Friars is a place of bounty, and it is known, amongst the poor, that Thomas Cromwell will feed anyone in need. It has been known for a Baron and an Earl to sit down with a one eyed carpenter, or a cobbler, down on his luck.

"If they grow more numerous, I might be amongst their number myself," Cromwell replies, laconically. He finds it hard to listen to a list of his own virtues, and is a very modest man, considering his high station in life. There is a grain of truth in what he says though, for he simply cannot refuse anyone in need, and a downturn in his fortunes will bode ill for all of the poor of the district.

"Never, my friend," Chapuys exclaims, in Spanish. "There shall always be a place in my house for you."

"Eustace… I own your house," Cromwell says. "Your precious Charles rents it from me on a four weekly basis."

Chapuys slips into English once more. It is a better language to swear in. He expresses his view that so short a rental indicates in what esteem he is held by his distant masters.

"They could, at least, allow me six months to complete my tasks!"

"The prime one being the saving of England," Will says. "If Katherine and the Pole clan fall to an assassin, the world will place the blame at Henry's door. Norfolk and the rest will see how the people react, and may be tempted into rashness. None here want to see a civil war."

"Though some of us would like to test our metal," Richard Cromwell says, boldly.

"Then '*some of us*' are damned fools, Richard." Will wants no one there to think he is keen to fight. "In Ireland, my colonel commanded me to fight, and I fought. The Irish are a great multitude, and do not understand the meaning of fear. A chief of a clan might lead a hundred men into a fight, and come out with ten, but if he has killed a few Englishmen, he rejoices as if winning a great battle. I have seen the grass turned red with blood. Imagine that blood to be English, or your brother's, or friend's"

"Will is right," Thomas Cromwell puts in. "Besides, war is very bad for trade. The ports close, and we can't get our wool to market, or import good wine. Now, how do we stop this madness before it takes hold?"

"We must protect the Pole family," Miriam says, coming in with another flagon of beer. "Forgive my interruption, Master Thomas, but it is my experience that men always talk too much on these occasions."

"Well spoken, Mistress Miriam," Chapuys says, clapping his hands. "If Cromwell permits... may we hear your ideas?" Cromwell smiles, and nods consent. In the few weeks that the Jewish girl has been under his roof, he has grown to love her almost as much as his own two, long dead, daughters, and wishes her to be treated as an equal.

"These Frenchmen have made a mistake," she says. "They have revealed their identities to us, and they know we will be looking out for them. They must hide from our wrath. I ask you, gentlemen, where would you hide a duck?"

"On a pond?" Richard asks, then blushes at his own stupidity. "Oh, I see. In a flock. You think they will flee to France?"

"Of course, but they must have money. To get it, they must finish what they have started." Miriam tells them. "They know they must act swiftly, else we will capture them. So, how many must we protect?"

"Three." The gathered company look at Cromwell with varying degrees of surprise. He shrugs, and explains. "Their leader, rather foolishly mentioned he had that number to deal with. I was confused at the time."

"Why so?" Chapuys asks.

"There are a dozen prominent members of the Pole family, and perhaps as many friends of the queen," Cromwell replies. "With both Katherine and Mary to murder… who, I thought, was the last one? Then it came to me. I have been a fool, and it may yet cost our cause dearly."

"You worry me, master," Rafe mutters through a mouthful of ham.

"How did our killers get to their victims?" Cromwell demands to know.

"Trickery. They present themselves as a travelling troupe of entertainers, and gain access to them," Will offers. "Who would suspect them?"

"Presumably, by walking up to the front door, knocking and advertising their presence," says Chapuys.

"Then how would they gain access to the queen, let alone poor Mary, who is under guard, and watched around the clock face?" Cromwell asks. "Royalty does not have the same privileges as others. Stewards would turn them away, or guards send them packing."

"This is true, Cromwell," Chapuys agrees. "Even I must beg for a few minutes with her blessed Majesty. These tumblers will fail in their intent."

"They never meant to murder Katherine," Miriam says, "nor poor little Mary. They are contracted to kill Poles, and Poles alone."

"Then which three?" Will ponders. "We know they must act swiftly, so can rule out any family members who live more than a day's ride. Gilbert Guyot is no fool. He will want to kill, and be on a boat to the continent that self same day."

"I agree." Cromwell stands and crosses to search out an atlas of county maps he uses when inventing new titles for Henry to scatter amongst his hangers on, and lifts down a leather bound book that is almost too heavy for him to lift. He places it on the desk, and opens it to the section covering the south eastern Shires, and their principal towns, great halls, and sea ports. The Cinque Ports seem an obvious escape route.

Then he takes down a second, slimmer volume. The cover bears a single word title… *Vindicatio.* It contains details of every person who Cromwell considers to be an enemy, of either himself, his family, or England. Percy is listed inside, as is Sir Thomas More, and two score lesser offenders. There is an entire chapter devoted purely to the Pole family, and their retainers.

"Are these the people you have marked down for death, Cromwell?" Chapuys asks, reading over his friend's shoulder.

"No, my friend. They are merely noted as being… less than sympathetic to my cause." He points to the first name on the page. "See? This fellow has his fortune abroad, and a son who skulks in Paris, blackguarding the king. But he lives near Carlisle. Too far for our purposes. The same as with Sir Adwulf Pole, who resides in Chesterfield."

"We must scour your little book, master," Rafe says. "though that may still leave us with too many names to save."

"Then we select the most likely few, and try to keep them safe," Miriam snapped. "With your permission," she adds, assuming a meeker tone. It is hard for her to remember her place in this strange new world. Under her late grandfather's roof, she was actively encouraged to take part in business matters, and speak openly about matters that concerned her directly.

"Oh, don't play all meek and mild with me, my dear young lady," Cromwell says, grinning. "Will, your blessed wife is too clever for us poor men. You should whip her more often,"

"I would rather face an army of Scots, sir," Will replies, and they all laugh. Miriam has suggested a workable plan, and it remains only for the details to be put into place. They talk on into the evening, and, just after midnight, complete their arrangements.

As they finish off the food and drink, then make their way to their beds, Cromwell takes Will Draper's arm, and begs him to stay behind for a moment. The soldier of fortune ushers his comrades from the room, then turns back to his benefactor.

"Is Miriam quite recovered, Will?" Cromwell asks. "I shall forever blame myself for the danger she had to face today."

"Forever is a long time, sir," Will says, easily. He is a fatalist, and believes that life is a constant struggle to stay on top. If bad things happen, then at least, he has the means to counter them with good. "Miriam does not blame you. She thinks herself to have been at fault. The friars are small, elderly men, and the two she saw were big fellows. She believes she should have suspected something was amiss at once, and cried outdoor help."

"As *I* should have suspected my first inclination," Cromwell says. "I assumed the Frenchmen were going to kill Katherine. I was wrong. However, whoever is behind the plot to kill the Poles will still want the queen and Princess Mary dead. They will see it as a simple solution."

"How so?"

"The slaughter will silence the Roman Bishop for a while," Cromwell explains. "Katherine's death will also free Henry to marry again. The mastermind behind the plot will expect the king's gratitude."

"Then you believe that the queen to still be in danger?" Will asks.

"Yes, I do…. somehow." Cromwell is thinking on his feet. Ideas, half formed, flit across his over-active mind. "After we have dealt with Guyot, we must look to uncovering the real conspiracy."

"With your permission," Will says. "Miriam's brother is back from Dover tomorrow, and I will employ his particular skills."

"Very well," Cromwell is trying to see things from his adversaries point of view. "We must dig down into the very root of the thing. There is a master's hand at work, and I want to unearth the whole plot."

"Mush has the face of an innocent," says Will, "and people speak too openly when he is about, as if he has a child's mind. He and his people will infiltrate the enemy, and help direct out attack."

"He has his own people?" Cromwell is amused. "The boy is only…"

"The *boy* drove a dagger into Harry Cork's heart, without a moment's hesitation." Will Draper has made his point, and his master bows to the truth of it.

"Have him be a little more subtle this time," Thomas Cromwell concludes. "We do not want the Thames clogged with too many bodies!"

*

Eustace Chapuys returns home to find his old servant has lit a good fire, and laid out his night attire, correctly. He smiles, knowing that the ageing Spaniard fears for his position, having been revealed to be a Cromwell spy, and decides that he shall have fun with the situation.

"Excellent, my dear Luis," he mutters. "I am travelling tomorrow, and will need my best riding habit, and the black boots I bought in Santiago de Compostela." He is going to look every inch the Spanish ambassador on the morrow, sporting the hand made leather riding boots he paid a king's ransom for, during his visit to Galicia, three years before.

"You are leaving London, *Señor*?" Luis is not a good traveller, and can foresee a few uncomfortable days ahead.

"Do not fret, old man," Chapuys replies. "I will be making the journey on my own."

"Alone?" Now he is *really* alarmed. Good masters are hard to come by, and he does not know how he stands with Chapuys just now. "Where to, sir?"

"Ask Thomas Cromwell, when next you report to him."

"Oh, forgive this humble man, sir!" Luis throws his hands up in real consternation. "I exchanged worthless gossip for some meals, and a few silver coins. You must expect such behaviour from a poor servant. I have the money safe still, and it is all yours, if you but say the word."

"I will deal with you on my return," Eustace Chapuys says.

"Then I hope it is a long journey, master," Luis Gomez grumbles, "for my back will not stand too harsh a beating."

"You sly dog. You know I will not thrash you, as you deserve!" The ambassador suddenly has an idea. "When next you go to confession, put the coins in the poor box."

"I will, your honour," Luis says. "On my life."

"Exactly," Chapuys says, and dismisses the old rogue from his presence. The man has been passed down from his father, and he can only guess at his age, which he places at between fifty nine, and sixty five. Old Luis knows he cannot go on for ever, and has even suggested his own replacement, a nephew, called Alonso, who is willing to travel at a moment's notice. Another Gomez in his entourage. Chapuys smiles, and then yawns. He must sleep.

On the morrow, he and Thomas Cromwell's young men will have a hectic time ahead. He likens himself to a pebble, thrown into a still pond. There will be a great splash, and a lot of ripples to watch out for.

If their counter plot works, Eustace Chapuys believes it will force the hand of his enemy... whomsoever it might be. He crosses himself, and prays for success. Then it occurs to him that he is asking God for something selfish, and adds an addendum, explaining that it is not for his own gain, but for the good of Katherine, the queen... and the perfidious, Godless country that is England.

"Bear with me, Lord," he concludes, " for it is all for the best, I believe.... Amen!"

9   The Court of Broken Hearts

"I have received a note, Your Majesty." Maria de Salinas, the widowed Lady Willoughby, puts the bowl of warm water, scented with rose petals, down by the queen's bed. Roses in March are a wondrous thing, made possible, she hears, by Thomas Cromwell. It seems he advises the gardeners to keep bushes, potted, and by the great ovens in the royal kitchens.

So, she has petals to smell, in March. Replacing the bowl each morning is her only real duty, and she fulfils it each day, with pleasure. Katherine is more than her queen, she is her confidant, her best friend, and she loves her for it.

Maria de Salinas' father had died when she was five, and she was brought up by a cold, remote uncle, who wanted her off his hands, as soon as possible. Entering the service of the House of Aragon was the perfect solution for everyone. She soon became devoted to Katherine, and witnessed all her trials and tribulations, with an angry heart.

"A note?" The queen pushes herself up into a sitting position in the huge bed, and removes her tightly knotted night cap. Her long, red hair, streaked now with white, tumbles free, over her white shoulders. "Is it a love note, Maria?"

"You must not make fun of me, Highness" Maria says, blushing at the notion. "The gentleman says he has written me a song, and wishes for me to hear it. He suggests a private meeting between the two of us."

"The poor fellow," Katherine says. "Does he know you are made of stone in the ways of love?"

"Madam, I am almost forty years old," Maria explains.

"Love does not count the years, my dear friend," the queen says. "I still yearn to have my husband beside me here. It is a large bed for so small a queen."

"Love leads only to pain."

"Yet your late husband, Willoughby, left you a wealthy woman," Katherine says, teasing her best friend.

"I thank him for that," Maria replies, "but I never truly loved him, my lady. Our marriage was more like a financial arrangement."

"That is a sadness." Queen Katherine crosses to the bowl, and dipping her fingers into the scented water, she splashes a few drops onto her face. "The pain of love is exquisite. Send your secret lover a note back. Tell him you will meet him here, in these very rooms, with a queen as chaperone."

"That is a gracious offer, my lady, but…"

"It was not an offer, Maria," Katherine says, casually. "It was a royal command. Thank him for his letter, and tell him you wish to hear these poetic words he speaks of. Is he handsome, my dear?"

"He is." Maria is uneasy. She is soon to be forty, and wonders what her admirer finds so attractive about her. "I think his age is no more than thirty."

"Wonderful. A young, lusty lover, Maria." Katherine pulls the lace bow at her throat, and her nightwear billows, and falls down to the floor. She is naked. "Imagine how strongly he will plough his furrow. Write back, at once. I am curious to meet this ardent young gallant. What is his name?"

*

"Richard Rich!" Barnaby Fowler slaps the young man of law on the back, and falls in beside him. "We are well met, sir. This is a good omen, and no mistake. Where are you headed?"

"Grey's Inn law chambers, sir," Rich replies, warily. The fellow looks well enough dressed, but has the look of a rogue about him. "Do I know you? The face is familiar, but I can't place it. Or think why I should."

Barnaby Fowler turns the cuff of his short, black doublet, displaying the embroidered letter 'C' that marks him down as a Cromwell man. It is a device becoming well known about the city, and usually inspires either respect, or fear.

"Then that is how I know you," Rich says. "I must have come across you around one of your master's most excellent breakfast feasts."

"Indeed, sir." Fowler takes his elbow, and steers him from the main thoroughfare. "The way you go is dirty, and overcrowded. I know a better, quicker way."

"But this leads only to the river," the young lawyer protests, growing a little alarmed.

"That is so, Richard," Barnaby Fowler replies, winking at the young lawyer. "I have a swift boat waiting at the dock."

"A boat?"

"Yes, it is one of Master Cromwell's own. He has given me use of it, whenever the need arises."

"A generous man, your Master Cromwell."

"Indeed he is, Richard." Fowler beckons to a big, rough looking boatman. "Let me introduce you to Master Henry Brough. Though folk call him Bad Hal, or Rough Brough, for some unknown reason. He is going to take you for a ride."

"What is this?" Rich is becoming even

more alarmed, and moves his hand to the hilt of his sword.

"Pray, do not make any rash moves, Richard," Barnaby Fowler mutters, "unless you wish to anger Bad Hal. He is as like to snap your blade, or even your back. Just get into the boat, and behave your good self."

"Where are you taking me off to?" Richard Rich is a lawyer, not a fighter, and he sits, meekly, down on one of the cross benches.

"Why, to see Master Tom, of course." Fowler has his instructions. He is to fetch Master Rich to a certain house on the river. Thomas Cromwell specifies that he is to be unharmed, but a little fear is quite acceptable, to help loosen his tongue. From there, he will be transferred to Austin Friars under guard. "Afterwards, my dearest friend Bad Hal Brough, will either row you back to the bridge, or drop you off it, after dark."

"Oh, Christ!" Richard Rich feels the hand of death on his shoulder, and begins to cry.

*

"You may invite him here, as my guest." Katherine is enjoying herself, for the first time in several years. "I will arrange for connecting rooms, and he can *slip into you,* after dark."

"Madam, have you no shame at all?"

Maria says, joining in the silly little game. "What if I cannot cope with his... great ardour?"

"That is true. These English all have very big pintles, or so I hear. I myself have scant knowledge, having dealt with but a solitary one."

"Hush, my lady. You make me blush. The boy may be even less competent than I, when it comes to making love."

"Then I shall hide behind a screen, and come out if either of you need support." The idea is so ridiculous that it sets both women off laughing again.

In their straight laced environment, even such a trivial event as a *billet deux* is extraordinary, and an event to be cherished. Queen Katherine, having been born the youngest surviving child of Ferdinand and Isabella, the joint rulers of Spain, has been swaddled, and protected all her life.

Her parents had, almost immediately, begun to look for a good political match for her. So it was that, at the age of just three years old, she was betrothed to young Prince Arthur, the son of Henry VII. When she was almost sixteen, Katherine made the long journey to England. She was married at sixteen, shut away in Ludlow Castle, and then, suddenly widowed. Less than six months after the wedding, Arthur was dead of the terrible sweating sickness.

"What if he doesn't come?"

"Then I shall ask Henry to cut off his head," Katherine says, sternly, then adds, with a smile, "or his prodigious pintle."

"I will fetch paper and ink," Maria de Salinas says. She is an attractive, well off, widow of a certain age, and if a young, vigorous man wants to court her... then why not?

*

"Master Rich, this is a pleasant surprise," Thomas Cromwell says, ushering the young man into his library. "All my young agents are away, performing certain duties I find thrust upon us, so I must attend to you myself. Let me make my apologies in advance."

Richard Rich freezes in terror as the tip of a very sharp knife touches his throat. Cromwell has conjured it from his sleeve in an instant, and has the man up against a wall. The ageing lawyer is reminded of his time in Italy, fighting for the French. He recalls, vividly, how he once fired a crossbow into the throat of a charging knight, and the bounty he reaped from robbing the still warm corpse.

"Dear God, sir!" Rich whispers.

"Do not dare to 'Dear God' me, young sir," Cromwell replies, harshly. He is in a hurry, and cannot afford to play silly games

with the fellow. "I will have either answers, or
your life. Sit down, and attend me well. I want
nothing but the truth from your lips. Do you
understand, or shall I have my boatman drown
you in my cellar?"

"Mercy, sir. How have I offended you?
What harm have I done that warrants such
harsh treatment?"

"Tell me about the note."

"Pray tell, which note?" Cromwell's
hand is a blur, and the dagger embeds itself in
the wood panelling behind Richard Rich's
right ear.

"Oh, yes…. You mean *that* note. Silly
of me to forget. You mean the one I sent to
Eustace Chapuys."

"To me, you damned idiot," Cromwell
growls. "You meant for the Spanish gentleman
to seek me out."

"Forgive me, sir. I meant no harm. I
only wanted to alert the proper people to
something I have heard about."

"You suggest that bloody murder is to
be done, sir," Cromwell says. "There is
nothing casual about where you obtain your
information. Who spoke to you about killing
the Pole family, *en masse*?"

"I was approached by a man in the
outer court," Rich confesses. "he fell in with
us, and spoke of politicking. He asked us, each
gentleman in turn, what would happen if

Henry died suddenly."

"That in itself is treason, Master Rich." Cromwell pours a single glass of wine, and hands it to the terrified young lawyer. "You know that. It is written into law, that talking of the king's death is an offence. Wishing for it, means the axe."

"You misunderstand, sir. The gentleman I speak of loves the king, as we all do. He meant... or so I took it... to wonder if Katherine would rule through Mary. We know the king's mind in the matter of the queen."

"You know the king's mind?" Cromwell grins through clenched teeth. "Even Henry does not know the king's mind, you damned idiot. What happened then?"

"A few of us, all lawyers, began to debate the legality of things, and concluded that Mary may well rule. Ogilvy suggested the king's bastard son be a candidate, but I could not see my way to that."

"Some could." Cromwell is thoughtful now. "The kingdom will be torn asunder, Master Rich. Is that what you wish?"

"Not I, sir!" He is affronted. "I am for Henry, the one, anointed king. There is enough legal precedent for him to set aside the queen, and marry again. A young, fertile girl will give him boys, and that will put paid to Queen Katherine and her papist daughter's claims."

"You said all this to your friend?"

"I did, and he told me that some like minded people had a mind to remove all obstacles in Henry's path, and that I was a welcome addition to their cause. I almost told him 'nay', but the lawyer in me, stayed my immediate refusal."

"Had you declared against them, you would have been killed too," Cromwell confirms. "You did the right thing."

"I knew I could not stop them, nor could I report openly to any of the king's men. For, who knows which of them are in the plot?"

"So, you chose to drop the mess in my lap?"

"I can only apologise," Richard Rich says. "I trust you, above all others."

"That is most reassuring, Richard," Cromwell says, disguising his contempt for a man who can be both a clever fellow, and a complete idiot at one and the same time. "Though I must disabuse you of your belief in self determination. Did you not wonder why they enlisted you in their odd little enterprise?"

"I believe they want my expertise, as a man, well versed in the law."

"Then you believe wrongly." Cromwell dampens down the anger which is swelling inside. He has a mind to beat some sense into the silly whelp, but decides, instead, to elaborate. "If one wishes to kill the beast, you swiftly cut off the head. You do not trim off the toe nails first. In other words, kill Katherine and Mary, and the rest wither away without a fight."

"Oh, I begin to see." Richard Rich is catching on, but does not like the way it makes him look.

"At last. The plotters wish to assassinate the queen, but fear my agents. I might find out, and stop them. So, they have devised a plan to divert me from my duty, and it has almost succeeded. They tell you some of their scheme, knowing you will inform on them, and I will have my people chasing about England, trying to catch a band of tumblers."

"But we do know Katherine is in danger," Rich replies.

"Yes, though not the how, where, and when."

"I see." Richard Rich frowns, and asks something that puzzles him. "How could they know for sure that I would warn you, Master Cromwell?"

"Because you are a coward, Richard. They led you to me, knowing you feared me, more than they."

"Led me?" Rich is sick with himself now.

"Yes," Cromwell is beginning to tire of the man's lack of imagination. ""Who fell in with you that night?"

"The Earl of Surrey."

"Who would as like scrape you off his shoe, as befriend one of your class. The man considers himself above all, save Henry. He even sneers openly at his own father. Norfolk would have drowned the insolent puppy years ago, were he not the first born son."

"I thought the boy liked me, sir." The last illusion is blown away, and Richard Rich must learn about humility.

"He picks you up, and suggests a visit to my dinner table. He is a part of it. You were given the opportunity of informing, and you took it. Surrey wants the queen gone, sooner rather than later. He does not wish for the law to work against Katherine. The devil's child is in a hurry to attain his true rank under Henry."

"I… I don't see."

"God's teeth, Richard! Katherine is dead, and Henry is rushed into marriage with Anne Boleyn… young Surrey's cousin. In gratitude, she elevates her supporters. When old Norfolk dies in a few years, his son will be more powerful than the king. Imagine the wealth he will command, not to mention the fifty thousand armed men at his beck and call."

"Then the Earl of Surrey is the leader of the plot?"

"No, he is too young, and too vain. Though only fifteen years old, he is already a hate mongering wastrel, and a notable drunkard. He is being guided, just like you, and Gilbert Guyot."

"Who?"

"Never mind. I have work to do, Rich. Get out."

"Yes, of course." He hesitates, almost too frightened to speak, then says, "You will not let the queen, Mary and Maria die, will you, Master Cromwell?"

The light of revelation suddenly shines down upon Thomas Cromwell. The young fool has little inclination to act either way, except for one, obvious thing. He is in love.

"Maria de Salinas?"

"She is the sun that warms my heart, sir," Richard Rich declares. "She is the morning and the night. The sun and the moon. She is..."

"At least forty," Cromwell says, cruelly. "You fear for her life, and that is why you sent the note. It is as good a reason as any, I suppose. Tell me, what is it, apart from her estates, and five thousand marks a year, that ensnares your heart?"

"I care not for fortune." Richard is greatly affronted.

"Why not... have you already one of your own?"

"No, I am in debt, but whom, apart from yourself, is not?"

"Lady Maria. She is worth a goodly amount in land and gold." Cromwell shakes his head, and places a blank sheet of paper before the besotted young man. "Write it all down, including the name of the scoundrel who tried to lead you into treason."

"Then I am not to be drowned as I leave?"

"What, and deprive the Donna Maria of her sweet young lover?" Cromwell sneers.

"You mock me now, sir."

"No, I envy you, Richard. You have found a woman you adore, and lust after, and she is very wealthy. It is a fairytale come true for you both, and I wish you every happiness. I hope she loves you back, as hard."

"Then I really can go?"

"As soon as you finish your confession." Cromwell delights in the look of horror which crosses his face. "Though I fear you might, through your innate sense of honesty, implicate yourself."

"I might word it carefully, sir," Rich replies, "avoiding anything that might incriminate me."

"Of course. Why did I not think of it? That is a splendid solution, but I must insist on a list of those who spoke of Henry's sudden, violent death."

"They are just young idlers, Master Cromwell."

"Oh? Are they indeed? Did you not mention that Harry Percy was in the group? And was not Stephen Gardiner, Thomas More, Tom Cranmer, my lords Surrey and Norfolk, and the king's own bastard son, Henry Fitzroy *all* present?"

"But Fitzroy is only ten years old, sir."

"He is a precocious child," Cromwell replies. "Put him on the list, just for form's sake. Do not date it."

"You would have me draw up a death list, Master Cromwell. I admire you, and trust it will remain unused?"

"It is merely a form of insurance, Richard," Cromwell tells him. By itself, a few names scrawled on paper, means nothing, but every little piece of evidence helps. A thousand scraps of paper might bring down a duke, or save a queen, one fine day.

"Shall I sign it?"

"Best not," Cromwell says, taking the goose quill pen from his shaking hand. "For I do not think you would stand up to a hard questioning. Run along now, and give my fondest regards to Lady Maria. Your puppy love for her may yet save many lives."

"I *do* love her," Richard Rich says, then adds, as a Parthian shot. "You *do* know what love is, don't you, sir?"

It is a loose stair tread on a dark night, a lie told sweetly, or a blade that cuts both ways, Thomas Cromwell thinks, but does not say. Happiness is a fleeting thing, and he has no wish to spoil the young man's dreams, unless he must.

*

Maria de Salinas is waiting. The queen has given her tacit approval of Master Richard Rich, and loaned her one of her best dresses. It is cut in such a way as to enhance the beauty of her neck and shoulders, and draws the eye away from her woeful lack of a large bosom.

"You have a fine face," Katherine says, hoping to be kind to her flat chested friend. "By the time he gets to thinking of your breasts, he will be too besotted to consider them as a drawback."

At almost forty, Maria is still most fetching, and has often been complimented by gentlemen around the court. Until know, she has resisted all blandishments, and remained an independent widow, but this poetic young man has touched her heart, and convinced her of his undying devotion. He is the only man ever to write a love song for her. So, she waits for him. Time passes, and she begins to fear that he has changed his mind, and lacks the courage to tell her that he is not coming. The clock says eleven, when she decides that she has been a fool, and begins to cry.

*

Richard Rich is still shaking with fear

as he leaves Austin Friars, and retires to the nearest tavern to buy a calming drink. After one and a half bottles of wine, his nerves are more settled. He knows he should be somewhere, but cannot think straight. One of the tavern wenches sits down beside him, and begins to stroke his thigh.

There are rooms, Richard is told, where a fine gentleman might take his ease with a willing companion. It strikes him as an excellent idea, and it is only after he has pleasured the raven haired tart a second time, and slipped her two silver shillings, that he recalls his promise to visit Maria. He dresses in haste, and expends another sixpence on boat hire, hoping to make up for lost time.

He arrives at the queen's private rooms two hours late, and smelling of drink. Maria receives him, but only to chide him for his appalling tardiness. He offers his apologies, claiming he has been on an errand of mercy for the ailing Duke of Surrey. Then he steps forward, kneels, and takes Maria's hand in his.

"Forgiveness is all a part of love, my sweetness," he purrs, kissing the hand. "I am younger than you, and more prone to silliness, but give me a chance, and I will shout my love for you from the highest tower in England."

Maria wants him. She is about to relent, when a traitorous draft, blowing under the door, wafts Richard's rancid aroma under her nose. She has been married to a man who, despite his years, was an ardent, though clumsy, lover. Master Rich smells, unmistakably of recent sex.

"Master Rich, I have a mind to lay with you," she says tartly, "but wonder if you have the strength?"

"You will find me a goodly rider, madam," he says, brazenly. "You have but to provide the mount."

"No sir!" Maria pulls her hand away from his. "I will not be your second conquest this night!"

Rich stands, and steps back a pace. He sees that further words will only provoke her to greater anger. He bows to her, turns on his heel and strides out of the room.

Maria cries now, in earnest. She sees how foolish it is to trust any man, and vows to herself.

No more!

10 The Lady's Hebrew

"There is a strange young man, demanding to speak with you, madam. Shall I have him thrown out?" Lady Jane Rochford, is George Boleyn's wife, and a principal Lady in Waiting to Anne Boleyn. She has a curt manner, and often oversteps the bounds with her sister-in-law.

"How so… strange?" Lady Anne is bored, and wishes she were still free to mix with all her dear old friends, without Henry's sanctimonious disapproval. "Has he two heads, Lady Rochford?"

"The one is enough," Jane Rochford retorts. "It is the pet Hebrew of Thomas Cromwell."

"Master Cromwell is a friend to us, these days," Anne replies smoothly, and she glances down at the superb yellow stone which adorns her right hand middle finger. "and must have sent this monstrosity with an important message. Show him in at once."

"My lady, I don't think…"

"No, you do not, Lady Rochford." The Boleyn temper is never far beneath the surface, and besides, she roundly dislikes her brother's wife, who she suspects is a little prettier than she is. "Bring him to me, now!"

Lady Rochford pauses just long enough to show her displeasure, makes a tutting noise, and hurries outside. She will complain to George again, but knows it will do her no good. Her boorish husband has little affection for her, and seldom supports her in the constant sniping matches with his sister. The swarthy young Jew is still standing where she left him.

"Come." She leads him in to Anne's presence, and instructs him as they walk. "You address my mistress Anne as 'My Lady' at all times, fellow. Visitors must not approach, unless bidden, and remember to bow low. You do know how to bow, don't you?"

"The English bow, My Lady Rochford, or does the Lady Anne prefer the French style?"

Anne Boleyn catches the last few words, and smiles to herself. She understands that a clever man might be employing a witty *double entendre*. For the French style is, her brother tells her, much employed by the city whores these days. It is safer, they claim, and allows them to get through more customers each evening.

"Master Mush, Lady Anne. A messenger from Thomas Cromwell's offices," Lady Rochford announces, and moves to one side. Anne Boleyn is immediately struck by the almost feminine beauty of the olive skinned young man, and beckons him over to stand closer to her. She looks at him, and he holds her gaze, most brazenly for so young a man.

"Master Mush?"

"Just Mush, Lady Anne." Moshe ben Mordecai is now used to being known as Mush Morden, to conceal his otherwise transparent state of Jewishness, and thus preserve his life. English law still demands the death penalty for his race. "It is what my friends call me."

"Cromwell's pet Hebrew, I am told," Anne says, glancing over to Jane Rochford, who squirms uncomfortably. "What message have you for me?"

"I am instructed to remain in your company for this day, my lady. Master Cromwell says I must ignore all your protestations, and stay close by your side."

"His impertinence is astounding," La Boleyn says, but not unkindly. In fact, she is intrigued, and Mush's unexpected presence has lightened her mood considerably. "Does he deign to say why this must be so?"

"Yes, madam, he does." Mush leans closer, and drops his voice to a husky whisper which sends a thrill down Anne's spine. "A word alone, if I may?"

"Out of the question!" Lady Rochford has heard enough, and comes roaring from her dark corner, intent on expelling this upstart youth at once. "Alone indeed… why I have never heard…"

"Leave us."

"What?" Lady Rochford halts in mid flurry. "You can't mean to be left alone… with… a … he is a …"

"Oh, Jane, you are such a prig. Stand outside. Leave the door open, so that you may see me, yet not hear this dark secret I am to be told. Go on… run along."

Lady Rochford obeys, reluctantly. She stands, observing the rest of the meeting, and tantalisingly out of ear shot. It is humiliating, but then, her life is one long humiliation, thanks to her marriage to a man who does not want her.

"Well?" Lady Anne says. "Explain yourself, Cromwell's little pet."

"Master Cromwell says he is about to uncover a wicked plot against the crown. It is just possible that your own life might be in some kind of danger."

Anne Boleyn feels a tightness in her stomach for a brief moment, then recovers her composure. She is intelligent enough to know that she has made enemies, and she fears an assassin's knife more than anything. Mush pretends not to have seen the slight flicker of fear in her eyes.

"Who means me harm?" the lady demands. Mush shrugs his shoulders. He is a foot soldier, and has not been made aware of all the details, the motion says.

"I am to keep you safe, Lady Boleyn."

Lady Anne, despite finding the youth attractive, would rather be surrounded by trusted men, with swords and pistols. She fears Master Cromwell has taken leave of his usual good sense, for once.

"How so, Master Mush?" she snaps. "Have you a hundred armed men outside?"

"Just one Mush, lady." The movement is a blur. Anne flinches, and stares at the bowl of green apples set on the table by the far window. One of the fruits has been skewered by a slender Spanish throwing knife. "I can outreach any sword, madam, and kill a man at thirty paces, even before he can think to unsheathe his weapon."

"Might not a lady occasionally enjoy an *unsheathed* weapon, Mush?" The youth's face remains impassive, and Anne decides that he means nothing more than he says.

"I shall stay out of your way, but always within reach, Lady Anne." He bows. "By your leave?"

"Very well," she replies. Thomas Cromwell is no fool, and if he says she is to be guarded, then let it be so. The boy is both unusual, and good looking. She might as well spend the day drinking in his prettiness. "Do you know any poetry, Mush?"

"No, not in English, Lady Anne."

"French?" He shakes his head. In truth, he can speak French, Spanish and a little Italian but, like Eustace Chapuys, he prefers to keep such a talent quiet.

"I know a rude song in Irish, taught to me by my brother in law, madam."

"Then you must entertain me in English," she says.

"What the hell is this?" George Boleyn, the Earl of Rochford, alerted by his scornful wife, is suddenly there, hand on sword hilt. "Alone, with a ... a ... a Jew!"

"He is to be my new bodyguard," Anne Boleyn says, enjoying her pompous brother's upset. "He will attend to my body, and keep it preserved, George. I would take your hand from your hilt, brother... if only for safety's sake."

"Are you mad? Alone, with a man?" George Boleyn can contain himself no longer, and seeing the youth is unarmed, draws his sword. "Away with you, Jewish dog, or I will forget myself, and gut your worthless body!"

He is not quite sure how Mush has managed to get inside the range of his sword, nor how he has managed to grasp his wrist, but the pain is real enough, and he cries out as his blade clatters to the floor. Mush twists, hard, then steps back, and smiles at the man.

"My apologies, Lord Rochford," Mush tells him, coldly. He stoops, and retrieves the sword. "No edged weapons are allowed within this chamber, by order of the Privy Councillor, Master Thomas Cromwell. The next man to draw on me, in this room, will die. Is that clearly understood?"

"What right have you to…."

"Oh, do shut up, George," Anne snaps. "If you value my honour so much, you may stay. You can even invite that dried up prune of a wife of yours back in."

George Boleyn swears to himself that he will get even with the upstart Jew, but accepts Anne's terms with ill grace. He calls his wife in, and bids her to stay, as chaperone to his sister. She is a valuable commodity, and if there is a hint of scandal, Henry might drop her for another. With Lady Mary Boleyn already compromised by Henry, the family are running out of viable females to throw at the king.

"There, now we are four," Lady Anne says. "Shall we play cards, or hide and seek?"

"I can play cards," Mush says. It is a safer option than allowing Lady Anne to conceal herself about the court. "Shall we play for pennies… or shillings?"

George Boleyn has a deck with him, and as he deals, Anne acquaints him with Thomas Cromwell's worry for her safety. He frowns, and speculates as to who might wish to harm her.

"Who would dare?" he asks.

"Take your pick," she says, bitterly. "Am I not the French whore, hated by all of England?"

Mush picks up his cards, and spreads them, fan-like in his hand. He has a knave, and two queens. He thinks of the queens as Katherine and Anne Boleyn, and wonders just who the knave will turn out to be.

"It will all change, once you are queen," George grumbles.

"Will it ever really change, whilst Katherine and Mary still draw breath?" She grins then. "Perhaps we could convince dear Mush to throttle them for me?"

"It is against my faith to kill women," Mush replies. "I am much more likely to stab a bad card sharper."

"What sir?" George stutters. "You dare to call me a sharp?"

"Shall I cut your sleeve, and let the card fall?" Mush asks him.

"I thought this was to be a friendly game," Rochford mutters, replacing the stolen card in the deck.

"It is sir, which is why I have not slit your throat." Mush smiles at the ladies. "Who shall lead?"

Two hours later, George Boleyn takes his leave, his purse lighter by almost two pounds. His sister is delighted, and even Lady

Rochford manages a smile.

"You teach my husband a lesson in humility, Master Mush," she says. "Thank you, for that at least, my clever Jew."

"Madam, the jest grows a little weary with overuse. I am an Englishman, and my name is Moses Morden. I hail from Coventry, where the darker skin is prevalent, due to the local charcoal making. The smoke tans us at birth, My Lady.

"Then I shall call you Master Morden."

"Just Mush," the young man says, as he pockets the silver coins. "Just Mush will do."

*

It has been a long day, and Thomas Cromwell is tired from his exertions. He has concluded his business with Richard Rich, set Mush to guarding La Boleyn, alerted the queen's swarthy Moroccans to be extra vigilant, and sent his agents out into the unknown, on a quest to save a family he would rather see broken, or even dead, for political reasons.

It will be a difficult night for the lawyer, as he sits up in his library, waiting for a hard riding messenger, bringing him news. He is particularly worried about Eustace Chapuys, who has become a good friend during the last week.

The Spanish ambassador is a

determined sort, and has insisted on riding out to warn one of the plot's possible victims. Cromwell is worried, because he thinks the man may well be a target too. Destroy the Pole clan, the queen, and her closest advisor, and the job is done. Above all men, Chapuys has the queen's confidence, and may therefore be a target.

"Go warily, my children,"he mutters, and reaches down a volume written in Italian. It will pass the time, he thinks, until news comes … god or bad.

*

The snow of January and February has given way to an almost constant rain, and the roads to the south coast are softening into cloying mud. Night falls swiftly on the downs, and it is a brave, or foolish, man who travels after dark.

Eustace Chapuys is neither a hero, nor a fool, and he stops at an inn outside the tiny, well kept village of Chiddingstone. It is close by the great rolling acres of the Ashdown forest. He knows that, at first light, he must traverse the wide forest, which spreads across a quarter of the shire, and provides excellent hunting forays for King Henry, and his rich, aristocratic friends.

The innkeeper is, at first, wary of the little foreigner, who travels alone, but warms to him when he asks for his best room, and a good meal. There is the smell of money in the air, and customers have been few and far between of late.

"I have a haunch of venison," the man says. "It has been hanging this month past, and is ready for the spit. My wife will dress it with vinegar, if you wish."

"Have you no garlic?" Chapuys asks, more in hope than certainty.

"Bless you, no sir. My customers are honest folk, and don't like that French muck. I'll rub her down with salt instead, if you like, or roast some onions with it."

"Your wife wishes to be rubbed down?" Chapuys is confused by the man's way of talking, and imagines the stout woman by the fire, being treated so.

"My wife?" The innkeeper is becoming as confused as the ambassador. "If she takes your fancy, I could have her warm your bed tonight. Though I must wonder at your taste in women, sir. My pot girl is but fourteen, and much more comely."

"No, no!" Eustace Chapuys has finally unravelled the convoluted misunderstandings. "Cook the animal any way you care, my man. As for your wife, I mean no slight to her, but I am very tired, and must decline your kind offer."

"And Tilly? She is an eager and pleasing girl." He leans forward, and winks.

"She can just as easily go atop, as below. I can vouch for her most readily, sir, if you get my meaning?"

"Food and a bed," Chapuys repeats, this time much more firmly. The innkeeper shrugs his shoulders, and retires, muttering about strange foreign folk, and their strange, foreign ways. An hour later, and Eustace is presented with a platter of steaming meat, and roasted vegetables. The serving girl smiles, and pouts at him in what she thinks is a lustful display, until he slips her a silver sixpence, and chases her away.

The food is warming, and only serves to enhance his drowsiness. He eats his fill, and washes it down with a nice, malted ale. Though not up to the standard of Cromwell's fine kitchen, it is good enough, and he retires, content.

It is a little past midnight when he finally slips into his bed. He has a full stomach, a room to himself, and a straw filled palliasse, which is very comfortable and, mercifully, free of fleas and lice. He blows out his single candle and, in moments, he is fast asleep.

Eustace is walking down a delightful wooded valley, back in his beloved Savoy. He can see the little house, at the edge of the trees, where he keeps his mistress, safe from prying eyes. He sighs, longing to be there, and in his lover's arms. He is at the door. There is something wrong. Marianne is long dead, of course, and the door is leaning out, covering him. His chest is constricted, his head swims, and he cannot breath. He is on the edge of oblivion.

He comes full awake then, feebly kicking, and thrashing his weary arms. There is something soft pressed over his face, choking his very life away. He cannot fight anymore, and feels his head thumping. So, he thinks, this, at the end, is what death is like. Then the pressure is suddenly lifted, and the room is in black, noisy tumult. Someone cries out.

Eustace fumbles to light the candle, then staggers across the room, and throws open the wooden shutters. Moonlight pours in, illuminating a scene of savage carnage. A huge man is rolling about the floor, locked in a violent embrace with a second, slightly smaller man. They roll again, and the smaller of the two is on top, and strangling the man beneath. With a gasp of horror, Chapuys recognises the bigger man as Richard, the huge nephew of Thomas Cromwell.

Just when it seems the assailant will triumph, Richard grabs the man by the chin and the back of his head, and twists, as if drawing a cork from a bottle. There is a loud snapping sound, and the man flops over to one side, quite dead. Richard gets to his feet, rubbing his neck.

"My God, but he was a strong enough bugger, Master Eustace. Thanks be, I have a neck like a bullock's, else it would have gone bad for us both."

"Master Cromwell.... Richard," Chapuys gasps. "I praise God you came when you did. I thought myself a dead man."

"Not on my watch, sir," Richard Cromwell replies. "My uncle fears for you, and set me to follow on. I saw this wretch climb in another window, and knew him for a villain."

"Is he dead?"

"If not, he will walk bent sideways for all eternity," the big man says, and smiles at his clumsy joke. "The neck is broken, and that usually suffices in these cases. Shall I stab him a few times, just to make sure?"

"Pray, not on my account," Eustace Chapuys replies. He does not like being near a dead man, and does not wish to compound the horror by seeing blood spurting. "Then I was on these fiends list all along?"

"It seems so, sir. I think this poor, undone thing will prove to be one of the brothers Vernay. It is as we feared, and the troupe have split apart, with each one on a separate mission of murder."

"We must get on then."

"No, sir. I must apologise to you, for the ruse, but it was for your own good. Master Thomas suspected you to be on the death list, as a close friend of the queen. So he gave you a task, contrived to flush out the killers."

"I was bait?"

"You might well say so, Master Eustace, but there was no other choice," Richard Cromwell kicks the body at his feet. "This one followed you from your house, and so, I followed him. I misjudged his fleetness of foot, and arrived later than I should. I would have been mortified, had he completed his murderous task, before I got to him."

"I concur," Eustace Chapuys says, understanding how close to death he had been. "Let me call for the innkeeper, and rouse him from his bed. We shall have wine."

"I have not eaten all day, sir."

"Then you shall have venison, until you cannot stand!" says Chapuys. Richard Cromwell grins. He is a simple soul, and wants only to do his duty, and feast at any opportunity.

"Sir, I fear I might consume the entire beast."

"What about the body?"

"What body, Señor Chapuys?" Young Cromwell drags the corpse over to the open window, and throws it out. "There, now we can eat. Gomez and I will bury it in the forest tomorrow."

"Luis Gomez is with you?"

"I followed you, and he followed me," says the young Cromwell. "He is tending the horses, and would not be deflected from his duty."

"You amaze me."

"How so? Luis loves you, sir, as if he were a father."

"Then I must cherish his devotion, and reward it."

"Serving your family seems reward enough," Richard replies. "Besides, he's probably robbing you blind as it is!"

"Then I must overlook it, for he pecks a few grains, and never devours the whole crop. And what of tomorrow?"

"Back to Austin Friars," Richard Cromwell replies. "My uncle is closing in on the real quarry, and will have need of us."

"What about Guyot, and the surviving Vernay brother?" Chapuys asks his saviour.

"Do not concern yourself about those two rascals," the big man says, and grins broadly. "Thomas Cromwell, like your Pope Clement, is infallible!"

"Sir, you blaspheme!" Chapuys says, somewhat shocked at the statement.

"Oh, I do?" Young Cromwell asks. "Is the pope not then infallible, sir?"

11 Baying the Hart

Claude Vernay has ridden hard. He skirts the outlying farms and tiny village, coming, at last to the sprawling, half decayed castle. If he expects more difficulty in his approach, then he is pleasantly surprised to find the grounds unguarded.

It is a simple matter for him to cross the shallow, dry moat, and scale the buttressed outer wall. Once on the battlements, he crouches, waiting for a sign of guards. He is French, and does not understand the King's peace. For over fifty years it has not been necessary to retain armed men so far south of the more dangerous Welsh border country. The castle's defences have been sadly neglected.

Margaret Pole, Countess of Salisbury, has another reason to avoid having heavily armed men stationed about her rambling country home. She is badly out of favour at court, and King Henry does not need his suspicions aroused against her. The king fears her Plantagenet family connections, and keeps a wary eye out for any sign of fomenting rebellion.

Claude Vernay is oblivious of this, and has but one thought in his mind. He must do away with the elderly countess, as fast as possible, and make his escape. There will be a hue and cry raised, and he wants to be long gone, sailing back to France, with a heavy bag of gold at his belt. He drops from the battlements with practised ease, and makes for the great house.

Somewhere, a dog barks. He crouches, and waits for the beast to come at him, but is again surprised. The animal is kennelled, and unable to do ought but yap at the moon. He scuttles onwards, and reaches the inner sanctum. It is easier than he thought. Once over the low sill of an unguarded window, or past a door, he will have the house at his mercy.

He sidles along the red brick wall, until he comes to a lower floor window, lavishly glazed with square panes of blown Venetian glass. The assassin opens up the ground floor window with his blade, and is about to climb in, when dark shapes suddenly loom from the shrubbery, and fall on him. He swears, and lashes out with his knife, but it slices through empty air. There is a curse in the dark, followed by a flurry of heavy blows landing on flesh. The Frenchman manages to scream, once, before his head caves in.

It is only a matter of a few desperate moments, and all is over. The second Vernay brother lies dead on the carefully mown lawn, clubbed down by Rafe Sadler and Barnaby Fowler. Lights appear, and servants come running from the house and the stables, armed with an array of weapons. The countesses private secretary leads the way, sword in hand, and makes as if to fall on the two Cromwell men.

"Stay, sirs. It is done," Rafe shouts, and holds up his hands, as if to show he means no further mischief. "Your mistress is safe from a murdering rogue. May we leave you to dispose of this offal?"

*

Things are not so clear cut with Will Draper. He is in Sussex, ready to protect Lady Ursula Pole, daughter of the Countess of Salisbury, but she will have none of it, and deeply mistrusts Thomas Cromwell's man. The Privy Councillor is for the king, and therefore, against all who might oppose his rule. The Poles are descended from the last Plantagenet king of England, and have a strong claim to the throne, should it ever become vacant.

"Master Cromwell bears us nothing but malice," she says sharply. "Why should I believe your preposterous story?"

"I swear it is so, my lady," Will Draper says. "Someone is coming to kill you, and I must stop them. Tell her ladyship, Miriam."

"Each minute lost now brings you nearer to disaster later, Lady Ursula. I am not a paid Cromwell agent, and seek only your safety. Let Will Draper guide you in this, and

you might well survive to see another day."
Miriam Draper's argument seems to work, and
her husband is pleased he let her come with
him. In truth, he would have to have tied her
up in a cellar to keep her away. She is part of
this mad adventure, and wishes to see it
through to its bitter end.

"What must I do?" Lady Ursula asks,
warily.

"Undress," Will says," and let my ...
Miriam... put on your finery. I think you have
very similar figures."

"Might I ask you to turn away?" Lady
Ursula says. She finds the young man
attractive, and wonders about Miriam. As she
undresses, she concludes the olive skinned
beauty is either a wife, or his lover. Either
way, it would be dangerous to try and seduce
her companion away from her.

Miriam steps forward, and helps,
unlashing the cords at her back. She sees Lady
Ursula, who is an attractive thirty year old,
admiring Will out of the corner of her eye.

"Do not think it, madam," she
whispers into the woman's ear. "I have fierce
and jealous blood in my veins."

Lady Ursula gives a slight nod. She
has had many lovers, and is practiced in the art
of romance. She fully understands that Miriam
will fight for this man, and so withdraws from
the field. Her dull husband to be must content

her for now, despite his complete lack of artistry.

The dress is finally off, and Miriam puts it on. Will hurries them, then insists Lady Ursula Pole locks herself away in another room. Whatever the outcome this night, she must live. Cromwell demands it of him. Under other circumstances, they would be foes, and quite able to inflict harm on one another's causes.

"Light the windows well," he commands, and an elderly servant bows, and sets about the task. Miriam takes a seat in one corner, and starts to embroider at the hooped wooden stand Lady Ursula usually employs. She looks amazing in her borrowed finery, and Will sees that she can easily pass for a fine lady. A window is left unlatched, as if missed by a lazy servant.

"There, the trap is set," Will says to his wife. " Let us Bay this Hart and take his antlers as a trophy."

"Is that how you think of Gilbert Guyot?" Miriam asks. "You see him merely as an animal, to be hunted?"

"I see him as a great stag, rampaging his way through a forest. It is my task to pen him in, until he turns, at bay. Then I must deal the death blow."

"Can you not simply take him captive?" Miriam asks.

"That would be cruel indeed, my love," Will replies. "For Master Cromwell would be forced to question him then, and the pain would be unbearable, even for a strong man. At the finish, he would have to hang by the neck. No, Gilbert Guyot must die by my hand this day. Besides, he threatened you... the most precious thing ever to befall me."

"You must not kill on my behalf," Miriam tells him. "That would not be to my liking."

"Then he must die for the murders he has already done," Will replies, " though Cromwell would like one prisoner, at least. I cannot deliver him up to such cruel treatment... even if he did offer you harm."

"He may not even come," Miriam says. "We might spend the night waiting for something that is not ordained."

"True enough."

They lapse into silence then, both wondering if the Frenchman will come that night, or not. It seems to be an age before anything happens. Will fancies he hears a floorboard creak, and puts a hand on the hilt of his sword. Then, all of a sudden, Guyot is there, in the room. His approach has been so stealthy that he is just feet away from Miriam before he gives a great cry of anger.

He recognises her, and turns to see where the danger lies. The traps sprung, and now, the beast must turn, and fight for its life.

Will Draper steps from behind a tapestry, and draws his blade. For a moment, Guyot considers snatching the girl in his arms, to use as a hostage again, but she has conjured a wicked looking *Basilard* from somewhere, and is pointing the slender, double edged knife at him. He backs out of her reach, and grins.

"So, English... you think to stop me?" he asks.

"I do." Will holds his sword ready,

"Let me go, or I will spit you, like a pig, then kill the woman anyway."

"You French dog," Will replies. "By now, your friends are both dead, or taken. Defend yourself, for one of us must die tonight."

Guyot draws his sword, and has a short dagger in his left hand. Will is familiar with this way of fighting, and knows the Frenchman will try to draw his attention with the dagger, before thrusting home with the sword. It is not the way a gentleman fights, but then, Will is not a gentleman either. He has fought in the bogs of Ireland, and faced the fiercest Welsh outlaws in his day.

Even with this knowledge, he is almost caught out, as the Frenchman's blade passes under his armpit. Will turns aside, and feints. Guyot parries, but cuts through empty air.

"Clever, sir," the Frenchman says, and

leaps forward once more. The sword passes Will's shoulder by inches, and the knife is suddenly coming up in a vicious thrust.

Will Draper dances backwards, as nimbly as he can, and the sharp dagger point cuts only his doublet front, sending a small ivory button skittering across the room.

"Too slow, sir," Will says, executing a deft right, left cross cut. The long blade swishes through the air, and the Frenchman is once more out of range. The Englishman dances away, drawing his enemy to him, and practices a few more swift cuts with his fine German made weapon, taken from the body of a slain Irish warlord, some years before.

He never allows his eyes to flicker, not for one instant, as he waits for an opening. That it must come soon is obvious, for both are fighting men, and know how energy sapping single armed combat can be. String the affair out too long, and you risk tiring, or making a simple mistake. Either will kill you.

In Ireland and the Welsh bandit country, Draper has learned to attack quickly, and kill in what ever way presents itself. Once, after losing his sword, he had fought on with a handy rock, and crushed his opponent's skull in. The Frenchman is moving his left hand right and left, in an almost spellbinding way. The dagger is moving like a viper, waiting to strike.

Will keeps his eyes on Gilbert Guyot's blade, and retreats yet another step. Then he is where he wishes to be. The great inglenook fireplace surrounds him on either side, so that he has only his front to protect. The fire is roaring at his back, but he hardly feels the tremendous heat it throws off.

Gilbert Guyot realises his error in letting the soldier of fortune choose the killing ground, so smiles, and taunts him.

"Do you feel the heat, *mon ami*?" he says. "It is almost unbearable. I shall keep you here, fenced in, until you can stand it no more. Then you must come at me, and that is when I will kill you."

"You talk a fine fight, Guyot," Will snaps back. "Yet I seem to have you just where I want you."

"Come, let us be done. Afterwards, I will find the Pole woman, and kill her," Guyot snarls. "Then I will take your woman, and teach her how a Frenchman uses such a slut."

Will's face becomes a picture of rage, and he lunges, madly, stupidly at the man. Guyot ripostes, aiming at the heart. Draper is not there. His uncontrolled rage is mere fakery, and he rolls aside at the last moment. Guyot's killing momentum sends him crashing headlong into the fire.

The Frenchman screams as the flames lick at him, and leaps to his feet. He comes out of the fire, rushing at Will, swinging, and cutting for dear life. Guyot's left sleeve is ablaze, and he knows he must finish it now, or die. Will dances backwards, parrying each attack. Finally, he side steps the enraged Frenchman, and lets him crash into the wall.

Gilbert Guyot is entangled in a rich, very dusty tapestry, which wraps about him, and bursts into flames. The assassin is engulfed in fire, and screams in agony. Will cannot be so hard, and lunges forward, skewering his foe, just under the heart. He withdraws the long blade, and the flaming bundle that has been a man, crashes to the floor.

Miriam is already at the door, ordering the lurking servants to fetch water, else the great hall be engulfed. She grabs the first bucket, and throws it over the burning wreckage. Will pulls her aside, as others appear, and begin to beat out the fire.

"Let the woman's servants save her precious house, my love," he tells her. "We have saved her life, and that is enough!"

The air is filled with the pungent smell of roasted flesh, and one young serving girl wretches in a corner. Will Draper sheathes his sword, and puts his arms about his wife. She has proven her bravery beyond all reason, and he loves her more than ever. Lady Ursula appears at the door, sees what has come about, and falls down in a dead faint.

"Let's hope Rafe and Richard have faired equally as well," Will says. "Pray the Vernay brothers have not drawn any Cromwell blood this day."

"I hope not," Miriam whispers, "for the god of Abraham has already been given His burnt offering."

*

Thomas Cromwell is content. Messengers are here, sent ahead by his men to proclaim their complete success. His nephew, his task completed but a few miles from London, is just now riding through the front gate of Austin Friars. Eustace Chapuys and his faithful old servant are just behind.

"Eustace, my dearest friend," he calls, "come inside, and take breakfast with us all. And you, loyal Luis... you shall sit by our side." The old servant bows, and beams his gratitude at his master's neighbour, but Chapuys is still feeling a little peevish.

"Would you not prefer to take me fishing, Cromwell?" he says, dismounting. "I am, after all is said and done, the most excellent bait."

"Would you rather be dead?" Richard Cromwell says, and is admonished by his uncle for his abruptness.

"Enough of that now, nephew," says Thomas Cromwell, sharply. "The ambassador has made a good point. I gambled with his life, in order to save it. In truth, Eustace, these fellows would never have stopped. Sooner or later, they would have slipped a knife into your back, or slit your throat open, even as you slept."

"Please, let me simmer, Thomas," Chapuys retorts. "Once I have let my feelings out, and partaken of your fine ham and bread, I will come around."

Cromwell is happy. The Spanish ambassador, though a comical figure in some aspects, is an intelligent man, and one he wishes as a friend, rather than an enemy. When the time comes to gently displace Queen Katherine, he will need his support.

Chapuys will never betray his queen, of course, and Cromwell admires him for that, but he must be shown the way forward in the king's great matter. Katherine has to go, but there are two ways for her to choose. Fight, and spend her later years in a nunnery, or some damp castle, or comply, leaving her with titles and rank, as Princess of Wales.

"I am half starved," Richard Cromwell announces. "Let us see what there is on the table!"

"The man is a phenomenon," Chapuys says, following his companions through the labyrinthine corridors of the big house. "He ate a haunch of venison, an entire loaf, and a half dozen fried duck eggs. All this after dealing with my would be assassin. He killed the fellow with his bare hands, Thomas. I swear I have never witnessed such a feat of strength in all my days. He is a veritable Samson."

"Without a Delilah," Richard says.

"Let us pray that we have seen the end of these strolling players," Cromwell says. "For they met with some success, and stretched my people thinly."

"From your lips to God's ears, my friend." Chapuys sits at the long table, flanked by Thomas Cromwell, and his aged servant, Luis. "Is that bacon I smell? Come, Luis, help yourself. It is not like you to hold back."

"It is not poisoned," Cromwell says, "Else my nephew would be a shade, these long years past. Eat well, my friends, for we still have much to accomplish."

Thomas Cromwell is a very rich man, but recalls his hungry days as a child, and enjoys watching those about him eat well. There is never a beggar turned away without a full belly, and neighbours cherish an invitation to dinner as if it were gold. He is looking forward to the change of season, when his table will bear fresh apples, damsons, and ruby red cherries once more.

A young servant, Meg, one of the many homeless strays Cromwell employs, enters, and gives a small, clumsy, curtsey. Her job is to sit by the rear door, and attend to any stray visitor. In return, she eats well, is safe from lustful exploitation, and has a warm bed at the start of each night.

"Begging pardon, master, but there's a strange foreign gentleman, 'as come around the back. He is asking after *Master Charpoose.* He says he's a doctor, but he looks ever so foreign to me. What am I to do wiv'im, master?"

"Ah, I quite forgot," Eustace Chapuys, rises, apologising for the interruption. "It is my day to receive Doctor Vargas. Will you forgive my absence, Thomas?"

"Bring the fellow in," Cromwell declares. "There is food for all... if Richard does not get to it first!"

"No, I must decline your kind offer," Chapuys says, hurriedly heading for the rear entrance door, "but the man is a terrible boor, and has no conversation to speak of. I see him only out of pity."

"Pity?" Cromwell smiles. "Then he is a pitiable doctor, old friend. Do ask him in."

"No, I will not, for he is a boorish fellow with nothing to say."

Or he has much to say that is not for our ears, Cromwell thinks. Poor Chapuys has been forced to lie to him, in order that the queen's physician's mission is kept quiet.

"That is odd," Richard Cromwell says, tearing off a huge piece of bread. "I trust your friend is not unwell, uncle."

"Doctor Vargas is Queen Katherine's own most private messenger; a conduit between her royal lips, and Ambassador Chapuys' ears. Eustace will glean what he can, and put it in his secret letters to the Emperor Charles."

"Do we not open *all* his letters?"

"No, I let the Lord Chancellor's men do that," Cromwell replies. "For they contain nothing of any interest. Eustace has another, more secret way, of sending his real news."

"The crafty fellow," Richard says, swallowing down a boiled goose egg. "Have we not uncovered this hidden channel, sir?"

"I have not looked." Cromwell sighs. His nephew is a strong, reliable, and loyal young man, but he has no head for the business of state. He explains. "If we look, we will find, and Chapuys will have no safe way to converse with his master. In that unhappy event, he will become useless to Charles, who will recall him, and send a wilier ferret."

"Then you let him keep his secrets?" Richard is somewhat confused, but that is a common state with him. He is slow, but gets there in the end. He shrugs for now, and rips off a chicken leg, which is then shredded with the greatest gusto.

"For now," Thomas Cromwell replies. "One day, there will be no need for any of this stealth. I shall so regulate the affairs of England, that the people will live under a benign, and open governance. There will be no one to object, or seek to further their own ends, and peace will reign supreme over the land."

"I'll most certainly drink to that, uncle," Richard Cromwell says, gulping down a huge cup of watered wine in two great swallows. "For do you not say that all this constant strife and unrest is bad for trade, and hurts our profit margins?"

"My God," Thomas Cromwell mutters, "the boy actually understands!"

*

Eustace Chapuys laments his missed breakfast, especially when Doctor Vargas has nothing but trivia to report. The queen's lady, Maria is upset, though he does not know why. The queen wishes to express her disapproval of a gentleman of the court. Poor Richard Rich, he thinks, what have you done?

"Is that all, Vargas?" he asks.

There is something else. Vargas is nervous, and seems uneasy. Chapuys pours him a glass of Spanish wine, and sits patiently, whilst the medical man composes his thoughts. At last, he speaks.

"I have told you all that Queen

Katherine says. What I now say, comes from my heart, *Señor.* I see the guards are more attentive, and the queen's household are alert to any danger. You fear for her safety. Do not deny it."

"There is always danger, my dear Dr Vargas," Chapuys says, noncommittally.

"I should have been told, sir." The doctor is clenching his fists, open then shut, in agitation. "What if something evil befalls Her Majesty, and I might have prevented it? I am in her company almost every day."

"Your loyalty does you nothing but credit," Eustace tells him, patting his arm. "I have her ringed about with guards. The two infidels stand by her door day and night, and her ladies take turns sitting with her."

"You might deflect a dagger, sir, but have you considered another method?"

"Another method?"

"Poison, sir."

"Poison?" Eustace Chapuys is momentarily horrified, then shakes his head. "No, it cannot be. The queen never eats a meal alone. There is a different lady at her table for each meal, eating the same dishes."

"Of course," Doctor Vargas stands to leave, and bows to the ambassador. "Forgive me, *Señor* Chapuys, but I seek only to cover all of the possible contingencies. With your permission, sir, I will visit the queen's kitchen often, and inspect the prepared food at random."

"Granted, Dr. Vargas."

"God be with you, sir."

"And you, my loyal friend." Eustace Chapuys had not given any thought to poison, and is relieved that Katherine's physician is fully alert to the danger. As he waves the man off, his stomach grumbles, and he regrets his missed meal once more.

He recalls what Cromwell has said, just a short while before, when urging everyone to eat. His kitchen is safe. Pray to God, the Savoyard mutters, "that Queen Katherine's is as sacrosanct!"

12   Inquisition

Will Draper, his wife Miriam, and Rafe Sadler arrive back at Austin Friars a little after noon, and are greeted by the news that everything has gone to plan. All three of the would be murderers are dead, with no cost, other than a torn doublet, a scratch on Barnaby Fowler's upper arm, and some slight loss of Eustace Chapuys dignity.

"You should have seen his face," Richard Cromwell laughs. "He must have thought two bears had jumped in through the window."

"Poor man," Miriam chides. "Do not mock him so, Richard Cromwell, for, unlike you, he is not the killing sort. He is a gentle kind of man."

"I take no pleasure in it," Richard mumbles. "Only pride in how I do it. The man was beaten, fairly and squarely. My strength against his, and God favoured me."

Will Draper smiles. Miriam is, in truth, loved by everyone at Austin Friars, and brings the feminine touch, where it is lacking. He knows that Master Cromwell once had a wife, and daughters, but he has never pried. Some wounds run too deep, and Will knows how losing Miriam would affect him.

Thomas Cromwell has a living son, but keeps him well away from the intrigues of court, and allows him only brief visits to the great house. The boy is almost eleven years old, and is being educated in the country, learning the fine art of being a Tudor style gentleman, with greyhounds to course, and falcons to fly. He will be the gentleman his father never was, and no one will dare remind him that his paternal grandfather was nothing but a mere blacksmith.

In truth, Thomas Cromwell is afraid of loving the boy too much. His wife, Elizabeth, and the girls, Grace and Anne, almost broke his heart when they died of the sweating sickness, and he cannot face another such loss. Each night, he prays that Gregory will outlive him, if only by a few years.

"A job well done," Rafe Sadler says, and he drinks from his mug of frothing ale. "Here is to us, dear comrades."

"A job half done, is no job at all," Tom Cromwell says, coming into the huge kitchen. "Eat up, boys, and let us have a council of war. Our tumblers were paid by someone, and he is the next rung on the ladder."

"Have you a name, sir?" Will Draper stands, and rests his hand on the hilt of his sword. "Speak it, and I will deal with him this very day."

"Brave words, Will," Cromwell replies, pouring himself a goblet of wine. "but I want this particular scoundrel alive, and in my power. There are many ways to catch a rat, without hitting it with a big stick."

*

Sir Edward Prudhoe smiles, admiring the excellent cut of his new doublet. The short leather garment has slit sleeves, to show off the lining which is made of Cathay silk. It has cost him half a king's ransom, but he does not begrudge it.

In the last month, he has become a man of means. The knighthood, bestowed unexpectedly at Yuletide, has come with the rent and income from a couple of small estates in Cheshire, and so he is elevated to the level of middling gentry.

It is a rapid ascent, made possible by an unexpectedly generous benefactor. He is not ungrateful to his new patron, and when it is suggested that he speak to certain people, and arrange for certain events to happen, he is happy to oblige. For a patron can bestow, and just as easily, take away.

The Pole clan are the king's most dangerous enemies, and deserve their fate. Sir Edward is now well placed to spread rumour, and mingle with useful people, both high and low. His tastes are perverse, and it is not uncommon for him to frequent the bawdiest of establishments in search of his pleasures. It is in one of them that he comes upon Gilbert Guyot, a cutthroat of the first order.

Under pressure to enlist some useful men, he recognises a dangerous rogue when he sees one, and enlists his aid with the promise of riches to come. It is a simple matter to spread around a little silver, and suggest that there is much more to be had. If only the Frenchman and his men might see their way to performing a favour for him.

"What favour?" Guyot demands to know.

He hesitates to suggest murder, but Gilbert Guyot is not the squeamish sort, and falls in with the plot readily. It is a small step from planning, to bloody action. Two Poles are already dead, and the rest of the list will soon follow. His master will reward him well, and he is more than content with his lot in life.

He is unaware that his carefully arranged plans have foundered on the great Cromwell rock, and is pleased with himself, beyond measure. It is in this frame of mind that he decides to take a walk down by the river. His purse is full, and he is in need of some lively, youthful, company.

Despite it being proscribed in English law, and punishable by impalement on a sharpened stake, Sir Edward Prudhoe is overly fond of dalliances with pretty young boys. There is nothing so fine as a doe eyed youth to play with, and the young catamites often hang about the ferry boats, plying their saucy trade.

If he is careful, a gentleman can enjoy the delights of Sodom for but a few shillings.

There are a few such boys about, but they are of the lowest type, and he has used them too often before. His new status demands he find himself a better quality youth to take into his bed. Perhaps a young man who scrubs up well, and might also act as his page? Then he stops, stares in wonder, and smiles.

The youth pauses on his way, and smiles back. Sir Edward notes that he is quite well dressed, and indescribably attractive. He decides that he must have him, as soon as possible.

"Good day to you, young fellow," he says, falling in with the boy. "Do you know the best way to Putney?"

"Why, no sir, I do not."

"I do. I have a house there. Would you care to see it?"

"You are a stranger to me, sir," the boy replies, lowering his eyelids coquettishly. "I do not, ordinarily, give my company to men, unless they be both kind … and generous."

"Ah! I knew you to be a sweet little catamite." Sir Edward tells him. "Come home with me, and I will love you, end to end."

"What a saucy fellow you are, sir," the youth giggles. "Shall we walk? For I might not be able, afterwards. From the cut of your hose, I fancy my hands will be full."

"Not just your hands, I pray," Sir Edward says, linking the youth. "I have a full purse, and would gladly empty it under your sweet caresses. My name is Sir Edward, my sweet child. Pray what shall I call you, in my driving throes?"

"My people call me Mush, sir. Shall we away?"

*

"He wanted to what?" Richard Cromwell says, shaking with laughter. "I thought one only did *that* to sheep."

"If you think the fool's words were bad, you should have heard what Lady Boleyn did suggest."

"What? Lady Anne spoke to you of…"

"No, you idiot," Mush replies. "Not that Boleyn. It was afterwards . I spent the day, as ordered, protecting the king's lady. As I left, a beautiful woman pulled me into a side room, and demanded I satisfy her deepest wants."

"Never!"

"Truly," Mush smiles at the recollection. The frantic fumbling of clothes, and the swift, shuddering coupling, over in moments. "Lady Mary has a wicked tongue."

"The sister?"

"None other," Mush replies, with a lewd wink at his comrade.

"Have you told my uncle?"

"No."

"No matter, he will already know. I wager he was aware, even as you displayed your tiny Jewish pintle to the woman"

"Very funny," Mush retorts. "At least, I may see mine, when I look down. Now, shut up, and help me unload the cart."

Sir Edward Prudhoe is bundled up in sackcloth, and his mouth is bound, as are his arms and legs. The ride across town has been bumpy, and he is shaking with fear. One moment he is in a narrow, deserted alley, running his hands over the boy he wants to buy for the night, and the next, he is battered, bound and gagged.

Rough hands grab him at shoulder and ankle, and he feels himself being carried. There are descending steps, and the smell of dampness. He thinks himself to be in a cellar.

"Tie this rope about him, and hoist him up on the beam." It is the voice of the catamite, no longer soft and inviting, but harsh and commanding. He is hoisted up, and finds himself swinging gently back and forth.

"Shall I drag the table over?"

"Yes. Is the spike fixed firm?"

"It is, and as sharp as a sword."

Sir Edward Prudhoe is shaking now, as realisation dawns on him. He wants to plead, or offer money for his life, but cannot speak through the rag jammed in his mouth.

"What is it that the damned man   is

is saying?" Mush asks.

"I don't know. He is gagged. Shall I remove his hose. They are a fine weave, and I could use them for myself. Besides, it will make it easier... for the spike to enter."

"No, let the damned things rip, even as he will, when the spike rams home."

Sir Edward Prudhoe finds enough strength to set himself swaying, and tries to scream. He is seconds from the most disgusting death allowed by law, and can almost feel the impaling spike.

"Now?" Richard asks.

"Not yet. Loosen the gag, and we will hear him beg for his depraved, and bestial life," Mush says, coldly.

"Can we not just drop him on the spike?" Richard Cromwell says, but he reaches under the sacking that masks Prudhoe's face, and pulls out the gag. "There, now he will babble like a madman, just to save his worthless skin from a just punishment."

"Please God, I pray save me. Listen to me, sirs. I have never lain with a boy before. I was misled by a pretty face."

"Oh, he calls you pretty, Mush. I do not see it myself, and would prefer the pick of the flock instead. Let me cut the rope, and so end his worthless life."

"I have money." Prudhoe thinks, frantically, what he might say to avoid a vile death. "I can find you a hundred pounds apiece."

"Perhaps two hundred," Mush says.

"I have land. I can raise a loan on it, and find you the gold."

"How long will that take?"

"A few weeks."

"Cut the rope."

"No!" Prudhoe is almost dead with fear. "I can get as much as you want, I have a powerful benefactor who will support me."

"Let me guess," Richard Cromwell says. "You work for a great lord, who does not mind you tupping boys, and he just loves throwing his wealth at you."

"I do, sirs. Please, listen to me. Hear me out, and you shall both profit from it, beyond avarice. I am employed by a certain influential man… to do … to arrange matters. I speak of political things, good sirs, beyond our understanding."

"This great man… he values you so much?" Mush affects curiosity.

"He values what I do for him, and fears what I know about him."

"He sounds like a complete knave," Mush says, softly. "I suspect you mean Thomas Cromwell, for he is the greatest knave in the land, and must have the most wicked secrets to be kept."

"No, it is not Cromwell," Prudhoe

replies. "I cannot speak his name, but he will pay well for my safe return, and my continued silence."

"Riddles, and more riddles" Richard says, giving the hanging man a small shove. "Give us proof, fellow. Something to bind us together."

"Do you know the Pole family?" Prudhoe plays his last, and best, card.

"I do," Mush says. "An ill-omened clan. They have been sadly diminished these last weeks."

"All my doing. My master demanded their deaths, and I arranged matters. Even now, my men are scouring the Pole name from England's shores. They have a list, such as will please even the king ... if he would but admit it, like an honest soul."

"That is surely enough to hang you, sir," Mush replies, coldly. "There is but one more thing. I *will* have a name."

"I cannot!"

"Cut the rope."

Richard saws at the heavy cord, and a strand snaps. Sir Edward screams, and gives a name. Mush smiles, and nods, then says:

"I do not believe your cowardly lies. Now, Richard, cut the rope!"

Sir Edward Prudhoe screams, and the sound reaches the very rafters of Austin Friars. Even Eustace Chapuys, who is strolling in his garden next door, looks up, crosses himself, and shudders. There are things that happen in Austin Friars that will never be really known, and sins committed that, surely, will never be forgiven.

*

Thomas Cromwell studies the report, speedily written by Mush, and nods his approval. It is he who, through his wide range of agents, discovered the secret of Sir Edward Prudhoe's peculiar sexual tastes. It is he who asked Mush to play the part of bait.

"A fine job, my dear boy," the lawyer says. "I trust you were not too disgusted by the role I cast you in?"

"I am yours to command, Master Thomas," Mush replies, openly. "My family owe you our position, and our gratitude. You found my grandfather's murderer, and gave him to me. You have but to ask, and I will do it. I might not be as great a fighting man as my brother in law, Will, but I can serve in many other ways."

"Quite so. I hear you served well the Lady Mary Boleyn, but yesterday. She is a dozen years older than you, and will make a dangerous bed mate."

"In truth, sir, a wall sufficed. The lady was in sore need of a man and, as a gentleman, I was forced to oblige her until she almost passed out with joy. It will not happen again."

"On the contrary," Thomas Cromwell says, "it shall. The lady is easily seduced, and has a head full of secrets. You must invite her to visit you here, at Austin Friars, and satisfy her needs. In this way, we will have a clear window into the hidden lives of the Boleyn family. Can you do this for me, Mush?"

"It is an arduous task, Master Thomas, but I will rise to it," Mush replies, smiling. "I will ask her, when next we meet."

"Caution her to secrecy," Cromwell advises. "If her sister finds out, she will have her locked in a nunnery. Tell her that, if I am pleased, I will find her another husband, and a small estate in Suffolk."

"Suffolk, sir? Why Suffolk?"

"Charles Brandon is with us." He does not bother to explain that the Duke of Suffolk is some thirty odd thousand pounds in debt, and owes his continued good fortune to Thomas, who waives the interest, in return for his servile devotion. "He will have a spare farm or two, I think, and the weather is clement."

"What about this Prudhoe?"

"He is recovered?"

"Still shaking. He actually believed there to be a spike on the table. The fool landed on a bed of straw, and wept great tears of gratitude. He has told us all he knows, and made up even more to keep us happy. Shall I give him a quick death?"

"That is your Jewish blood talking, my dear Mush," Cromwell replies. "Sir Edward is a useful sort of a fellow, and must be kept safe, for now. Have him locked up in one of the attic rooms, and fed well. Fat men cannot run."

"And the name he gave us?" Mush is still dubious. He cannot quite understand why the man would take so great a risk as to order a half dozen murders. "Can you believe it?"

"I can." Cromwell sighs. "It is a name I suspected almost from the start."

"Will we kill him too?" Mush asks. It seems the quickest, and surest way of solving all their problems. The king will not be too upset, and Katherine will be grateful. "I can slip past his defences, and slit his throat, whenever you command it of me, Master Thomas."

"Enough of killing." Tom Cromwell says, wondering if the youth is the most cold hearted killer he has ever known. "We must lay a careful trap. I can do nothing without proof."

"There is Prudhoe."

"A disgusting sodomite who orders murder, and will say anything to save his own worthless skin?" Cromwell shakes his head. "I do not think his testimony will carry much weight in a court of law."

"You mean to go to law over this?"

Mush is amazed.

"Perhaps it might be the only way," Cromwell mutters to himself. "I fear no man, but our foe is, perhaps, my match."

"Never,"

"I thank you for that," Cromwell says. "I pray that you are all backing the winning horse."

"Horse?" Richard comes into the library at that moment. "It must be nearly dinner time. I have fed Sir Edward, and cautioned him to silence. I swear his hair has started turning grey."

"I would age too, if suspended over a spike." Cromwell puts the report to one side.

"The spike is not real," Richard says.

"In his mind it is," Cromwell tells them. "Make a man believe something, and it is as real to him as if he could hold it in his hand. The power of...." He tails off, and smiles. "Yes. The truth is that which you can get most men to believe. Thank you, nephew."

"For what, sir?"

"For showing me the way ahead."

*

Maria de Salinas gives a small curtsey to Lady Mary Boleyn as they pass. The queen's lady in waiting has no choice, as to ignore a Boleyn will only bring more trouble down on them. Besides, it just a small curtsey, and will not change the world.

"Good day, Lady Willoughby," Mary says, in as friendly a voice as she can manage. "I trust your mistress is well?"

"I am on my way to fetch her doctor, Lady Mary," she confesses. "It is a small disorder, but an uncomfortable one."

"Oh, you mean the curse?" Mary says. "Have the queen try mulled wine with a grain of arsenic. It eases me greatly."

"Thank you, madam. I will let the doctor do his business."

"As you wish. By the way, my dear, I hear about the court that you have been treated badly in love."

"You go too far," Maria says, giving Mary a sharp look.

"Often, and with many men," Lady Mary replies, smiling. "I have no reputation to speak of, but regret the loss of yours."

"I have nothing to be ashamed of, my lady," Maria tells the Boleyn woman. "I am as blameless as can be."

"Yet Richard Rich claims to have lain with you."

"What?" Tears well in her eyes. "How could he be so vile? I spurned him, because he lied to me. The most he did was touch my hand, and that in the presence of the queen. How shall I ever clear my reputation now?"

Lady Mary Boleyn is genuinely sorry for the woman, and is in the mood to help. She has just heard from Mush, her new, young, lover, and wishes the world to be a happy place. She comes to a decision, and resolves to help the woman, come what may.

"I will stop the rumours," she announces. "Master Rich is a swine, and an inconsiderate lover. I tried him once, and will not waste time on a second visit."

Maria is wide eyed. Lady Mary talks like a common whore, and she is scandalised. The idea that such a woman can help seems preposterous, but she has no other way to vouchsafe her virtue.

"I will be in your debt, Lady Mary. I regret my mistresses current troubles, but do not wish ill on your family. The king is like a ship, blown hither and thither by the precocious winds. When next he veers, it will be into Queen Katherine's safe harbour."

"Let the best woman win, eh?" Mary smiles, and continues on her way. At the end of the corridor, a guard opens the door, and she enters the large outer court, where courtiers, hangers on and unattached ladies congregate.

"Lady Mary, I hear you have a new friend. Do we know him?" Lady Margaret Norris asks.

"A passing fancy," Mary says, dismissively. She wants Mush, and knows she must keep him a secret. "Though I have heard news of another lady. Do you know Maria de

Salinas?"

"Lady Willoughby? Master Rich says he has prised open her particular treasure chest, and found it wanting."

"Then he is a lying dog, and no gentleman," Lady Mary tells the gathering. "The truth is, he tried to seduce poor Lady Maria, but she refused him, having found out that he is enshrined in poetry."

"What ever do you mean?"

"Have you not heard it?" Lady Mary asks. "The king says it is a timely warning against sin. It goes thus:

When goest ere to fulsome rise,
For to plunder her Rich prize,
Wary be, in fortune's lap,
Or take no heed, and court thee clap.

It is one of Master Tom Wyatt's little verses, and speaks well of the price of random love."

"Rich has the clap?" The Duke of Norfolk is standing near by, and cannot hide his pleasure. "That is wondrous news, my dear niece."

"Uncle Norfolk, I did not see you there," Lady Mary Boleyn's mother is a Norfolk, and the duke is a patron of the Boleyn clan. "Forgive my most unladylike coarseness."

"Oh, it is forgiven, my girl," Norfolk says. He is delighted because Rich is going about with his son, and he hopes his youthful heir has shared the same pox ridden little doxy. "My son will be horrified at the news, God rot the impertinent little bastard's hide. Now, when will you call on me, sweet girl? Of all my nieces, I am most fond of you, my dearest Mary."

"You honour me, Uncle Norfolk," Lady Mary tells him, but thinks how to avoid a private meeting. Norfolk is an old goat, and if he wants his way, she must, for the families sake, endure his disgusting sexual advances. "Though I am a little worried, as I have been... close... to Master Rich myself."

The duke steps back, as if the sickness will leap from Lady Mary to himself, and bows a hasty good day. It is one thing to laugh over his son's misfortune, but quite another to contract so vile a sickness from his own sister's daughter.

The little knot of ladies have dispersed at Norfolk's approach, and are happily spreading the new rumour throughout the court. Master Rich will soon find himself a laughing stock, and Maria de Salinas' honour is restored.

Another time, and Lady Mary Boleyn might need some willing help. It is good to know that the queen's closest friend is now in her debt.

13 Invitations

Stephen Gardiner is somewhat puzzled. One of Thomas Cromwell's young men has just delivered a note from the fellow. It is, rather curiously, an invitation to dinner, that very evening, in honour of St. Eustace. He crosses to a bookshelf, and takes down a book, so old that it is hand written in Latin. He opens the velum covered tomb, and starts to read out aloud.

"St. Anselme, St. Augustus, St. Stephanus, St. Matthias the Lesser... ah, here we are. These damned monks must never have heard of alphabetical lists."

St. Eustace, he reads, is the patron saint of hunters. For a moment he ponders the incongruous nature of this titbit, then smiles. The great, all knowing Thomas Cromwell has, he perceives, made a silly mistake. How unlike him.

St. Eustace is to be celebrated with a feast at Austin Friars, on completely the wrong day. The blessed man's day is the twentieth day of September. Cromwell is either too late, or far too early. Stephen Gardiner will rib him mercilessly over so glaring an error.

"Shall I send back word that you are busy, sir?" his new secretary says. He knows his master wishes to steer clear of the war that is about to erupt between Austin Friars, and

Utopia.

"What, and miss a fine dinner?" Stephen Gardiner enjoys a good table, and Cromwell sets a finer one than Henry. "Let me advise you, sir. There are two men in England one must never refuse an invitation from. One is Henry, because he is king, and one is Thomas Cromwell, because he *is* Thomas Cromwell!"

*

The Dukes of Norfolk, Suffolk, and Surrey also receive an invitation, but care nothing for dates. They know that the wine will flow freely, and even a lord of the realm enjoys a *gratis* meal. When the venison is as good as Cromwell's, one can turn a blind eye, and even sup with the devil.

"The butcher's boy says I may bring a friend," Norfolk bellows, waving the invitation at his son. "That will *not* be you then, sir! I shall take someone that I actually like!"

"I have my own friends a plenty, father," the Earl of Surrey replies. "You do not possess a single one. Not even Thomas Cromwell, who is actually a lowly blacksmith's whelp, calls you 'friend', sir. It was fat old Cardinal Wolsey who was the son of a butcher."

"I thank you for the correction," Norfolk says. "Does a Smith outrank a butcher of sheep? Will you be bringing your mistress?"

"And spoil a damned good drinking session?" the Duke of Surrey replies. "No, I shall take along Master Rich."

"Ah!" The Duke of Norfolk simply cannot contain his pleasure at this. "Your new pet poodle. I hear you two often swive the same doxies?"

"What is that to you, sir?" Surrey replies, haughtily. "There are sheep in Kent who hide at your approach, father. I know all about the dirty sluts *you* keep about the county."

"Do you now?" Thomas Howard, most eminent lord in the realm, is shaking with suppressed laughter. "Then you will know that they are free of the pox ... unlike Master Rich!"

"That is a scandalous remark, sir," Surrey says, but he still feels a coldness in his stomach. "Where is your evidence?"

"God's teeth, my boy, the man is clapped, on the word of your own cousin, Mary Boleyn. She let this particular cat out of the bag yesterday, and has a certain knowledge of these things. You have gone ashen, sir. Perhaps an urgent visit to the court physician is called for?" Norfolk grins, as his son almost runs in search of medical help.

He will attend Cromwell's feast, if only to further irk his ungrateful son. There is the slight problem of finding a guest to take, as he believes men hold him in such high esteem that they stand back, in awe. The truth, that he is a loud and obnoxious bully, disliked by all, will never cross his aristocratic mind.

Then it comes to him. Tom Wyatt, the saucy writer of love poetry is back from France. He will do nicely, and shall earn his dinner by spouting off a few ribald rhymes.

*

Charles Brandon, Duke of Suffolk will attend, and has no shortage of friends to take along. He is a weak man, prone to many vices, and this seems to engender deep affection in other men's hearts. Even Thomas Cromwell, he fancies, has a soft spot for him.

"Who, by Jesus' Cross, is this Sainted Eustace fellow, Roger?" he asks, showing the invitation to his dice partner.

"Patron saint of buggers, drinkers and fornicators, with any luck," Roger De Crecy replies. "Shall I join you, Charles? I fancy a good meal, and Cromwell knows how to entertain. His cook used to work for Cardinal Wolsey before he was killed."

"Almost all his servants did," Suffolk says. "The cardinal died of an illness, and was not executed. Master Cromwell is a decent sort of man, and did not want them to suffer for their master's stiff necked disobedience of Henry."

"Come, sir. You are as a brother to the

king, so tell me true. They say he was about to forgive the man."

"Yes, that is so. He told me even as the cardinal was being marched back by Harry Percy. The king near wept when news came of the old man's sudden death."

"He blames Percy yet, does he not?"

"When he is in a black mood, he curses the man, and says he was given poor council."

"Which is why he favours Cromwell so much, I wager?"

"Then you would lose your bet, sir," the Duke of Suffolk responds, heatedly. "Master Cromwell has the sharpest wits in England... perhaps Europe. He gives sound advice, and has progressed the matter of Henry's separation from Katherine far more than the Lord Chancellor ever could."

There. Charles Brandon's duty is done. He is wholly owned by Thomas Cromwell, and must honour his name at every opportunity. One day, he will be debt free, and able to become his own man again, he thinks. It is a childish dream, and deep inside, he knows this. There will ever be a Cromwell to contend with.

*

"An urgent communication from Privy Councillor Cromwell, My Lord Chancellor." The herald bows, and places the note on the desk before him. He turns to leave, and is not surprised to see the king studying Sir Thomas More's amazing map of the world. A second, deeper bow, and he is gone.

Henry shakes his head, and comes to join More at the large desk. He is considering the map, and wishes to ask something.

"Is my kingdom so small, Sir Thomas?" he asks. "It is but a thumb's length, and is dwarfed by the mass of this New World."

"Ah, the Spanish lands, sire." Thomas More steeples his fingers, as he does when about to impart some profound piece of knowledge. "It is rich in gold, and savages. My agents say the Emperor Charles has three thousand men there, just to keep the peace."

"Still, sir, I am informed that it brings in a great deal of wealth," Henry replies. "Thomas Cromwell says we should be building ships to explore its length and breadth, for our own ends."

"Cromwell is a dreamer, Your Majesty," the Lord Chancellor explains. "The Emperor would see such an action as an insult. We would be faced with a war against Spain, and the rest of the Holy Roman Empire."

"I see. Cromwell tells me that there is enough rich land to increase my kingdom a hundred fold."

"No land can be that vast, sire," More tells him. "The map maker has exaggerated the

New World's size to aggrandise the Emperor Charles. It is but the most easterly end of the Indies, and probably hemmed in by the vast lands of Cathay."

"I must speak with Cromwell at greater length." The king is restless. Lady Anne is indisposed, and her sister is suddenly coy, and less free with her favours. He is bored, and wishes a diversion. Even Brandon's company is not what it was. He spouts on about Master Cromwell to excess. "What have you there? Is it a response to our letter to my Brother France?"

"It is not his seal, sire," More says, throwing the note aside, unopened.

"Then whose?" More is cornered. He opens the note, and reads.

"It is an invitation to dinner, Your Majesty. From Master Cromwell. He says he is celebrating the feast day of St. Eustace."

"Never heard of him," Henry says. "I hear he sets a fine table, Lord Chancellor."

"I have no use for fancy food, sire. Bread and a little gruel suffices to keep me alive. Cromwell seeks to far outdo your own kitchens." It is a clever thing to say. Henry is jealous of his supremacy in all things, and will begrudge Cromwell's culinary aspirations.

"Does he now?" Henry takes the invitation and reads it aloud. "You are to bring a guest, Sir Thomas. I have a mind to sample

Master Cromwell's feast. We shall go together."

"My Lord!" More is flabbergasted. "You must not. Think of the danger to your person. There is not time to gather enough guards, and the food is untested."

"I am sure Thomas Cromwell has his own tasters, my Lord Chancellor. Will you gainsay me my pleasures on so little account?"

"Of course not, sire. I will have my own people escort us to Austin Friars. As for the food... I will taste every dish, as a precaution."

"A daring promise, Sir Thomas," Henry says, laughing softly. "For Master Cromwell might well want to poison you!"

"I am glad to see Your Highnesses mood is lightened at the prospect of my doom. Let me write, and warn Cromwell, that he might ensure your perfect ease."

"No, do not. Let us take him unawares, so I am not given any particular preference."

"As you wish, sire." Better still, More thinks. Let us see how Cromwell copes when caught off guard. The man is a master of forward planning, and might be thrown by Henry's sudden appearance, to the extent of making a social blunder.

"Is the conversation good at Austin Friars?" Henry asks his Lord Chancellor. He never ventures out in such a way, and he is expecting some wondrous things of the evening.

"Not good, Your Royal Highness, but certainly very sharp, and interesting to an intelligent man. The talk is often about politics, or religion, and food is discussed *ad infinatum*, as is diplomacy. Sometimes Master Cromwell allows a woman or two to attend, though they are usually the clever sort, rather than women of easy morals. I fear that Eustace Chapuys, the Savoyard diplomat, will be there."

"The Spanish ambassador?" Henry is taken aback, and wishes to know more. "Cromwell has befriended him, you think?"

"In the hope of being given a fine pension by the Emperor Charles, no doubt." More cannot resist the jibe, but immediately regrets his words, for the French king sends him generous gifts of money, in the hope of winning him over to the French cause.

King François believes diplomacy and bribery are horses from the same stable. He secretly endows one of More's precious colleges with six thousand silver marks a year, and sends gifts of jewels for his wife. In return, he wants the Lord Chancellor to sway Henry's choice of any future bride. A French queen would suit François well, drawing the house of Tudor closer to the house of Valois, presenting a powerful front to the emperor.

More accepts the gifts, but writes to François, saying the matter is most delicate, and cannot be rushed. He writes the same thing to the Holy Roman Emperor, who, in the guise of the King of Spain, has granted him an enormous pension of ten thousand *ducets* a year, for his natural life.

"Thomas Cromwell has no need of other rulers pensions," Henry growls. "He must be making a most tidy sum of money from my patronage alone. And you, sir? Does your fortune grow apace?"

"I can present Your Majesty with a set of my accounts at a day's notice," More replies. "My entire fortune, for what it is, I would gladly put at your disposal."

"I am glad to hear it, Tom," the king says, showing by this unusual familiarity that he trusts the man's word. "Now I must summon my Master of the King's Wardrobe, and change into my best finery."

"Simple dress is the accepted standard, sire," Sir Thomas tells the king, "Although, Ambassador Chapuys does tend to turn up wearing the most ridiculous hats."

"He does... silly fellow," Henry says. "Though that reminds me that I have some new made hats, just in from France. My Master of the Wardrobe tells me that the peacock and ostrich feathers are simply divine."

'Oh, feathers, sire?" Sir Thomas More's heart skips a beat, and he offers up a silent prayer that the ambassador and the king do not exchange millinery secrets. "How absolutely delightful!"

*

"Oh, Sweet *Jesu* on his Cross," Harry Percy, Duke of Northumberland moans. Life is becoming more intolerable with each passing hour. He struggles to read the invitation again, and shakes his head in despair. "The man is a complete monster. Why, when he so hates me, does he bid me come to dinner?"

"I'm sure I don't know, my pet." The willing tavern girl says, emerging from beneath the bed covers. The duke's ardour has wilted, and she cannot blow embed onto his flickering coals."Mayhap he wants to feed you up… put some vigour into your pintle?"

"Quiet, you filthy little trollop," Percy says. He racks his brains, wondering what Cromwell's game is. The man is his Nemesis, and brings him nothing but ill fortune. "Am I to be hounded for ever because of one old, fat, priest?"

Percy had Cardinal Wolsey under arrest for treason, some four months past, and the man simply died of an ill humour picked up on the road to London. Henry now uses the event to punish him, transferring his own feelings of guilt to Northumberland, and

Thomas Cromwell shows him nothing but utter disdain. Now this is thrown at him, and he expects it is but another attempt to blacken his already sullied honour.

"I care not what his motives are," Percy declares to the girl, who is trying to rekindle his passion with deft fingers. "Two may play at that little game. I shall make him look a fool in front of all of his guests."

"How so?" the girl asks, trying to slip her tongue into his unreceptive ear. He shrugs her off, and starts to look about the grim little room for his discarded clothes.

"Get your clothes on, slut," he demands. "For I will fit you out in a silken gown, and present you as my dear friend, Lady Something or Other. At the height of the evening's festivities, I will reveal you to be nothing but a low born jade, who is any man's ride for a silver shilling, and a glass of cheap wine."

"Will you pay me well, sir?" the girl asks. These nobles are a funny sort, she thinks, but they have money, and she is willing to participate in any silly mummery, if it pays its way in silver.

"Two shillings," Harry Percy offers.

"Five, and I get to keep the gown."

"Such a gown might cost me nine or ten pounds," Percy snaps at her, though he will simply borrow one from his mother's wardrobe. "That is a great outlay, especially on a little trollop like you... no matter how pretty you are."

"It shall be well worth it," the girl tells him. "I dress up well, and I shall play my part to perfection, sir. Your friends will think I am of noble birth, once they have a drink inside them, and act accordingly towards me. I shall have your Master Cromwell kneeling at my feet, and paying court to my beauty."

"Very well." Percy thinks of their surprise, and humiliation, once he reveals his little game, and decides to meet the girl's rather stiff price. "What is your name, by the way?"

"Purity," the girl says, with a knowing smirk. Harry Percy throws his head back, and laughs.

*

"Remove your hose, My Lord Surrey." The rotund little man rubs his hands, to make them warmer to the touch.

"Is that really necessary?" Young Howard asks, his face blushing the colour of a ripe cherry.

The court doctor sighs. It is ever this way with the aristocratic ones, he thinks. They believe they have special rights when it comes to any form of illness. Still, the fee will be a good one, even if he must go to the father to collect it.

"Yes, it is, My Lord Surrey. I must examine your... the *affected* part, sir." The doctor picks up a long metal instrument, with a forked end to it, and hovers over his cowering patient. "If you please?"

"My friends say the sickness rots you away," young Howard says. He is, despite his philandering, still only a young boy, and prone to all sorts of terrors, real or imagined.

"Your friends are absolutely correct," the ageing doctor replies, gravely. He stoops, and examines the exposed, quite flaccid little member closely. "Though it is not something for you to worry about, My Lord Surrey."

"What say you?"

"There is no discharge, My Lord, and a distinct lack of other symptoms. In short, you are clean." The doctor is somewhat perplexed as to why the youth has sought him out, but still resolves to charge him two pounds, infected or not. "Why ever do you think you were diseased?"

"Richard Rich and I have shared ladies favours," Surrey admits to the amused doctor.

"And Master Rich is infected?" he asks.

"So it is rumoured, about the court," Harry Howard replies, a little abashed.

"Has he confirmed this to you?" the doctor asks. He is beginning to sense some sort of a misunderstanding. "If he is infected, there is a wonderful new cure. It combines leaches fixed upon the scrotum to draw away the bad vapours, and mercury, which is injected into the pintle by means of a hollow needle."

"Dear God, it sounds most painful," Surrey crosses his legs, subconsciously.

"Very. I think it would deter most men from drawing from a tainted well." The doctor starts to pack away his instruments, a little sorry at not being able to practice with his leeches on so obnoxious a young man. "I doubt it is a treatment Master Rich can afford. Where shall I send my account, sir?"

"To my father," Surrey says, maliciously. He has caused the consultation with his wicked jest. "Double charge the old goat, doctor, and I will vouchsafe it."

The young earl is relieved. The idea of mercury coming into contact with his private parts is horrifying. It will not stop him enjoying his nights out though, and he is looking forward to the Feast of St. Eustace that very evening.

He lacks even a rudimentary education, and does not know his saints days, else he would wonder why the feast was being celebrated either five months late, or seven months early.

"Ah, Rich," he cries, swaggering back into the great outer chamber of Henry's court.

"You will come with me to Cromwell's feast tonight... health willing."

"You are feeling sick, sir?" Richard Rich asks. He does not want to lose so wealthy a friend, and the sweating sickness is abroad again, but not yet in London.

"Not I," Surrey says, with a twinkle in his eye. "Though it is rumoured that you are."

"Of what, sir?"

"The clap."

"Sweet Jesus!" Rich is horrified. If such a tale gets about, he will be hard pressed to find a willing bed mate, and his father, a God fearing sort, will cut his already meagre allowance to a beggar's pittance. "Where do you have this from, sir?"

"My father, Norfolk," Surrey says, "and he has it from Lady Mary Boleyn. She swears it to be true."

"Then I am utterly undone," Rich groans. He cannot call the Duke of Norfolk, or his niece, liars. "I might as well leave court at once, and go home to my father's dreary farm."

"Not so fast," Surrey says. "Their humorous prank has caused me some upset, Richard. We will look for a chance to bait my father this evening."

"And Lady Boleyn?"

"I shall pay her a visit," Surrey replies. "I shall remind my cousin how she favoured me two years ago, whilst still married."

"Favoured you?" Richard Rich smiles. Here is a piece of fine gossip to throw back at her. "How so?"

"In a way that the ladies of the French court favour, for it keeps them free of childbirth."

"You are too knowing for a fifteen year old, my friend," Richard Rich tells him. "Still it will make for some ribald conversation this evening."

"Yes, I cannot wait to see old Cromwell's pudding face when we dun him and his guests in his own lair."

"Go easy on him," Rich says. "He is not as bad as you think, and might one day prove of some use to you."

"Really, Rich," Surrey snipes. "Do you owe him money? Is that why you speak well of him?"

"My Lord Surrey, do not you owe him?"

"A mere trifle," Surrey sneers.

"Seven thousand pounds, I hear," Rich replies. "Can you pay it back, on demand?"

"Well… not at once.'

"Then go easy, sir… for your own sake," Richard Rich says, but he fears the words will fall on deaf and stupid ears.

14   The Feast of St. Eustace

"Our first guests are arriving, Master Cromwell," Rafe Sadler reports. "The ambassador is here, as is that cocksure turd, Richard Rich. He is with Norfolk's spavined brat."

"Keep Surrey and Norfolk apart at the tables," Thomas Cromwell replies. "With two long tables set parallel, there should be no quibbling over who has seating precedence."

"Assuredly not," Will Draper says, hurrying into his master's library. "The Lord Chancellor is even now in the courtyard, and he has brought a surprise guest. You will never guess who, Master Tom."

"Ah, then Henry has come," Cromwell says. "I rather hoped he would. My invitation was delivered in his presence, quite on purpose, and he has a healthy curiosity."

"You knew?" Rafe makes a mental note to bring out the very best silver, and warn the kitchen staff to be on their very best behaviour.

"I hoped." Cromwell picks up a pen, and makes a couple of alterations to the table plan on his desk. "There, that will do. We might yet find a king next to a commoner, but it will only serve to make the conversation more piquant."

Rafe Sadler scoops up the plan, and

hurries off to arrange matters. The cook is still being awkward over disclosing his menu, as he hopes for a last minute delivery of truffles from Kent. The ground has been hard, and the truffle hunting pigs have struggled to find the delicacies, so early in the season.

Sadler is torn between greeting the king properly, and his kitchen duty, but is saved by Eustace Chapuys, who springs forward, and bows to Henry, almost before he is in the door.

"God save Your Majesty," the slightly built Savoyard says, bowing low. He is primed not to mention anything at all to upset the king. "Saving my own lord, you are the only monarch in Europe who is so loved, that he may walk freely amongst his subjects, as you now do."

"Yes, Chapuys," Henry replies, patting him heavily on the shoulder. "My people hold me in the greatest esteem, which is only fitting. I am told that Master Cromwell keeps a better table than mine. Can that really be true, sir?"

"I have eaten at the finest tables in Europe, sire," Chapuys replies, "and am well placed to give a truthful reply. I find Master Cromwell's fare to be wholesome, and filling, but in comparison to your own, it lacks that certain … *je ne sais quoi*."

"Ah! Exactly what I said to the Lord

Chancellor," Henry declares. He is delighted with this answer, which serves to bolster his unchecked ego.

"Sire, I see you favour the French style of headwear," Chapuys says. "I must compliment you on your most superior taste. Do you favour ostrich, or peacock feathers?"

"Both, sir," Henry glows. "Both. For can one have too much of a good thing? You know Sir Thomas More, I take it, my dear *Señor* Chapuys?"

Chapuys bows to Sir Thomas, and the three men pass pleasantries as to the opulence of Cromwell's great dining hall. It is large enough to accommodate thirty guests, and has been panelled with a dark stained oak.

"Good timber," Henry declares. "My ship builders would have use of this quality."

"Then Your Majesty is building more warships?" Chapuys asks, ingenuously. The Lord Chancellor leaps in, to minimise the damage done.

"The king has commissioned three merchant ships, Ambassador Chapuys," he says, casting a warning look at his master.

"Of course... merchantmen, what else" Henry agrees, stumbling over the clumsy lie.

"Then your foundry in Cheapside is casting nothing but church bells?" Chapuys cannot resist a gentle goading of the king, and his chief minister, for the cannon makers are working at full tilt of late. "There will not be a single cathedral in England without a fresh peal."

*

Rafe is safely in the kitchen, and has finally extracted an idea of the evening's menu from the cook. There is a thin vegetable soup to start, followed by cold lamb in vinegar sauce, roasted venison with a medley of pot roast beets, and other, broiled root vegetables. Then there is a dish of hare, stewed in red wine, and a selection of hot mutton, beef, or game pies.

The centre piece of the evening is an amazing platter of stuffed swan, which sees birds, in descending order, stuffed one within the other. On cutting into the dish, one will go through layers of swan, goose, duck, chicken, and quail. This last main dish is to be served up with a rich truffle sauce.

"And in between?" Rafe Sadler asks. "The king must not be kept un-amused."

"Goats cheese, hard Dutch, and soft French cheeses, served with unleavened bread," the man replies. "Then there are various poached fruits, custard tarts, plum puddings, honcyed dumplings, marchpane delights, and other sweet things. Master Cromwell's vintner has laid on suitable wines, ales, and beers, to compliment each course. Five dozen bottles of wine, and three firkins of ale should see us through, with enough for breakfast too, sir."

"Our guests must never have an empty dish in front of them," Rafe says, and pads off to make sure each man is in his rightful place. He arrives back in the great hall, to find Henry has usurped the role of Chief Steward.

The king has taken the place of honour, as is his right, and is busy placing each guest as they come in. He puts More to his left, and Norfolk to his right, then decides to shuffle the duke down by one space. This means Norfolk's guest, the poet, Thomas Wyatt must be shuffled down on the other side of the table.

"I want Tom Cromwell by my right hand side," the king declares. "You there, stop skulking around like a dog. Who are you sir?"

"Richard Rich, sire." Rich bows, and his knees are shaking at being so directly addressed.

"Never heard of you, fellow. Poet, layabout, or lawyer?"

"Lawyer, Your Majesty." Rich squeaks.

"Lawyer, eh? End of the table, sir," Henry says, brusquely. "Take young Howard with you, and keep the silly coxcomb as sober as you possibly can."

The guests are getting into a horrible muddle, when Rafe steps in and, with a few quiet words and nudges, seats them without any further upset. As the last one takes their place, Thomas Cromwell makes his appearance, and bows low.

"A happy surprise, Your Majesty," he says, holding his arms wide. They embrace, and More frowns at the overt show of royal approval. "Your royal presence honours my humble home."

"Not too humble, I hope, Thomas," the king replies, smiling at his own remark. "For I am looking forward to a fine dinner. In honour of St. Eustace, I'm told?"

"It was to be a small, unassuming dinner, given for the ambassador, sire," Cromwell explains. "I thought it only apt therefore, to feast the patron saint of hunters."

"Apt?" Henry is confused. Although he prides himself on his pious knowledge of all things religious, he has never heard of this particular saint. Sir Thomas More leans over, and whispers, explaining that Chapuys' given name is Eustace.

"Droll, my friend," Henry says. "You liken the man to a saint, though some might think our *Spanish* Eustace to be more of a devil!" He laughs, as if it might soften the mild insult, and Chapuys smiles. Great men make small jokes, he thinks. It is ever thus.

"You know my lords Suffolk, Northumberland, Norfolk, and Surrey, Your Majesty, but might I name Master Rich, who works diligently for you in the law courts, and

Dr. Adolphus Theophrasus, a learned visitor from the Hellenic lands. I also see we are to be joined by Master Wyatt, whose often unbridled... sometimes thoughtless... wit is renowned right across Europe."

The king waves his fingers in slight acknowledgement, but is more interested in the females seated about him. He nods to Lady Mary Boleyn, smiles at Miriam Draper, and her husband, and asks who the beautiful, raven haired, young woman is, sitting opposite the already drunken Harry Percy. Thomas Cromwell shrugs his shoulders, and turns to Percy for clarification.

"My Lord Percy, pray acquaint the king with the name of your ... most delightful... dinner companion."

"Might I then name, and recommend to you, my dearest cousin, sire... Lady Purity Percy, of the Lower Putney branch of the family." Northumberland says, stone faced.

"A rare sort of a beauty," Henry replies. "Where have you been keeping her hidden, Harry?"

"In some low tavern, no doubt," Surrey whispers to Richard Rich. "Do we not know her, in every sense, Rich?"

"I suggest a sudden loss of memory," Richard Rich hisses in his ear. "If the king thinks he is being made fun of, it will go badly for all those concerned. Let Lord Percy have his puerile little joke, and let he alone pay the price of it. The man is a fool, and invites disaster with every word he utters."

"Alas, the girl has been receiving a fine education in a local convent, sire, and I have but just released her from the imminent threat of having to take holy orders." Percy is convincing enough to fool Henry, but Tom Wyatt has to hide a wry smile at the man's foolish audacity. It is but a couple of days since he was tupping this particular novice nun, and he admires Percy's almost suicidal sense of humour.

"And the gentleman by your side, my lady?" Henry is in full flirting mode. "Please, do not say he is your betrothed, lest it breaks my heart."

"Why, no sir," 'Lady' Purity replies, blushing. "I am well acquainted with many gentlemen of the court, Your Highness, but I fear he is a stranger to me."

"What's this?" Henry taps a spoon on the table. "Name yourself, sir. Is it meet that you should remain anonymous, yet still have the pleasure of taking a seat by so regal a young lady?"

"My name is Sir Edward Prudhoe, sire." Sir Thomas More looks up, for the first time, and sees the man staring back at him, his face a mask of cold fear. He turns then, to see that Cromwell is smiling with pleasure at the springing of his little trap.

"Not a prude by nature oh?" Henry says, and is surprised when nobody laughs. Perhaps, he thinks, I have too subtle a sense of humour. "Prudish ... Prudhoe... a play on your name, see?"

"Very good, sire," Edward Prudhoe mutters. "The jest is new to me, and I commend your quick wittedness." He sits still, as if the sword of Damocles is suspended above his head.

"Sir Edward is lately back from France, sire," Cromwell explains. "He was of a mind to import their culture, for our entertainment, but found it not to his taste."

"What news of France, Prudhoe?" Will Draper asks. He is primed by Cromwell, and ready with his questions.

"I did not visit Paris, sir," Prudhoe replies. He is still nervous, and expects to be choked to death at any moment. "I toured the outer provinces."

"Have you a patron?" Will prompts.

"No longer," Prudhoe says. "I fear I am currently looking for gainful employment."

"Come to me tomorrow," Thomas Cromwell says, enjoying the contrived conversation. "I am sure to find a use for so well travelled, and knowledgeable, a gentleman, sir. I wager you have much to tell me that might be used to good ends."

"My humble thanks, Master Cromwell." Prudhoe lowers his gaze, unable to face the withering look directed at him by the infuriated Lord Chancellor. If looks could kill, he believes he might already be dead on the floor.

"Enough of dreary diplomatic business," Henry cries. "How is life treating you, Mistress Miriam? I trust Master Draper is a good, and *loving* husband?"

"He is, my lord. Our happiness is due to your generosity, and we cannot thank you enough." Henry is a little confused, but Tom Cromwell whispers in his ear, reminding him of how he has granted Draper's wife the right to live in England.

"Ah, yes." Henry is uncomfortable, for he knows the woman's grandfather, a Jewish banker, died in his place. "You must ask, if there is ought else I can grant you."

"Peace of mind would be nice, sire," Miriam says, sighing and fluttering her eyelashes. "I worry about my neighbours, who seem to have offended the crown in some way."

"Oh?" Henry is not a stupid man, he senses a trap of some sort, and looks to Cromwell for support. He cannot allow a woman, no matter how beautiful, to dispute state business with him.

"Enough, Mistress Miriam," Cromwell

snaps. "It is not your place to petition the king, no matter how worthy the cause. Forgive her, Your Highness, she does not understand these things."

"There is nothing to forgive," Henry replies, smiling at the girl, dazzled by her beauty. "Is it a matter for the courts, Thomas?"

"I do not think so, sire," Thomas Cromwell says. "I think it is a matter of conscience, best left to the churchmen to decide. Let us not discuss it tonight. I will call on our dear Lord Chancellor tomorrow, along with Prudhoe. Sir Edward has a good head for ecclesiastical problems, I believe."

"Let me put your mind at rest, my dear Tom," More puts in. "Is it about the people my men over zealously took up, last week?"

"Concerning the ownership of certain religious books, I believe." Cromwell says, pointedly. "There is some rash talk of serious charges being laid."

"Let me put your mind completely at ease," More replies. "Having looked into the matter, myself, I find there is no case to answer. The men will be home for breakfast."

"Unharmed?"

"Of course. I am not a monster, Thomas." More is not happy. The first racking was to take place the next morning.

"There, Mistress Miriam, I told you that the rumours are false. Sir Thomas More is an absolute stickler for the laws of the land, and will not see any man condemned unjustly."

"Then we are now comfortable with Tyndale and his doctrine?" Henry asks. He is a little surprised at More's sudden change of heart, but is content that no bones have to be broken over the issue.

"In this particular instance," More says, hurrying to repair the breach in his defences. "Each case must be looked at independently, sire … by commissioners, appointed by…"

"The Privy Council," Cromwell interjects. "I will see a select group is put into place at once, sire."

"Is that hare?" Henry is no longer listening. Talk of the minutiae of law bores him, and he has lost all interest. "Move down a place my dear Lord Chancellor, and let Lady Purity sit by me. The poor child looks famished."

*

The meal progresses well, with small islands of diners living out their own small lives with gossip. Lady Mary Boleyn asks Sir Roger De Crecy if he has heard about the certain gentleman who has brought the clap into court. He can hardly contain his mirth, and, staring across the table, wonders aloud who it might be.

"Look not at me, dear lady," Tom Wyatt calls out to her. "For I am a poet, and poets, it is well known, are impervious to the ailment. Else how could we write of love so easily?"

Now they are there, neither Surrey nor Richard Rich have the courage to confront the Boleyn woman, and lapse into a sullen silence. Lady Mary sees she has the advantage, and presses on.

"Perhaps these things are best kept secret, Master Wyatt" she says, fluttering her lashes at Richard Rich. "For well born ladies always admire discretion in a gentleman's nature. It can be a two way thing, can it not, Master Rich?"

"I agree, Madam," Rich says, nodding his consent to the deal. He will say no more about Maria de Salinas, and expect to hear nothing more about his imagined ailment. It was stupid of him to boast falsely, but he did it out of spite, and without thinking through the dire consequences.

"The Clap!" Dr. Theophrasus says, rather too loudly. "Now, there is an interesting ailment."

"I am itching to find out about it," Richard Cromwell calls from the end of the table, and a ripple of laughter runs around the room.

"I believe it to be caused by bad

humours in the womb," the doctor proclaims for all to hear. "The lady, being out of sorts, passes the sickness on to the man. One seldom hears of sodomites falling ill with the clap."

Sir Edward Prudhoe shudders, and reaches for his cup of wine. In the space of a single day, his world has turned completely upside down, and he is contemplating ruin and disaster henceforth.

Sir Thomas More nibbles at some dry bread, but is seething inside at his apparent defeat. Cromwell is in possession of Prudhoe, and knows about the plot against the Pole family. He must release a few heretics as the price of his immediate silence.

"Cheer up, Sir Thomas," Cromwell says. "You have done a good day's work, to offset the bad. I pray you understand this."

"I do," More nods, and smiles thinly. "You have me at a disadvantage, Master Cromwell. I can but bow to your superior abilities, on this occasion. I take it there will be no entertainers tonight?"

"I regret not, Lord Chancellor," Cromwell replies. "I fear their permits have been revoked... permanently. My fool is somewhere about, should you wish to match wits with a jester."

"I thought I already had," More replies, testily.

"*Touché*, sir," Cromwell says, and

smiles at the remark.

"You must come to see me tomorrow, Master Prudhoe," More says, pointedly.

"I regret not, sir," Prudhoe says, noting his sudden reduction in rank. The knighthood seems to have vanished. "Master Cromwell insists on my constant presence."

"Stick with old Tom, sir," Wyatt says. "That is... Master Cromwell, for I have never known a truer friend."

Cromwell is content. He has thwarted a series of heinous, politically motivated murders, and forced the release of some common men, whose only crime is to have read William Tyndale's writings. The evening progresses well, until the kitchen porters come in, bearing the stuffed swan.

Thomas Wyatt leaps to his feet, and launches into an impromptu, and somewhat lewd ode, dedicated to the various ways a man might stuff a plump bird. Henry is pleased with the young fellow's sharp wit, and insists he must return to court.

"We've missed you, Master Wyatt," Henry says. "What has France got that we lack?"

Safety, Wyatt thinks to himself. Thomas Cromwell has warned him that Percy was disposed to ruining Lady Anne Boleyn with rash comments alluding to her virginal state. It is a wise man who knows when to make himself scarce. The poet has often written lurid lines of love to Anne, before her elevation to King's fancy, and it would go ill with him if the king suspects more has happened than an exchange of mere poetic couplets.

"I must return, on business, sire," Tom Wyatt replies. "Though my heart is ever here, in England. I shall return at some future date. I promise."

"If not, I shall send Cromwell to hit you over the head, and drag you back," the king says. "More wine!"

The Earl of Surrey, wishing to keep up with his elders, has drunk far too much, he vomits, and slides under the table. This is an affront to the king, who sneers at Norfolk.

"The fruit is rotten, Uncle Norfolk," he says. "You must wonder if he is really yours."

Tom Howard flushes a bright purple. That Henry feels able to comment so, shocks him. The king has taken twenty five years over the business of producing an heir, and is yet to come good. He is about to reply, but Cromwell squeezes his arm under the table.

"Do not lose your head, Lord Norfolk," he says. "For once lost, even Dr. Theophrasus might struggle to put it back on your shoulders."

"Butcher's boy!" Norfolk growls.

"You confuse me with Cardinal

Wolsey again, sir," Cromwell whispers back. "I am the blacksmith's lad, and a much tougher proposition for that. I am told that your great grandfather was a peat cutter, and the illegitimate son of a wandering priest."

"He was a bishop," Norfolk whispers back, then grins. He is beginning, in a perverse way, to like Cromwell, very much. "It will be a sad day when I have to have you killed, Master Blacksmith."

Harry Percy is drunk, and becoming quietly furious. Henry has stolen his latest bed companion, and is running his hand up and down her thigh. Suffolk makes to stop him rising, but he shakes him off, lurches to his feet, and shouts down the table.

"Pray, sire, when you have done with my whore, might I have her back?" The room fall silent. Lady Boleyn suppresses a giggle, and Stephen Gardiner clutches at the golden cross hanging about his neck.

"Have a care, Percy," Henry says, his voice grown cold, and furious. "remember where you are, and in whose company you eat."

"You mistake me, *cousin* Henry," Percy replies, lurching to his feet. "I mean no insult to the girl, for that is her trade. Purity is a working girl, and will lay down for any man who has a silver shilling."

Thomas Cromwell makes a small

gesture, and two of his young men appear, take Percy under the armpits, and drag him from the room. Rafe Sadler approaches the girl, takes her elbow, and gently draws her from the king's side.

"The lady's attendants are here, sire," he mutters in the king's ear, and takes her from the room. Once outside, he gives her five shillings, and sends her on her way. He returns to find Lady Mary Boleyn in Purity's place, running her fingers across the king's chest.

"A pretty evening's work, Master Cromwell," More says as the evening stutters to a close. Guests have split into small groups, and are finishing off the last of the good Flemish wine. "Are you proud of yourself?"

"I am proud of stopping your wicked plot," Tom Cromwell replies. "You set yon Prudhoe on the Poles, without mercy."

"Not so. I merely mentioned that the family are a nuisance, and he took the wrong end of the stick. What evidence you have will not stand scrutiny in a law court. Sir Edward will be called upon to swear against the Lord Chancellor, and the full might of his high office."

"You will not hold that position long," Cromwell replies.

"No?" Sir Thomas sniggers. "Henry wants his annulment, and I will get it for him. Afterwards, I will suggest that you might need a long rest from your duties. He will agree, out of gratitude."

"Gratitude?" Cromwell smiles. "It is a dangerous thing to remind a king that he should be grateful. Wolsey forgot that, and seemed too haughty. So, you all pulled him down."

"Is this what it comes to?" More asks. "Revenge? Suffolk is your lapdog, Percy is shamed before the king again, and Norfolk is reminded of your brute power. You behave like nothing more than a common thug, sir!"

"I am a common thug," Cromwell replies, staring the Lord Chancellor down. "I use brutish force to get my way, and try to keep order in England. You will have us tied to Rome again, and the king a servant of the corrupt Bishop of Rome."

"If it saves his immortal soul... yes."

"I despair of you, Tom," Cromwell says. If he can only show the man the right path for England, he thinks. "Can we not pool our resources, and work together?"

"Never."

"Then you intend baulking me at every turn?"

"It is too late, Cromwell," More says. "I do not dislike you. I simply cannot walk the same path. Your road leads to heresy."

"And yours to murder." Thomas Cromwell watches as his one time friend leaves, and shakes his head. The king is in a better mood, and he and Lady Mary are ready to be escorted back to Whitehall Palace. Harry Percy, Duke of Northumberland, is in the kitchen, sobering up. On the morrow, he will ask the king what to do with him. Henry will be inclined to forgive, once more, but a price must be paid. Perhaps some more of his dangerous border land might be allocated to Suffolk? After all, is not Charles Brandon a true and lifelong friend?

*

Cromwell spends a few moments with Stephen Gardiner, preparing him for the news of his new position. He will not want to go to Paris, but it is the safest thing for him. He has a conscience, and must be away when it matters, if only to protect his misplaced innocence.

"Paris?" Gardiner says. "Do you hate me so much, Master Cromwell?"

"On the contrary, Stephen," Cromwell replies, trying to reconcile him to the move. "I hold you in high esteem, and believe you will do good work for us. You shall negotiate the marriage between Princess Mary, and a suitable royal prince."

"Henry will not allow it'"

"I know, but we must be seen to be taking the matter seriously," Cromwell explains. "The French king will try to put forward a replacement for Queen Katherine instead. You must seem to like the idea, but sidestep it."

"You wish to keep France in our circle of friends?" Gardiner begins to understand. "Then you have another in mind. A Spanish princess, perhaps... or a German?"

"The situation is volatile, Stephen," Cromwell replies. "Once Henry chooses, the rest of Europe will want our blood."

"He will marry Anne Boleyn."

"Perhaps." Thomas Cromwell hopes not, and he prays the woman will surrender that which Henry craves, before any ill advised marriage takes place. There is far too much gossip about her and Percy, Wyatt has almost certainly had her, and several gentlemen of the court are too friendly for their own good.

He is tired of all the political chicanery, but must continue to support his view of what England requires. Then he shakes Gardiner's hand, and escorts him to the front door.

"The world changes, my friend, and we must change with it. Today's flight of fancy may well become tomorrow's rightful queen, and the day afters discarded whore. Goodnight to you, Stephen."

Rafe Sadler calls for a palanquin, and helps Richard Rich load the Earl of Surrey into it. The boy has his father's overweening arrogance, but none of his wits, or head for strong drink. He will wake up tomorrow morning, unable to recall any of the long night's events.

Suffolk hovers, wishing to bid a personal farewell to Cromwell, if only to assure himself of the man's continued patronage. Sir Roger De Crecy lingers too. He owes ten thousand to Cromwell, and does not wish to offend him in any way.

Cromwell sees this. He crosses to them, uttering words of friendship, and reassurance. They must not worry about their overdue loans, he tells them. The price of wool is going to go up another sixpence a bale, he explains, and their vast flocks will be worth so much more. Another loan to tide them over, just until the next market day comes around again... why not? What are friends for, my dear Brandon? Come back another day, and he will have one of his young men broker a fresh deal, and calculate the current loan rate.

Tom Howard, the garrulous Duke of Norfolk, is amongst the very last to leave. He has cornered Rafe Sadler, and demands to know where the girl, Purity, has gone to. He has a mind to make himself known to her.

Rafe shrugs his shoulders, and explains that she has melted away, into the night. Norfolk frowns at this news, and offers a small bribe, but Sadler must, regretfully decline it.

He *really* does not know where she will be. There are a dozen whore houses within a few minutes walk.

"Damn your eyes, but that's a waste," he cries. "Never mind, take the coins anyway. It will help to keep you honest, my young friend. Plenty more little fish swimming in Old Father Thames, what?"

"My thanks to you, My Lord Norfolk," Rafe Sadler bows, and slips the silver coins into a pocket. He will add them to the Austin Friars fund later, and expect only his fair share.

"And a fond goodnight to you, Master Tom Cromwell, the blacksmith's son … from the Bishop's grand bastard son."

Cromwell bows, and waves the great man on his way. It is only when Eustace Chapuys, deep in a philosophical conversation with Adolphus Theophrasus, sets out to leave, that a niggling worm of doubt crawls into his mind. Something has been said. Something he should have picked up on earlier. He is too tired to pin down the elusive thought.

It is in the deepest part of the night that he comes suddenly awake, and curses. The Lord Chancellor was not half as angry as he should have been. The curtain is finally drawn aside, the shadows melt away, and he can see clearly, at last.

Sir Thomas More has fooled him.

15　A Worm in the Apple

That the most obvious course is often the right one, is a truth that Thomas Cromwell often pounds into his young men's heads. It is easier to tell the truth, because a lie has to be remembered, and can often trip a man up.

"Stick as closely to the truth as you can," he tells them. "If you must lie, make it small, and hide it deeply within reality." Now he sees that he has allowed himself to be fooled in just that way by a cleverer mind.

It is not that Sir Thomas More is more intelligent, he is simply, in this instance, more devious. Cromwell accepts this, and realises that it is only because he has allowed himself to retain a scrap more morality than the Lord Chancellor. He rises with the sun, washes in water warmed by the kitchen girl, and calls for a council of war.

It is mid morning before Eustace Chapuys arrives, coming in with Will Draper's pet doctor, who has stayed the night with the Spanish ambassador, playing chess, and exchanging tales of their various travels about the world. Miriam and her husband are present, as requested, and Richard Cromwell is there, fresh from a huge breakfast of blood pudding, bacon and eggs. The council is complete when Rafe Sadler arrives in the cramped library.

"Good day, Master Cromwell," Adolphus Theophrasus says, taking the most comfortable looking chair without waiting to be asked. "Am I here in a professional capacity?"

"You are here for advice, sir," Will says, handing him a mug of ale, heated with a hot poker from the fire. "Pray sit in my comfortable chair, and listen."

"I am beginning to worry a little, my dear Thomas," Eustace Chapuys says, with a nervous laugh. "Each time I visit you, it ends in some form of mayhem."

"Then you will not be disappointed today," Tom Cromwell replies. He sits behind his broad, cluttered, desk, and steeples his fingers in thought. The strands of an idea are still forming in his mind, and he needs these people to properly assess that which he only suspects.

"Are there more heads to break, uncle?" Richard Cromwell asks. "It is my forte, after all."

"Ah... forte... from the French, Richard," Chapuys says, hoping to lighten the mood. "It is our word for the part of a sword that runs from the hilt."

"The part that does most damage,' Richard chuckles, and helps himself to a mug of ale.

"Perhaps. Sit, all of you, and let me

explain." The older Cromwell takes up a fine Venetian glass, and sips wine from it. "Last evening, we contrived to embarrass the Lord Chancellor, and force him to release a few of our persecuted friends. The price will be high, no doubt. Sir Thomas will have noted down each of us, and our part in his defeat, and then he will take his revenge… if we should let him."

"He cannot harm me," Chapuys says.

"No?" Cromwell shakes his head. "He can tell Henry you hate Anne Boleyn, and he will have you recalled, in disgrace. The good doctor will find his papers are no longer in order. He might be revealed as a Jew, taken up, and burned at the stake."

"Dear God!" Theophrasus exclaims. "This is the most barbaric nation on Earth, sir. Even the Turks leave you alone, if you pay them enough."

"He will turn his scorn on me, and on my people," Thomas Cromwell continues. "I will be turned out of office, and my young men forced to work for lesser men. Our fortunes will go, and some of us may even face the axe. Do I make myself clear?"

"You do, sir," Will Draper replies for them all. "I am minded of the old saying about dogs eating dogs. Sir Thomas is a beast, but we must be bigger, and better dogs."

"You mean to kill him?" Miriam asks,

and the small chamber falls into silence.

"We dare not," Cromwell tells her. "Henry would know it to be my doing. Then More's people would simply continue to fight against us. In killing him now, we sew the seeds for our own demise later."

"Then what do you propose?" Eustace Chapuys is mortified, and fears for them all.

"What I have always intended," says Cromwell. "We must undermine his position. Make him seem unfit for high office, or too grand, and Henry will drop him, as he once dropped Cardinal Wolsey. Once brought down, all More's power will ebb away, and we will be safe to continue with the great work."

"What must we do?" Will Draper asks. He is a man forged in battle; a man of action, and he wants to get at the enemy, as fast as is possible.

"It is a slow process, and might take a couple of years," his patron replies, taking some pleasure in their obvious support. "Let us ponder more immediate events if we may."

"You mean Sir Thomas More's humiliating climb down, last night at dinner?" Miriam asks. "It seems to me to be a very easily won victory, Master Tom."

"Most astute, my dear girl," Thomas Cromwell says, and he is delighted that she is quicker witted than the men. "I knew something was wrong last night, but could not think what. Then it came to me in the small hours of the morning."

"You speak in riddles, Master Cromwell," Adolphus Theophrasus says. "What has disturbed your sleep so? There are powders I can prescribe."

"He did not mind." Cromwell looks from face to face. Only Miriam nods her head in understanding. She thought it at the time, and can now put her thoughts into words, amongst her friends.

"The Lord Chancellor considers himself to be the finest intellect in all of Christendom," she explains to the gathered company. "Yet he accepted the utter confusion of his plans far too easily."

"Just so, Miriam," Cromwell says. "He frowned, and growled a little to be sure. He even allowed us an easy victory over the prisoners he meant to torture, but he was not overly put out by my seeming coup. He fooled me, you see."

"We won, Thomas," Eustace Chapuys mutters, unable to understand his new friend's chagrin.

"No, we did not, my friend. He did. He let us hint at the truth, and coerce him into the right path. In the middle of it all, he hid his great lie. He made us believe we have won the day, and yet, his great... and may I say, astoundingly bold... plot goes on apace, unhindered by our too feeble efforts."

"You mean the queen," Eustace Chapuys says, and he feels his heart begin to race in his chest. "Then the danger to Her Majesty is not yet over?"

"The threat to Katherine was the only real thing about all this," Cromwell replies. "We were meant to uncover the threatened danger to the Pole family, and the wicked attempt on your own life, my friend. More cared not if this chimera of a plot succeeded, or failed. It was a very clever trick, done with smoke and mirrors, my friends. The man is a clever magician."

"Then Katherine is still in danger?" Richard Cromwell asks, and he makes a note to ask what a chimera is at some later date, when Mush and Will can bait him over his thickheadedness. "Sir Thomas still thinks to remove her from the court... for good?"

"She has been under a constant threat to her life from the very outset." Thomas Cromwell has stated the facts, and must now put forward a theory. "It seems that More has a plan that will remove Katherine, yet not arouse suspicion against himself. He cannot be seen to have her blood on his hands. The king will not countenance that which reflects badly on him, and would dismiss him to save his own reputation. Thomas More is obviously confident of his scheme. There will be a certain subtlety about it."

"Then it will not be the knife from a dark corner," Will Draper says. "Nor the garrotte in the night. There can be no obvious signs of foul play on the body. More knows that clever, independent minded, men will view the corpse. *Señor* Chapuys will see the marks of murder, and shout it from the very roof tops of his empire. Until the king's name is mud, and More's reputation is in ruins. Why, even the emperor would rise up at such a crime, and order his forces to war."

"Correct, my friend. It would mean war, and on an inconceivably bloody scale." Thomas Cromwell turns then to look at Dr. Adolphus Theophrasus, who is sitting quietly, sipping his warm, spiced ale. "Well, sir, what say you?"

*

The doctor frowns, then puts his cup down. He composes himself, and prepares to give his opinion, but must clearly understand what is being asked of him.

"May I speak openly?" he asks.

"You are amongst friends," Will Draper tells him. "This meeting is secret, and will never be alluded to outside this room."

"Very well. Master Cromwell, are you then asking me how I would murder the Queen of England?"

"I am, sir." Thomas Cromwell leans

forward, directing every sense into what the man has to say.

"Poison." The doctor sits back, and spreads his hands wide, as if to say *'what else would a clever fellow use?'*

"Impossible... utterly impossible!" Eustace Chapuys cries, and is waved into silence by Thomas Cromwell, who then plays the devil's advocate.

"The food is tested as it is cooked," he tells the doctor.

"Then I would poison it afterwards," he replies, and shrugs his big shoulders.

"Lady Maria de Salinas, a person above reproach, usually eats with the queen," Cromwell explains. "If not her, then another lady in waiting. Surely, Lady Maria will sicken, and die too?"

"She would." The doctor frowns and strokes his flowing, white beard. "Does she drink at all, Master Chapuys?"

"Her Majesty enjoys a glass of red wine from her own native country," Eustace Chapuys tells him. "Spanish wine is, of course, the best in the world."

"Does this Lady Maria woman drink too?" the doctor asks of the little Savoyard ambassador.

"Usually." Chapuys says, but shakes his head. "The bottles come from the queen's own cellar, and are not opened until they are placed on the dinner table. The task always falls to one of her two Moroccan body guards, or onto dear Lady Maria herself. Even I have performed this cork pulling duty… on the odd occasion I have been honoured enough to have eaten with the queen."

"Then, if this is so, there is no way her food, or drink can be poisoned," Adolphus Theophrasus says, and strokes the bridge of his long nose. "What about her ablutions? What about the water she washes in?"

"Scented with rose petals. Brought in each morning by a servant," Will Draper reports.

"It might be poisoned, I suppose." The doctor says it, but does not give it much credence. "The lady swallows a few drops as she washes her face and, after a few days of this, she falls sick."

"I doubt the same servant brings the water to her chamber each day," Draper replies. "Usually it is whomsoever is on duty that morning. It is why Henry's would be assassin did not strike sooner… for he was not always on duty. Besides, it is far too hit and miss. If I were Sir Thomas More, I would want something that was foolproof. A way of poisoning the queen over a few weeks, that seems quite natural to the casual onlooker. A poison that took its time, and looked like a hundred different ailments."

"What might do that?" Cromwell asks the doctor.

"Arsenic can be administered in small, regular doses. It builds up, until the victim convulses, and dies. In the early stages, it might be mistaken for the sweating sickness, or even cholera, as the victim sweats profusely, and is constantly being sick. Slow poisoning, over a period of a few weeks, or even months, might well escape being detected."

"Anything else?" Cromwell demands.

"Lead," Theophrasus replies.

"Lead is a poison?" Miriam asks. She is surprised, as she has cosmetics made from white lead powder.

"Yes, my dear. It is highly poisonous, if administered in a large enough dose," the doctor replies. "It is much slower than arsenic, of course, and there are tell tale signs if the dose is hurried... such as a greyness in the finger nails, or a wanness of complexion, but one can always increase the size of the dose to compensate, and hope the symptoms are confused with a consumptive disorder."

"Two terrible ways to die," Chapuys says, "but we must discount both. How would they be administered? Besides, there are extra safeguards in place that no one knows about."

"Is this so, Eustace?" Thomas Cromwell is taken aback at this news, for it is not something his own spies have picked up on. "How do you mean?"

"The two Moroccan guards stand over the queen at all times, even when Dr. Vargas is examining her." Chapuys smiles, for he sees that his friend's eye is not so all seeing after all. "Why, the doctor even makes unannounced visits to the kitchens. He warned me against poison a while ago, and asked that he might take extra measures to safeguard Her Majesty. the man is dull, but completely devoted to Katherine. He will let no other doctor near her."

"By the Body of Christ!" Thomas Cromwell lurches to his feet, and slaps his hand down on the desk top, dislodging a rather fine copy of '*The Prince*' by Machiavelli. "I see it now, my friends. Let us drink to success, before I explain all."

Everyone in the room drinks from cups, goblets or glasses, except Cromwell. He simply sits down again, and smiles at his own slowness in realising the danger.

"Master?" Will Draper cannot understand. "What is it?"

"Do you trust me, Will?"

"I do."

"And you, my friends? Do you all trust me?"

There is a chorus of fervent consent, and Tom Cromwell nods his head, as if well satisfied. He stands, and walks over to his nephew.

"How are you feeling, Richard?" he asks, solicitously.

"Well enough, sir."

"Really? That is odd, considering I have put poison in all the cups. In two minutes, you will all be dead."

Eustace Chapuys lurches to his feet, clawing at his throat, as if he is in the last throws of his life. He stares, wide eyed at so calm an announcement of his imminent death.

"Impossible," Miriam says, calmly. "I prepared the wine myself."

"Of course you did, my dear," Cromwell confesses. "I lied to you all. You must see what I mean though?"

"I do," Miriam replies. "Everyone trusts their doctor."

"Especially one who goes out of his way to inspect your meals, and insists on administering medicine personally." Thomas Cromwell looks to the doctor. "Well?"

"If it were I doing the poisoning, I would make everything I do seem as clear as day. I would express my concern about the chance of poison being used. Then I would demand extra checks on the kitchens, and even more rigorous searches of any chance visitors. Finally, I would prepare a potion."

"A potion?" says Cromwell.

"A sweet, honeyed syrup," Dr Adolphus Theophrasus says to his host. "Something that will go down easily. In each draft, I would put a tiny amount of arsenic. Over three or four weeks, the queen will start to inexplicably sicken. It might be put down to the bad air about the palace, or perhaps, less delicately, attributed to a woman's monthly troubles. Katherine is of an age when they most rear their heads."

"If the queen is ill, Lady Maria will call for her own private doctor," Chapuys says. "If what you claim is true, the patient will be attended by her own murderer. Vargas is a sullen man, God knows, but I would never suspect him of so horrible a crime as this. What reason could he have?"

"He is in Thomas More's employ, of course," Tom Cromwell reasons. "God alone knows why he would wish to kill his own queen though. Can it be as simple a thing as money?"

"I will find out his reasons," Will Draper says. It is time for him to step up, and take his place on the stage. "All I need is access to Queen Katherine, when this devil Vargas is there."

"Can you arrange it?" Cromwell asks of the ambassador.

"I can," Chapuys replies. "It must be soon, for I have reports of the queen being ill these last couple of days. Lady Maria says the doctor is being most attentive to her needs."

"I wonder how much Sir Thomas More has promised the wretch?" says Will.

"Enough, for now I suspect the true reasons behind his treachery." Chapuys is thinking fast, and wonders how he could be so blind. "Vargas is bonded to the church, and would need a fortune to buy his freedom. He talks of returning to the south of Spain, where he can live out his own life without fear."

"Fear?" Cromwell asks. "Fear of what?"

"Yes, I should have realised what he was telling me during his ever so dull and rambling reports. He comes from the province of Granada, an area that, until recently was a vast Moorish emirate. Vargas grew up in a world of infidels, and may even be one of their number, and no Christian at all. No wonder he is so much liked by the infidel Moroccans. They understand that he is, in some way, of an affinity with them."

"Loyal men who probably do not suspect his wicked game," Thomas Cromwell says. "You must get our own man into the queen's presence, my dear Eustace, and you must do it today!"

*

"Arms are not allowed in the same room as either the king, or the queen," Will says. "I must think how to get my sword into Katherine's rooms without raising some alarm."

"Leave that part to me," Miriam tells the company. "I will contrive to get your sword into the queen's private chambers."

"How can you, safely?" Thomas Cromwell is unsure. Miriam Draper is a woman of infinite ability, but spiriting a yard long German sword past a dozen household guards, and two armed Moroccans, will be a most difficult task. Besides, he fears for her being taken, as even a woman might face the headsman's axe.

"Trust me, Master Cromwell," the girl responds, earnestly. "This is woman's work, and I will not let my husband down. The sword, and whatever else he needs, will be there, waiting for him."

"Then I will arrange a visit for us both, today," Eustace Chapuys tells Will Draper. "Is that suitable for your needs, Will, or do you need longer to prepare?"

"No, I am ready now," Will says.

"Best that you make the audience for three persons, *Señor* Chapuys," the Greek doctor says, lumbering to his feet. "Unless either of you know the symptoms of, or the proper antidote for, something akin to arsenic poisoning?"

Eustace Chapuys nods. He is fearful

that they might be too late, and Vargas has already administered enough poison to complete his task. Once more he curses himself for not realising that there was a worm in the apple. Vargas, for whatever his motives, could affect the entire history of England, with his one simple act of wicked murder.

Thomas Cromwell issues a few last words of advice, and lets his people go about their business. He has done all he can, and must wait now, to see who will come out on top. It worries him that More might still have his way, and drive Henry into the arms of yet another Catholic Spanish princess.

Chapuys master, the Emperor Charles will be pleased, of course, and the King of France infuriated. Neither nation will make a good bedfellow, Cromwell believes, and he wishes to steer Henry onto an altogether different course. The German states are solid and reliable, but above all... mostly Protestant.

Given the chance, Cromwell will wed Henry either to a pliable English girl of good family, or into a powerful Germanic alliance with the teutonic emperor, Karel. The two great powers, thus allied, will cow the French and Spanish into peace, and trade will flourish across Europe. For, when all is said and done, peace really is good for business.

16   The Midnight Queen

"Arsenic is the queen of poisons," Adolphus Theophrasus tells a fascinated Eustace Chapuys. "It was known of in the time of the old Roman Empire, but defined by a great German scholar called Albertus Magnus, about two hundred and fifty years ago."

"It is a grim discovery to have to your name," the little Savoyard says, shuddering. "I wonder how many deaths it has caused over these last centuries?"

"Hundreds, perhaps even thousands, I would guess," the doctor replies. "It was seen as an easy remedy to ease the path of succession in royal circles. I believe the French court often dispose of unwanted heirs by slipping it into their food. They see it as a way of ensuring the right fellow ascends to the throne, no doubt."

"Is it hard to prepare?" Will Draper asks the doctor. He is a fighting man, but knows you cannot defeat something you cannot see, or even taste, until it is too late.

"The first precise directions for the preparation of metallic arsenic can be found in the writings of Paracelsus, a notorious alchemist who lived about a century ago," Dr Theophrasus tells them. "He distilled it into a white powder, that could be sprinkled on to prepared food, or simply mixed into a drink.

His wicked preparations must have fetched a high price from those in need of a silent way to murder their enemies."

*

Chapuys pauses at the outer gate, and shows his credentials to one of the guards. The man, who cannot read or write, examines the royal seal, and is satisfied that everything is above board. Besides which, he knows Chapuys, and has seen Will Draper about the place often enough. He takes the small silver coin he is offered, and waves the three men through into the inner sanctum.

"Just down this final corridor," Eustace Chapuys tells his companions. "There is one more guard to pass, and then we are in the queen's private state rooms. Everyone you meet after that man will be one of Katherine's own people."

Will Draper follows, but feels naked without his sword hanging by his side. The weapon is dear to him, as he captured it in the heat of battle. The Irish lord had fought hard, and died well, and Will was proud to take his sword. A small dagger is hidden in the folds of his cloak, but it will be of scant help in a real brawl.

The final guard, a sergeant at arms, can read well enough, and it will take more than a small bribe, if he becomes suspicious of their motives. He raises a hand, and halts the small party.

"Your business, my good sirs?" he asks, and notes their lack of arms. They have their cloaks thrown back, showing that nothing is concealed about their bodies, and he nods approvingly. If only all these fine gentlemen were so amenable, it would make the job easier for him.

"I am the Spanish ambassador," Chapuys tells him. He uses this title, ratherthan the Holy Roman affectation, as it is better understood, and has less connotations with the Roman church. "I have an urgent matter to discuss with the queen."

"I recognise you, sir," the sergeant replies in an affable enough manner. "And these gentlemen?" The guard is suddenly of a mind to be a little awkward. He is not fond of foreigners, and the fat one has a distinctly Jewish appearance.

"Tad Beaton?" Will Draper says, hardly able to believe his luck. "Can that be you?"

"And who might you be?" The big man peers into the gloom of the ill lit corridor, then gives a great oath. "By all the saints in God's Heaven! Is that you, Captain Draper?"

"It is, you old fraud," Will replies. "Last time I saw you, the Colonel was deciding whether to flog, or hang you."

"And you says... 'beggin' yer pardon, sir, but Tad is the only man I have who knows his way out of this be-damned bog.' By sweet Jesus, but you saved my thick hide that day, and no mistake, sir."

"We must have a few drinks, for old time's sake, Tad," Will says, moving towards the door. He hopes that the half remembered friendship will be enough to grant them safe passage into the queen.

"Sorry, sir, but I has to have papers for you all... not just the Spanish cove. Orders is orders, after all," Will is considering how best to overcome the big mans stubbornness, when the door opens from within, and Lady Maria de Salinas appears, fluttering her arms at them all, and brushing the surprised guard to one side.

"Why do you delay, you oaf? Ah, Ambassador Chapuys, at last. You have the doctor with you? Good. Hurry, for Her Majesty is gravely ill. Guard, do not let anyone else enter, unless it is Dr. Vargas. You know him, of course?"

"Yes, Milady," Tad growls, somewhat put out at another foreigner putting him in his place. "but these people do not..."

They are inside, and the door closes before the guard can object any further. He shrugs, thinks what a small world it is, and returns to his solitary guard duty. Draper was a decent sort, he recalls, and thinks back to the long months spent chasing wild haired Irishmen across a merciless land. There can be no harm in him entering, and besides, he was unarmed.

"Well done, Lady Maria," Eustace Chapuys says. "How ever did you know we were coming?" In answer, Lady Maria de Salinas crosses to a huge tapestry hanging on the wall, and rummages behind it for a moment. She emerges, bearing Will Draper's precious sword, belt, and scabbard.

"How is this miracle possible?" he asks the helpful Spanish woman. "Did Miriam come to you?"

"I do not know of whom you speak, sir," Lady Maria replies. "I was approached by Lady Mary Boleyn. She begged a favour of me, saying it will help the queen. She told me a friend had given the sword to her, and asked for it to be delivered to me. It came in to these chambers, hidden under her skirts. Even the bravest guard will not venture there."

"Then Miriam must have gone to Lady Mary," Will decides.

"I think not," Chapuys says, smiling at the cleverness of it. "I think Miriam went to her brother, Mush, and sent him to his new lady friend."

"What? Mush and Lady Mary Boleyn

are... lovers?" Will is already buckling on the sword. "She must lack any taste at all. Still, I cannot complain."

"This way," Lady Maria says. "The queen is waiting for you all, in her bed chamber."

They follow Maria, and come into a luxuriously furnished room that serves both as Katherine's bedroom, and her receiving chamber. She is sat on a stool by the bed, looking ashen faced, and does not attempt to rise as they enter.

"Have you been sick, my lady?" Theophrasus asks in excellent Spanish. She nods, but it is only with an effort. "Did you take your tonic?"

"Every day," Katherine replies, "but it seems to do me no good at all."

"I can well believe that, madam," the doctor says. He crosses the room, and takes her wrist in his big hand. "Pulse erratic. You have grey patches under the eyes, and your general pallor is most unhealthy. Have you eaten any food today?"

"Nothing since last evening," Queen Katherine tells him. "I fear I am dying, sir."

"Nonsense, Your Majesty, I am the only medically trained man in these chambers, and, for you, Death is not invited today." The doctor opens his bag, a leather satchel of large proportions, and searches inside it. "Ah, the very thing. Take this, Lady Maria, and mix it with a little wine. Give it to Her Majesty to drink down at once, but make sure there is a large bowl close by. It is an emetic, and will help her empty her stomach… most violently."

*

"Will she live?" a distraught Eustace Chapuys asks the doctor, a few minutes later, as the queen retches up the contents of her stomach.

"I doubt that she has been given a lethal dose just yet," Adolphus Theophrasus explains to the concerned ambassador. "Once the stomach is completely empty, we will administer nothing but fresh milk, dry bread, and cold water. The water must be boiled first, and then allowed to cool. This removes all of the bad humours from it."

Will glances about the room, and sees the two huge Moroccans standing stock still by the door. They are watching him, warily. The younger one gestures to Will's sword, and seems as if he is about to demand that he remove it, but the older man speaks in a foreign tongue, and his companion settles back into his previous stance. They continue to glare at all that is going on, and mutter darkly when the doctor starts to treat the queen.

"The Mussel men don't seem too

happy," Will Draper says to Eustace Chapuys. "I wonder what they are chattering about?"

"I know a little of their tongue," Chapuys tells his companion. "The older one is telling his friend to keep out of this."

"A wise man," Will replies. "I think our doctor has a mind to empty the queen of all the bad vapours, and have her convalesce on milk. It must, I suspect, sooth the stomach."

"Arsenic is a kind of metal," Theophrasus says, reverting to his ponderous, heavily accented, English. "It finds its way into the blood, and settles where ever it might. I have found arsenic in a corpse's hair, under the fingernails, and in every major organ before now." He draws his two companions to one side, away from the queen, who is busy heaving into a bowl. "I cannot cure her, Chapuys. I can halt the poisoning, and hope she has not ingested too much yet. At best, she will be an invalid in her later years... at the very worst.... she may be dead inside a week."

"Dear God," Chapuys crosses himself. "What can we do to save her, doctor?"

"We have done all we can for the queen," the doctor tells them. "It only remains for us to now stop this murderous Vargas in his tracks. Is he due yet?"

It is then the bed chamber door swings open, and Dr Vargas is framed in it. He is a little taken aback by the scene, but soon recovers his composure. He glances at the queen, who is still retching, and nods his understanding of what is afoot.

"I see you have guessed all about my little game, Ambassador Chapuys," he says. "I hope your physician is too late, for it is my avowed intent to destroy that wicked woman. May Allah curse her soul."

"Wicked?" Will steps forward, and rests a hand on the hilt of his sword. "How can you say so, after what you have tried to do to her, fellow?"

"Her family now rule my homeland," Vargas replies. "They persecute all of those who will not convert to Christianity. I am of the true faith, and follow the teachings of the great prophet, Mohammed."

"Then you always wished her dead?" Chapuys asks.

"From the start," Vargas says. "Imagine my delight when an Englishman offers me a fortune to kill her. His master wants it to be slow, and look like Cholera, or the sweating sickness, he tells me. I am only too glad to oblige, for it is the Will of Allah, and my own wish too."

"Your plot is undone," Will says. "I am here to take you away, Vargas."

"Have I any hope of surviving the night?" The Spaniard seems unconcerned for himself. "*Masha Allah.*"

"You must make peace with which ever God you wish, sir, for I am to be the guide to your executioner," Will replies. "This shocking evil cannot go unpunished."

"Such a pity, sir," Vargas tells him. "Though I doubt one armed man will be enough to stop me. My Arabic is quite good, you see, and it has enabled me to speak with these two Moroccans at great length, and bring them over to my side. It will be an honour for them to help kill an oppressor of our faith. Should they die, they will be welcomed into Paradise, for all eternity."

Vargas speaks rapidly in Arabic, explaining the predicament to the guards, and the two Moroccans draw their wicked, curved scimitars. Will is suddenly at a disadvantage, needing to defend the queen, whilst contriving to best three armed men. The Spanish turncoat draws a stiletto blade from his sleeve, and crouches into a low, defensive posture.

Draper sees the older Moroccan moving to his left, and knows it is a feint, meant to draw his attention from his comrade in arms. Maria de Salinas begins shouting for help at once, and the lone guard outside comes in to see who is causing such an infernal row. He is a wily old soldier, with long years service in Ireland, and is alert to any danger.

"Look to yourself, Tad," Will cries, and the old veteran brings his halberd up, just in time to block a vicious stroke from the younger Moroccan. He cannot swing his own unwieldy weapon in so confined a space, and must be content with pushing his attacker away. The older man takes his chance, and lunges forward, sweeping his sword down in a great arc.

Will Draper drops to one knee, and takes the force of the blow on the hilt of his own sword. The Mussel man's blade slides off, without doing any harm, and Will turns his wrist, sending the point of his own sword up, under the man's left arm pit. He screams, and jumps back, from the questing blade. There is a rent in his gold brocaded jacket, which is seeping red.

Will steps back too, and watches, as the second attacker tries to get past Tad Beaton's guard. The old soldier blocks again, and twists away from the blow. The young Moroccan advances, exposing part of his back, and his right flank to Will. Draper is far too good a soldier to miss so open an invitation.

He drives home his attack, pushing the point of his blade into the man's right shoulder. The traitorous bodyguard tries to pull away, but Tad Beaton brings his six foot long halberd down in a heavy, two handed blow. The razor sharp axe head bites into the Moroccan's neck, just where it joins the shoulder, and cuts him down, almost to the waist. A spray of hot blood splashes across the queen's bed, a woman screams.

The older Moroccan watches, as his young companion topples over. He screams in rage, and rushes at Will Draper, cutting in a frenzy of blood lust. It is a fatal mistake. Will sways away from the wild slashes, and lunges, driving the steel point of his own German sword, deep into the man's heart. Even as he pulls back his blade, he feels a sharp sting in his own side, and turns to find that Vargas has struck at him from behind.

He steps back from the man, and tries to raise his sword in defence, but he is already beginning to stagger. The stiletto has gone deep, under a bottom rib. Vargas sees he has the advantage, raises the knife high, above his head, and prepares to deal the killer blow.

"No!" Eustace Chapuys cries out in dismay. He forgets his diplomatic training, runs at Vargas, and barges into him like a bull tackling a gate. The Spanish doctor crumples to his knees, and lashes out at this new, unexpected attack. His blade catches the little ambassador, and slices open his sleeve from elbow to wrist.

Tad Beaton lowers his halberd, advances, and drives the long, well sharpened point into the doctor's unguarded throat. The thrust is so powerful, that the point emerges from the back of Vargas' neck. He drops his blade, and grabs at the shaft of Beaton's weapon, as if he might draw it from his throat. There is a gush of blood, he chokes, and falls to one side. The eyes are already glazing over.

Tad Beaton stands athwart the body, ready to deliver a final death blow, but sees it is not needed. He glances across at the queen, who is still retching into a bowl. Lady Maria de Salinas has ceased screaming, and is patting her back, uttering soft words of gentle consolation.

"Bugger me," Tad exclaims, "but this is a real to do, an' no mistake. Have I killed the right one's Captain Draper?"

Will Draper, takes a quick inventory of the dead, confirms there are three, and swoons away, blood seeping from his side. The last thing he sees is the huge shape of Adolphus Theophrasus looming over him, and the last thing he hears, is the doctor's gruff complaint.

"May the God of Abraham be damned and damned again," he growls. "How many of these accursed Christians must I save today?"

17   Loose Threads

"There can be no doubt about arsenic's efficacy as a single large dose, Your Majesty," Adolphus Theophrasus explains. "It is the recent, regular administration of this poison to Queen Katherine which has provoked violent abdominal cramping, diarrhoea and vomiting."

"We thank God you were able to save the Princess of Wales, doctor," Henry replies. The battle to dissolve his marriage is entering a new phase, and Cromwell is advising him to use Katherine's old title at every opportunity, so that she might, in some way, become resigned to it. "She *will* live, will she not?"

"She will, sire, though I fear her health is not what it should be, and a period of isolation, and bed rest, might do her some good."

Thomas Cromwell has schooled the doctor well. He is giving the queen a clear opportunity to withdraw from public life, without losing face. Having delivered his report, and received a small purse of gold for his trouble, Adolphus Theophrasus bows, and leaves the two men alone.

"Perhaps a spell away from court, Your Majesty?" Thomas Cromwell says, once the doctor has left. "Somewhere in the countryside, with plenty of fresh air?"

"Have it arranged, Thomas," Henry

tells him. "It is for her own good. See what other onerous royal duties you might lift from her shoulders too. Do we yet know why this wicked Spanish doctor... Vargas... wished Queen... I mean Princess Katherine's death?"

"I regret not, sire," Cromwell lies. The blame is Sir Thomas More's, but there is not enough clear proof to make so dangerous an accusation. "It seems he and the two infidels were in cahoots with one another. Unfortunately, they are all dead, and we cannot question them. Who can fathom the convoluted minds of these strange heretics?"

"I believe we have to thank your man Captain Will Draper, once again?" the king says.

"By pure chance, he was with the ambassador," Thomas Cromwell says. "He and the guard on the door were able to overcome the would be assassins."

"Would that they had done it in a less blood thirsty way," Henry replies, a little pettily. "Lady Maria de Salinas informs me that a very expensive set of embroidered hangings, and the queen's...dammit... the princesses... best set of bedding were utterly ruined with the shedding of so much blood."

"The breaking of eggs, and the making of omelettes springs to mind, sire." Cromwell spreads his hands, as if to show that the blood letting was quite unavoidable.

"Yes, quite so." Henry does not know whether Draper has done him a service, or spoiled things. "We must think of a suitable reward for Master Draper. As for the astute guard... I will leave that to you, Thomas. My worry is that this will stir up great sympathy for Katherine's cause, and make the people think ill me. I foresee some difficulties over these events."

"The incident has been contained, sire," Thomas Cromwell says. "Captain Will Draper is a loyal servant, and the guard has been promoted to lieutenant, paid a small reward, and sent to augment the permanent garrison at Warwick castle. Dr. Adolphus Theophrasus is to be appointed as your new, personal Surgeon Practitioner, and I am assured that Ambassador Chapuys will not breath a word. It does his master no credit, as all three attempted murderers were the Emperor's supposedly loyal subjects. Eustace Chapuys does not wish any stain on his master's character, and will leave the event out of his latest report."

"Can we be sure?" the king asks.

"He sends his secret letters home via a banking house in the city, Your Majesty. It so happens that I am now a partner in the establishment, albeit a silent one."

"Ah, good fellow!" Henry is cheered up. "You are such a rogue, sir. A wonderful, loyal, rogue. Will it affect the annulment?"

"There will be no annulment, sire," Thomas Cromwell says, exasperated at the need to constantly reiterate his position on the matter. He decides to reveal a small piece of information to clarify the matter, once and for all. "There is a letter on its way to the Lord Chancellor, from the Holy See at Rome. In it, the self styled 'Pope' Clement, Bishop of Rome, refuses your request for an annulment, quite out of hand, and then actually threatens you with excommunication, if you persist in defying his wishes. He will insist you bow down to his demands, and return to Katherine's side, at once."

"What? The man actually says that?" Henry is shaken to the core. He has not been refused anything, save *la Boleyn's* sexual favours, since he was a small child.

"Not yet, sire," Thomas Cromwell explains. "The letter is still in transit. Sir Thomas will receive it early next week. I know of the contents, because I have a man in the Bishop of Rome's private office."

"You do?"

"I do." Cromwell cannot resist a small boast. "Saving yourself, sire, I have an agent watching every great man in Christendom. My agent in Rome tells me Sir Thomas sent a bribe, but it was considered woefully inadequate by the cardinals. My man in

More's office will let me know the very instant the Roman letter arrives. It will be a most revealing moment, no doubt."

"You think More will withhold it from me?" Henry is uncomfortable with this thought, as the Lord Chancellor has been a loyal friend for many years. "Would he dare do that, Thomas?"

"Possibly," Thomas Cromwell replies. "In that respect, he is not unlike Cardinal Wolsey, sire, who always did it for your own benefit. The cardinal always wanted to be a step ahead."

"And you, sir?"

"I think two steps is a better option, Your Majesty." Cromwell gives an ironic bow, and raises one eyebrow in comic fashion, to show he is jesting with the king.

Henry understands. The king throws his head back, and roars with laughter. He cannot help but like this new man. Since Wolsey's death, he has proved to be a constant source of loyal support. It is four months since the cardinal's death, and Henry has all but forgotten that he was the cause of his downfall. Instead, he chooses to salve his stricken conscience by blaming bad advice from lesser men. Percy, Norfolk, More and even Lady Anne Boleyn are to blame, he thinks. Had he been given all the facts, Cardinal Wolsey would never have been deposed. It is what Henry has taught himself to believe.

"Then tell me, Master Cromwell," the king asks, "where do I go from here? The Bishop of Rome means to break me. That is obvious enough."

"Then he is a damned fool, sire," Cromwell declares. "His word is law in Rome, but he has no legal rights in this realm. The Papal troops number less than five thousand mercenaries, and neither France nor Spain wish to test your mettle on the field of battle."

"Well said, sir." Henry loves his martial prowess being boasted of, and still remembers how he led his troops into action twenty years earlier, sweeping the French mounted knights from the field at the famous Battle of the Spurs. In truth, he had been hemmed in by a hundred knights, intent on keeping him safe, but he *had* been there, and the French *had* turned about, and fled the field.

"The throne is yours, by right, and English law says that makes you the supreme head of state. Every subject, you see, must be loyal to the king. That does not mean they can disobey you on certain matters, simply because the church says so."

"Rome will not allow my annulment, sir," Henry says. "That is their final word on the matter?"

"Yes, sire, but not yours." Cromwell

throws his chest out, and bangs a fist on the table. "Divorce Katherine, and do not refer the matter to Rome. To do so is tacit agreement that they can interfere. Do not ask permission, but take it, as your *divine* right. Do it, sire, and be damned to those dogs in Rome!"

"Divine right, you say, Thomas?" It is a heady phrase, and Henry can scarcely take it in.

"You are the one anointed King of England, by *divine* right, sire," Cromwell explains. "The oil daubed on your brow is a direct tie with God, who bestows *your* power by His will. Not the Bishop of Rome. Not the Earls of this realm. Not the Howard family, or the Percy brood. God grants you *direct* power. From God to king. Brush the Roman Catholic church aside, sire."

"They will excommunicate me, Thomas." Henry often has bouts of melancholy these days, and can feel sorry for himself at the drop of a hat. He pictures himself as a poor outcast, spurned by Mother Church, and reviled by the faithful masses, doomed to tread the road in bare feet, with all hands turned against him.

"Then excommunicate them right back, sire," Cromwell says, waving his clenched fist in what he assumes is a southerly direction. "If they try to brow beat you, turn on them like an enraged bull. I have started to put in place such laws, as will put you above a mere Bishop. Parliament will declare you to be head of the English church, and *insist* on your immediate divorce, so a male heir might be sired."

"Parliament will insist?"

"They will, Your Highness. You respect the law, so will bow down to their demands, and re-marry. The new queen will produce a male heir, and the future of England will be secured."

"You paint on a broad canvas, Thomas," Henry replies. "Can you really make it so? Will Lady Anne be my wife?"

"You may choose whom you wish, sire," Thomas Cromwell replies. "I am told there are some truly beautiful foreign princesses, eager to receive your attentions."

"I have made certain promises to the lady we speak of," Henry mumbles. "Can you really make all of this happen?"

"Only by your will, sire." Thomas Cromwell holds out his hands, as if in supplication. "Yours is the power… and yours shall be the glory!"

"What about Sir Thomas More?" Henry says. "He has been my conscience for many long years. A break with Rome is almost beyond comprehension for one such as he. The man will never stand for it."

"Then he has misled you," Tom

Cromwell says. "In the matter of your brother's wife, he failed you. In his dealings with Rome, he misled you, and in the matter of your divine right to rule, he will dare refute you. Some friend, sire."

"He will stand in our way, Thomas."

"I refer you back to the eggs again, sire," Cromwell tells his king. "We must break a few. It is the way of things. Your hands must remain clean though. Let me be the dog that barks for you, sire… as the adage goes."

"My bulldog, Thomas," the king says, and begins to laugh at his own feeble jest. "You shall be England's sharp teeth."

*

"How can I ever thank you, Ambassador Chapuys?" Queen Katherine says. She is somewhat recovered, and propped up in her bed. The blood stained covers and drapes have been replaced, at the expense of Master Cromwell's office, who will hide the cost away in the king's own accounts, and thus recoup the outlay, with a quite modest commission applied.

"I was just doing my duty, madam," Eustace Chapuys replies. He has his arm in a sling, despite the knife barely having broken the skin. "It is a cause of great sorrow to me, to find that the traitors were amongst our own people. I thank God I was able to foil their iniquitous plot, and so deliver my dear queen safe from their wicked treason."

"I knew it could not be Henry's doing." Katherine, despite everything, is still pathetically in love with her husband, and expects a conciliatory visit from him at any moment. "Does he know about this terrible business?"

"No, he does not, My Lady." Eustace Chapuys must lie, for the sake of everyone concerned. "Those who advise him will only use it to damage your cause. They will say the Spanish in England are untrustworthy, and urge him to ever greater folly. We must not give him cause to act ever more foolishly, My Lady."

"The king is not a fool, Ambassador Chapuys," Katherine says, protectively.

"He seeks to put you aside, madam," Chapuys replies, truthfully. "Is there then a bigger fool in this kingdom?"

*

Will Draper's injury is what soldiers in battle call 'a happy wound' or 'God sent'. The slim blade contrived to miss every major organ, and has left nothing more than a painful little cut, and a cracked rib. Adolphus Theophrasus has cleaned, and dressed, the injury, and advised a few days bed rest. His only concern is that any exertion might open up the six neat stitches he has applied with his catgut and needle.

Miriam Draper is happy to have her husband back alive, and moves him into their new home, a tall, sturdily built house on the banks of the Thames, without more ado. Once he is fully recovered, Will can stroll the short distance from the river bank, into Austin Friars, ready for the day's work.

In rapid succession she turns away Rafe Sadler, her brother Mush, Richard Cromwell, and even Master Cromwell. Will must have his rest, she tells them, sternly. No talk of business for at least another three days.

"You are too harsh, my love," Will complains, when he hears of his wife's actions, but she just smiles, and plumps up his pillows for him. He cannot be angry with her, and settles down to be an obedient patient, until the doctor says otherwise.

On the second day, two squires turn up at the new Draper household, on an errand from the royal residence. They deliver a basket of fresh fruit, picked from the king's own forcing houses in the grounds of Whitehall Palace, along with a purse of money. Miriam positively squeals with delight at the honour of being singled out by the king. She makes Will eat the fruit at once, whilst counting the bounty bestowed at the king's request.

"How much?" he asks, observing the small, neatly stacked piles of coins. Once, it would have been a year's pay for an officer in the king's Irish army.

"Ten marks of silver," Miriam tells him as she places the last coin on its stack. One hundred and thirty silver shillings in return for a quarter pint of her husband's precious blood. Enough for a new bed, and the running of the stables for six months, she decides. A fair return, if her man has to shed a little of his life's force. "I hope everyone has been paid out in kind. There are some who should be hanged for these past few days activities."

Will well understands her anger. Sir Thomas More is still the Lord Chancellor of England, and able to blithely condemn better men for heresy, and Edward Prudhoe is allowed to keep his life. The cowardly sodomite has been given a small purse of gold by Thomas Cromwell, and told to leave England at the earliest opportunity.

"Let sleeping dogs lie, my dearest love," Will says, as he pops another slice of orange into his mouth. "Master Cromwell knows what must be done, and will not let the guilty get away with things for too much longer. I dare say he has something up his sleeve, and will soon deal such a blow to Sir Thomas More, and his allies, as will make their very heads ring like church bells."

*

"You are no longer under our protection, sir," Mush tells a fearful Edward Prudhoe as they stand on the bustling Tilbury dockside. "Stay, and you will be fair game for the Lord Chancellor... who is a most unforgiving kind of a fellow."

"I could serve Cromwell in some capacity," the man begs. "I need not be cast out of England, sir."

"My master does not have enough men to keep you safe in England, Prudhoe," Mush says to him. "Besides, you will be much happier abroad, where they condone your odd ways." The young Jew has, over the previous few days, come to realise that Sir Edward is nothing more than a weak willed fellow, easily corrupted by stronger minds, and he feels a measure of sorrow for him now. "Here, take this, and may you take care."

Sir Edward takes the small purse of gold, and boards a ship for Calais which is to sail that same day. His chances of survival are slim, but he values his own life enough to at least make a run for the continent, where he might start anew.

News comes into Austin Friars, just two days later, that his body, run through a dozen times, has been found floating in the harbour at Calais. The Lord Chancellor's writ runs far afield, it seems, and the man's failure, and subsequent betrayal of More, has been duly punished.

*

The Duke of Norfolk is informed by Thomas Cromwell that his son has been meddling too much in grown up affairs. Despite his loathing of the boy, Surrey is his heir, and something must be done to reign him in, before Cromwell takes a hand in the matter.

"It is not my place to chastise him," Cromwell says, "but the king is pressing me for names, My Lord Norfolk, and your son has been most foolhardy. Pray, speak to him."

"You are insolent,Cromwell," Norfolk curses, but still resolves to have words with the boy.

"I hear you have been doing some small favours for Sir Tom More," Norfolk says to his son, that evening. "My family are no man's errand boys, save the king's. Your allowance is stopped, herewith, and you are to return home to live with your damned mother."

"For how long?" Surrey cries, petulantly. "She prays for my soul four times a day, and allows me no strong drink in the house."

"Until you are man enough to walk amongst your betters, sir!" The Duke of Norfolk's words are accompanied by a ringing cuff to the younger man's left ear that will leave him partially deaf for a week.

His return to the family home is a duel edged punishment, for the duke's wife only prays to excess when there are witnesses about. Once left to herself, she finds ways to indulge her libido that Norfolk does not yet suspect. For now, she must reign in her lust for virile young men, and play the wronged wife to her best ability.

"How tiresome," she says to the young blade who has most recently sated her passions. "The boy is bound to get under my feet!"

"Let me cut his throat," the young man whispers into her ear.

"Whose… the son, or the father?" she replies, and smiles. It is a temptation, and she can resist for only so long. "Would you could manage both, and keep me from the gallows, my fine boy."

*

Harry Percy receives a short, terse note, hand written by Thomas Cromwell. The king is most irate at being introduced to a common street prostitute, and deplores Lord Percy's poor sense of humour. Then, he is commanded to turn over one of his smaller border fortresses to Charles Brandon's men.

"For the *continued* safety of the realm," Thomas Cromwell finishes. He has put another nail in the Duke of Northumberland's coffin, and makes a note of it in his special book. The slim volume, entitled '*Vindicatio*' contains the names of all of his enemies, and each day he scratches out some names, and adds others. Sometimes, he muses, it seems like it will be a life's work.

Harry Percy helped bring Cardinal Wolsey down, and treated him badly whilst acting as his gaoler. Thomas Cromwell blames himself for not protecting the man who raised him so high, and will continue to exact vengeance on all who slighted the man, as long as he may.

For the moment, Sir Thomas More is safe, of course, but there is a strong wind coming. It will blow away the cobwebs of Rome, and be strong enough to topple even the greatest men in the realm. Cromwell sees that he must anchor himself, and Austin Friars firmly to the ground, whilst the savage storm of reformation sweeps over the land.

*

"One hundred and thirty shillings is a lot of money for a new bed, and six months worth of stable fodder," Will Draper says from his sickbed.

"Perhaps." Miriam smiles, and takes his hand in hers. "It is always wise to put a little on one side, against a rainy day, husband."

"Oh, there are a few of those coming,"Will tells her. "Though not for us, I hope."

"Twenty five shillings will buy the bed, and another thirty will keep the stables for a half year," he says. "Why can we not use the rest to have some pleasure in life?"

"Yes, that is one possibility," Miriam replies, with a coy smile about her lips."but I was thinking we might save the rest of the money to buy a really beautiful crib?"

"A crib?" Will frowns. "What ever for? I hope that Mush has not been indiscreet with Lady Mary to so daunting an extent. He is a young man, and too much bent on enjoying himself."

"Not poor Mush, my dear," Miriam says. "I fear it is we who have enjoyed ourselves... and there are certain consequences... or did you not know this?"

Will Draper, soldier of fortune, agent of Thomas Cromwell, and the king's sword of justice, smiles then.

He is going to be a father.

~End~

My special thanks to my wonderful, supportive partner, for all of the insightful comments, and other help in the writing of this, the second volume of my Tudor Crimes historical series.

The Tudor Crimes series of books, by Anne Stevens was first published in e-book form, and all fifteen of the books are available in that format through Amazon Books. The series is being published in paperback form, during the next twelve months, exclusive to Amazon.

King's Quest is the latest novel by Anne Stevens, and tells the epic story of Luke Boyd, raised as a tough Canadian frontiersman, and destined to serve his King and Country through the turbulent years of the Napoleonic era.

After being enlisted into the service of the English master spy William McCloud, Luke is catapulted into the heady world of the English aristocracy, where he rubs shoulders with the famous, and the infamous of the day.

The Prince of Wales - Prinny to his friends - has his own agenda, and wishes to see his ailing father declared insane and deposed, but William McCloud has other ideas. The spymaster weaves his way through the courtly deceits at Bath, and uses Luke and his comrades to good effect.

Along the way ... a way that leads to the king at Kew Palace... they fall in with a variety of people, from Pitt the Younger and Beau Brummell to Mr Fox, Charles Fortnum, and poor, half mad, King George III.

From the rough and tumble of a gentlemen's cricket match, to highwaymen, assassins, and wicked plots, Luke must emerge triumphant, and keep England safe from the evil across the Channel.

The First Consul of France, Napoleon Bonaparte, is intent on invasion, and his periodic appearances lend a depth to the history, and shows him to be quite different from his public face. Whilst he and Pitt see to the broad sweep of history, it is lesser known men, like Luke, who must get their hands dirty, for King and Country.

A huge epic of a novel... Ms Stevens latest outing does not disappoint ... all the usual wit and clever dialogue spills over from her TUDOR CRIMES series.....

Bel Ami (Critic)

Printed in Great Britain
by Amazon